EVERY VILLAIN HAS
THEIR STORY

I0654006

THE CIRCUS

A VILLAINOUS HEROS NOVEL

RUBY MEDJO

SUGGESTED READING ORDER
THE VILLAINOUS HEROES SERIES

Every villain has their story...

CONTENT WARNINGS:

This book is meant for an adult audience only.
18+. This book is not meant to be a guide to
BDSM, Kink, or any other sexual practices found
within. Please put your mental health first. This is
a dark book that deeply explores themes of loss,
grief, watching a loved one succumb to cancer, and
two teenagers who have been sexually abused
throughout their lives.
In this book you will find:
Dubious consent, breath play, blood play, knife
play, edging, cock warming, toys, forced orgasm,
primal play, anal, double penetration, risky sexual
practices, sexual assault (depicted on page),
homophobic slurs (said to main character), CSA
(discussed), blood, gore, murder, torture, cancer
(father figure), neurological disease (mother),
death of loved one (on page)

AUTHOR'S NOTE:

Although this book is not a standalone, it takes place thirteen years before the other books in the series. If you would like to read them chronologically, start with The Circus, then Folie à Deux, The Game, and Psychopathy. This is also where I will ask everyone to trust me again. *This book will hurt.* It deals heavily with trauma and watching a loved one battle cancer. If you don't want ANY spoilers, please continue on (stop reading this author's note, my brave little smut soldier) and enjoy Teddy and Eden's story. If you are like me and get a little bit of anxiety over these beloved fictional characters, if you need to know whether or not a story ends happily, sadly, or happy for now, the rest of this author's note is for you. This book does not end happily. It ends with unanswered questions and heartache. But there is something I can promise you, lovely reader.

This is not the end of Teddy's story.

Enjoy.

PLAYLIST

Circus Psycho by Diggy Graves

Annabel Lee by Nox Arcana

We Are Young by 3OH!3

Better Off High by Marcus Mumford

I'm Not Okay (I Promise) by My Chemical Romance

The Middle by Jimmy Eats World

Blinding Lights by The Weeknd

Bloodbath and Beyond by Ice Nine Kills

Come Little Children (From "Hocus Pocus") by Myuu

Cuckoo by Adam Lambert

Die Young by Ke$ha

Dragula by Rob Zombie

Helena (So Long & Goodnight) by My Chemical Romance

Sugar We're Going Down by Fall Out Boy

I Found by Amber Run

I Will Follow You Into the Dark by Death Cab for Cutie

Kids by MGMT

Run Away to Mars by TALK

Welcome to the Black Parade by My Chemical Romance

Little Talks by Of Monsters and Men

Rebel Love Song by Black Veil Brides

Mary On A Cross by Ghost

Bad Habits by Ed Sheeran FT. Bring Me the Horizon

Teenagers by My Chemical Romance

We Stitch These Wounds by Black Veil Brides

Devil's Choir by Black Veil Brides

Where Souls Linger by Nightfall & Nocturne

To those who waited in the darkness with me until
I found my light again

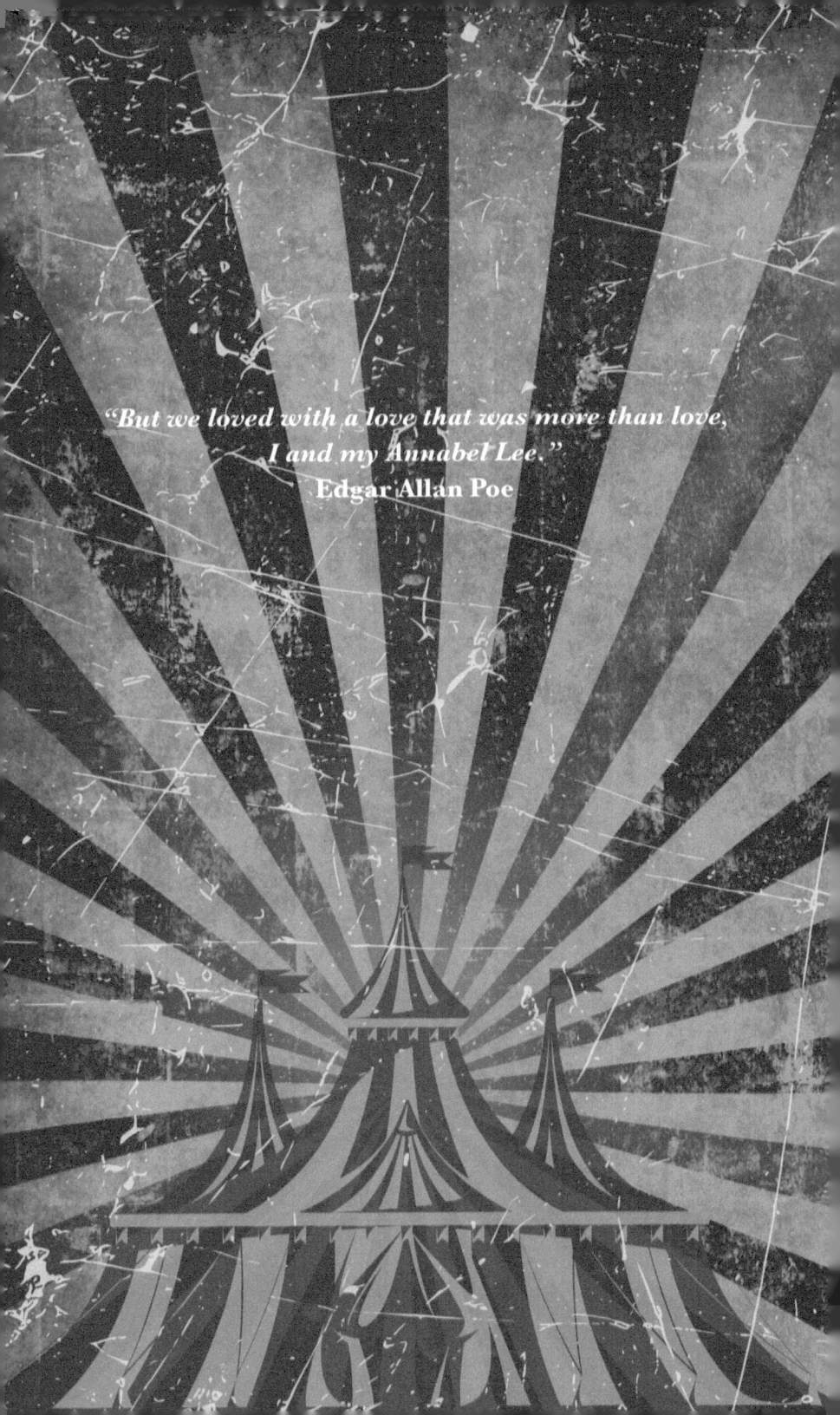

"*But we loved with a love that was more than love,*
I and my Annabel Lee."
Edgar Allan Poe

Before

ONE
TEDDY POE

Seattle, Washington
Thirteen Years Ago (Teddy is Eighteen)

NEON RED and blue lights swirl around the dusky street of an upper class neighborhood, blending into hues of purple when I allow my gaze to slip out of focus. My heart pounds in my chest so hard it shakes my frame, my tongue so dry it may as well shrivel up and turn to ash in my mouth. It would taste far better than the bitter hatred coursing through me. *Go have fun,* my mother had told me. *Go be a teenager for once.*

She underestimated just how vile teenagers are these days.

Cash stands beside me, lips pursed, hands clasped behind his back. I've already smacked the back of his head for his errant jokes at our expense, especially on the drive home in the cruiser. He's simmered down, reminded that for me, trouble with the law would be a one way ticket to death row. Only three people alive know my story in all its macabre abhorrence; my mother, Cash, and my step father Dick.

And only one of those fuckers is using it to blackmail my mother and I.

Eyes zeroing in on that dirty kiddie toucher, I can't help the sneer that paints my lips. Bloodlust is potent on my tongue, bringing it back to life. I salivate at the mere *thought* of plunging my knife into his throat, but he controls too much, and so I'm stuck in literal hell with my mom, and there's no end in sight.

We graduate in less than a month, and she keeps telling me to get out, go to college. But leaving her behind? With *him*? Fuck no. I'd rather perish alongside her, attempting to get away, than skip out and live my life, abandoning the woman who gave it to me.

Dressed in a matching pajama set, Dick stands on the steps to his upper-middle class home, a brick façade with ivy vines clinging to the mortar and window sills, gently waving in the breeze. He's speaking to two officers—the two dipshits who just arrested me and Cash at a party. A party we never would've gone to, if not for my mother's insistence. Through the darkness of midnight, my mom stands dutifully next to her paunchy husband, arms crossed, chewing her lip as she listens to whatever poisonous lies Dick is feeding the officers.

He'll do anything to get me off the hook, because it simply means he will sink those very hooks right back into me. I have to admire his cunning brilliance, no matter how much I loathe it. If blackmailing were a paid and reputable profession, Dick would be the CEO.

"Shit," Cash murmurs as my mother pulls away from the small gathering, eyes on the paved pathway as she makes her way over to us. I'm not afraid, not of her, because I know she will listen to our story and believe it. Unlike officers Tweedle Dee and Tweedle Dumb.

She pauses in front of us, her shiny black hair pulled back, streaks of silver woven into the strands. When she glances up, the teal hue of her eyes can be seen even in darkness, and I have to thank whatever god runs this universe on a daily basis that I look nothing like my abusive pig of a father. Killing him was pure bliss. I wish every night that I could do it again.

She clears her throat, and Cash folds before she even speaks, hating to disappoint anyone, but especially her.

"We're sorry, Mrs. Poe, seriously, it's not what it—"

She smiles softly, dimples forming near the corners of her lips, her eyes crinkling. Reaching out, she grasps Cash's arm, only trembling a little this time. I've been keeping my eye on those muscle spasms she claims she's having, demanding more than once that she go to a physician to figure out why.

"Cash, honey, I know you're teens and that experimenting with drugs is...just part of...growing up, but *cocaine*?"

His eyes widen comically as he begins to wag his hands and spit out an explanation, but I snort, crossing my arms and grinning at my mom. She tosses me a wink and pats Cash's shoulder.

"She's not serious, dipshit," I say, and he visibly relaxes.

"Thank fuck, because—you're right, Mrs. Poe—we do experiment with drugs but never that—*ooof*," he groans when I deck him in the shoulder.

"Can you be a little more discreet?" I hiss, eyeing the police, Dick's hands motioning around as he continues to lay on the bribes.

"I feel responsible," my mom says, chewing her lip again, a nervous habit she tries and fails to hide. "I told you two to go have fun."

"It was fun. Until Brant planted his coke on us and called the cops," I say flatly. He's next on my shit-list. With less than a month until graduation, my mom had all but forced Cash and me to go to our first high school party. Being the local freaks of Seattle Prep, we never get invited to anything, so we technically crashed it, hence why Brant played his funny little joke on us.

I hope he shits himself on Monday when we both show up to homeroom like nothing happened.

That alone may just make whatever punishment Dick is conjuring up for me worth it.

My mom's eyes widen briefly before they narrow. "Now I feel bad for making you two go."

"Nah, Mrs. P. 'Twas fun while it lasted," Cash says nonchalantly, slinging his arm over my shoulders. I swipe him away, top lip curling in annoyance. Cash is the little brother I never had, and the confidante I needed. Being sent to Seattle Prep and meeting Cash is the only good thing that's come out of the marriage between my mom and Richard. That, and the Mustang his dad gifted him for his sixteenth birthday.

It's been used in far more heinous crimes than I'm sure he ever envisioned for his son. Cash is simply a reliable and quick getaway driver, and he typically doesn't pester me for details after a murder.

"You should go on home, hon. It's late. Richard will...take care of this, I'm sure."

My teeth slide against one another, gritting so hard a headache blooms in my temples. The voices in my head begin to awaken, each one distinct and refined, but each one begging for the same thing.

Blood.

Because I know what Dick really wants from me. It's been obvious to me since the first time we met. I can still feel the way his beady little eyes slid over my adolescent body with far too much intrigue hidden in the depths of his gaze. As I've aged and filled out into a man, that intrigue has grown. I know I'm on the cusp of the age he prefers, but my youthful face is still enough to get him hard.

He knows I'd rip him to shreds if he ever dared to come onto me, which is why I also know he's circling like a shark, just waiting for the perfect opportunity to force me into it, to force me into perverted acts with him. He can't have me unless I'm compliant. There's enough at stake that I'm far too close to tipping over into that realm as is, so a night like this one may just be my downfall.

Cash glances at me, pulling me from my dark thoughts. "Let me know how it all pans out?"

I nod, pressing my lips into a thin line. "Yup. See you on Monday."

He gives my mom a bear hug, which she returns with a wide, genuinely happy grin, one that calms my heart a fraction. She's glad I found at least one friend in this world.

The absence of him is quickly replaced by a dark, ominous cloud in the form of Dick and the two idiots fresh out of academy academy. It's all I can do to bite my tongue and keep my insults behind my teeth. The tang of copper fills my mouth, and a shiver of pleasure rolls down my spine.

Dick adjusts his glasses before he speaks. "Apologize, Teddy, for being surly about this little...misunderstanding."

My eyes narrow on Dick's face. I have to wonder what angle he worked to ensure I stayed off the hook. Since I'm technically an adult, the consequences would have been far more dire for me. Mind still prodding at his defenses, I give my attention to the officers and say smoothly, "I'm sorry."

They're disbelieving, but the shorter one has been wearing a shit-eating smirk this entire time. Whatever Dick promised, it has to be sick and depraved. It's just the way he operates, and

I'm learning that just because people are granted positions of power, it doesn't mean they won't abuse it. Most salivate at the chance to walk through this world immune to consequences.

"Keep your nose out of trouble, kid," the taller one says, tapping my bicep with a rolled up piece of paper. The back side is blank, but the innards are shiny, colorful, like some type of flier. Dick must've given it to him, and though my eyes linger on the suspicious paper, I begrudgingly return my gaze back to the cop.

"Didn't you graduate from Prep two years ago?" I say blandly. His smile slips from his face like a droplet of water, and my smirk grows. Before they can say anything else, Dick barks at me to get inside. Casting one last glance at my mother, I silently obey.

Someday, I promise myself, I'll torture Richard Bird and all his cronies to death, and I'll grin as I do.

TWO
TEDDY

"AWW, MAN!" Cash whines, slamming his plastic tray the color of an evergreen tree onto the counter. Everything in this school is the exact same shade, from our uniforms to the lockers. Even our mascot is a green cartoonish spartan. "It's our last Mongolian Monday."

Giving him a sideways glance, I roll my eyes, shuffling down the line to scoop a ladle-full of white rice onto my plate. I'm eyeing the steaming egg rolls when someone bumps my shoulder a little too hard to be considered friendly. And since Cash is my only friend in this school full of entitled pricks, then I know without looking who it is that's attempting to torment me.

"Figured you'd be in jail, freak. Don't ya know, nose beers can kill you?"

Plucking an egg roll from its nest amongst the others with shiny silver tongs, I plop it next to the scoop of rice on my plate, ignoring Brant. His little prank cost me dearly. After the cops had left and Dick had ordered my mom to *her* bed (because, thank fuck, they don't share a room), he'd cornered me in the dimly lit kitchen and explained quite thoroughly how much of a disappointment I am and that I would need to repay his kindness of keeping me out of prison. I'm meeting him tonight at some warehouse on the outskirts of downtown Seattle. The little explanation I *was* granted let me know I'd be working for his son Daniel this summer.

Joy.

Continuing to ignore Seattle Prep's golden child, I toss a pile of orange chicken onto its bed of rice. Mongolian my ass. Our school reaches for diversity and falls flat on its face every single time.

"Hey, freak, I'm talking to you," Brant harrasses, following me to the corner of the cafeteria where Cash is currently moping over it being our last Mongolian Monday. I sit across from him, keeping my back to Brant. The last thing I need is more detentions and required meetings with the guidance counselor. That fucking bitch has it coming, too, and I cannot wait to carve her pretty face to shreds. If Brant keeps going, if he tips over into the realm of evil, I won't think twice about ending him. The only thing I will think millions of times about will be how I want to do it.

"Tedster, not to alarm you or anything, but you have a stage five clinger begging for your attention."

I snort, stabbing at a piece of chicken. Cash's eyes dance mischievously, shaded thanks to the mop of his dark brown hair. "I'm well aware, thank you. It must be tough, because he can't share his real feelings with me, ya know?"

My tone is smothered in sarcasm, and before he can bash my skull in with his own tray, Brant is called back to his table across the cafeteria, his groupies hooting his name. I glance over my shoulder, offering him a parting wink, and he steps backwards, pointing at me threateningly. With a sneer on his reddening face, he spits, "Just you wait, fucking freak."

He turns on his heel, ramming straight into a petite figure. She gasps, her tray hitting his arm full-force, sending all of her food flying onto her pristine but patched uniform. Brant gives her a look of pure disgust before storming off, leaving little Miss Eden Clemm to stand in the middle of the space, the cacophony of voices simmering down as everyone hisses in whispers to their friends.

If Cash and I are freaks, then she's the untouchable queen of misfits.

Sleek black hair braided down her back, ivory pale face turning pink in embarrassment, she stands amidst the mess of rice and orange chicken, her starched white button down now smeared with the sticky sauce and becoming more and more translucent by the second.

No one offers to help her. Not even the guidance counselor or the principal. Something nudges me to stand, to extend kindness to someone who doesn't ever receive it. But I don't, and the voices call me a coward for it.

Lips pressed together, her chin begins to tremble, and with her hands balled into fists at her sides, she storms out, leaving the mess behind.

"Ouch," Cash mutters around a mouthful of food. Everything returns to normal, the janitor slinking by with his mop in tow. "Poor kid. Mom isn't supposed to say shit about her patients, but her dad is on death's door."

My eyes cut to his, something twisting painfully in my heart. Eden always kept herself shrouded in mystery, and what few classes we shared together over the years, she never spoke to me. Hell, I don't think she ever even looked in my direction. The voices tend to calm in her ghostly presence, though, the haunting allure she exudes enrapturing. She's an enigma, and to a man like myself, that's very, very dangerous.

"With what?"

Cash slows his chewing, a sinuous smirk snaking its way onto his lips. There are two holes underneath his bottom lip that match mine. We'd pierced each other one night with safety pins while bored, and received a month's detention the next day for displaying them proudly. "Why so interested, Tedster?"

Leveling him with my own smirk, I say smoothly, "Just curious."

He rolls his eyes, pushing a piece of chicken around saucy rice. Just as quickly as our fun has started, it evaporates when the smile vanishes from his eyes. Cash has a big heart but plays the asshole jokester to keep everyone at bay. We both know one another's deepest secrets, though he thinks mine are way cooler.

My heart gives a heavy thump in that pause.

"Cancer. Pancreatic, I think. Terminal and near the end. He refused chemo or something."

My mouth fires off the next question before I can stop myself. "Where's her mom?"

He shrugs.

"Not in the picture, I think."

"Why?"

Slapping his hands on the table with an incredulous laugh, he snorts, "Jesus, Teddy, why do you care so much all of a sudden?"

I don't know why, and it's bugging the hell out of me.

I shrug, feigning nonchalance. "She's a freak, too. We know what it's like."

He crosses his arms and glares at me. "No."

"No, what?" I ask, brow crinkling. He motions to the doors she escaped through moments ago.

"No, she's not turning our duo into a trio the last few weeks of school. I have to draw the line somewhere for your compulsions."

Fucker.

"Then you'll understand they're obsessive, too, right?"

He grits his teeth, jaw flaring as he does.

"No."

I hold my palms up in surrender. "I have no choice."

"Yeah, you do. Get medicated like the rest of us, asshole, and stop catering to your impulses."

"Sounds boring," I say, looking at my cuticles. Cash huffs. He enjoys being my getaway driver far too much to deny me anything.

"Fine, whatever, but keep her away from me. She's freaky. As in...probably speaks to the dead and dances naked in the moonlight worshiping Satan freaky."

The smile that curls on my lips is predatory in nature, and I see it reflected in Cash's eyes.

"Perfect."

THREE
TEDDY

"PLEASE TELL me again why the fuck we're taking gym our senior year?" Cash grumbles shortly after lunch, tossing aside his khakis to pull on his ugly mesh shorts. Snorting, I shake my head and tug on my short sleeve shirt, sniffing at the collar as I do. I can't remember the last time I took it home to give it a wash, but at least I don't have major body odor like our other male counterparts.

Brant, naked as the day he was born, runs around the locker room, using his towel as a whip, his laughter boisterous as he snaps it at his best friend. I wonder when he will tell everyone he's gay. My guess is never, considering who his parents are.

"Because we failed freshman year and made a vow to retake it senior year for an easy credit."

Cash slams his locker shut and gives me a shocked look while I tie my tennis shoes. "Who's fucking idea was that?"

I smirk.

"Yours, dipshit, so stop complaining."

His grin flourishes, and he juts his thumb over his shoulder toward Brant. "He must've failed, too."

Meandering out the back doors to the track and field, I answer his sarcasm with my own.

"Nah, Brant just takes gym every year so he doesn't have to look more idiotic than he is. Brain versus brawn and all that."

"Sadly, his best idea was planting that coke on us."

We break out into a warm-up jog around the auburn-hued track, the day uncharacteristically sunny and humid, the boughs of heavy evergreens sweeping the freshly manicured landscaping. Behind us, perched high on a hill, the massive stone façade of Seattle Prep glares down at all of the students, its gothic architecture stunning, the gray foreboding building ancient and filled with secrets. The long glass windows glint in the rare sun, and sweat pools between my shoulder blades after only half a lap.

The students who have completed their warm-up gather in the center of the track where the grass is worn down to nubs. A few are stretching, some of the less athletic ones panting and red-cheeked. The only thing I do to keep myself in shape is stalk and murder people. Takes a lot more strength than one might think, or believe me capable of. I'm often teased for being tall and gaunt, having yet to fill out, but I've no doubt I could easily take on any of these assholes and win without even breaking a sweat.

Cash and I make our way over to the group, waiting for instruction from our two gym teachers. One, a young man fresh out of college, the new assistant coach for our lacrosse team, and the other, a wizened woman in her sixties who has worked here since the dawn of time. Her sour glance at all of us makes my stomach twist. She enjoys torturing her students as much as I enjoy lunging for the kill, but she's safe from the voices in my head. As much of a hard ass as she is, she's never been unkind to me, treating all of her students the same.

"This will be your last trail run of the year, kids. Partner up.

The team to make it back to me first will earn extra credit if they need it, and they won't have to dress down for gym the rest of the week."

"Fuck yeah," Cash hisses beside me, holding his hand low, palm open. I slap it, fighting my grin. It's not like we will win because we're fast and in shape, but because we will figure out a way to cheat just to piss off Brant. Everyone pairs off quickly, a group of bubbly girls flirting with said bully and his jock friends.

"Miss Peterson, Eden doesn't have a partner," Ashley points out. "Probably because everyone knows how slow she is."

The entire class collectively laughs, and even the new teacher fights to hide his grin. Fucker. I grit my teeth in annoyance, eyes finding Eden. She stands silently in the small crowd, skinny arms crossed, pale legs like twin sticks jutting out of her too-big shorts. Her shoes are barely clinging to life, old ratty Converse high tops.

Miss Peterson glances around the group of girls, searching for any other singleton and finding none. My body tenses, turning toward the freakish girl, and Cash punches my arm. "Stop it, asshole."

Our teacher's eyes land on me, and she nods her head in our direction.

"Eden, join Cash and Teddy today, dear."

Her eyes widen, and in the sunlight, they're the color of pale twin amethysts, round like a doll's in her porcelain face. The voices in my head perk up, and warmth flares through my chest. Blood would paint her skin so beautifully.

"Fucking hell," Cash mutters while I fight a grin.

"Get going!" Miss Peterson barks, ignoring everyone's shock. Brant and his pal Aiden jog by us, checking our shoulders as they go.

"It's perfect!" he calls, turning to jog backwards and grin at us. "A freak for the freaks to share!"

Cash, utterly annoyed, huffs and jogs off, leaving Eden and me alone with the teachers. She doesn't bother to even look my way, just sets her jaw and takes off into the woods, the trees swallowing her phantom-like form whole.

When I follow, the voices can't help but to paint a gruesome image in my brain, the kind where only one of us returns from the forest, her blood cooling against my skin.

WE CATCH up to Cash quickly, because of all the things he is, a runner isn't one of them. Eden remains silent, her pace light footed but nowhere near athletic. Stuck at the back of the pack, I don't mind; that prize was intangible for us, anyways. Brant is probably already back and asking if he can go again.

"Gettin' slow, Johnson," I pant, my eyes stuck on Eden's long braid, a few tendrils of hair snaking loose as it bounces against her bony shoulders.

"Fuck...off..." he growls, jealous that our time is being tampered with by Eden. For four years, it's been him and I and no one else. I suppose we've grown protective over one another in that sense, not keen to share when sharing would only bring us misery. But Eden...Eden has had no one throughout high school, and a sting of pity zaps through me. Pushing myself to jog faster, I catch up to the two, her sandwiched safely between us on the wide, dirt path, sunlight filtering in through the canopy above and painting the ferns a golden hue. The warm air is tinged with the scent of rot and dirt.

I glance down at Eden, who refuses to look at either of us.

"Brant said we could share you," I jest, prodding at her

defenses and seeing what will garner a reaction. Her cheeks instantly blot with more blood, her fists clenching so tightly her knuckles blanche. Cash's head whips in my direction, and he glares at me over her. Smooshed between us, she's nothing more than a tiny, defenseless mouse.

"Fuck no," Cash growls, then glances at Eden, his eyes softening. She doesn't bother to look at either of us, stone cold in her quiet anger. "I...I uh...you're pretty, but..."

I snort as he fumbles to retract his statement so as to not hurt her feelings, but her small voice lashes out, holding within it more ire than I ever thought her capable.

"Just leave me the hell alone."

She pushes herself harder, running a few paces ahead. Cash looks over at me, a mix of satisfaction and sadness creeping into the corners of his eyes. He doesn't want her to feel she has a place with us, yet he feels guilty at shunning her. I know my best friend all too well, and therefore know he will get over it eventually.

I wink, jogging ahead to catch up to her, the predator in me satisfied as her body tenses when my shadow falls over her.

"We don't have to share if you don't wanna. You can choose either one. Just know Cash likes his balls played—"

She halts mid-stride, and I nearly tumble into her, Cash flipping us off as he passes us and jogs away. In his absence, her fury grows, and her thinly arched brows pull low over her doe eyes. When she glares at me, heat rushes to my cock, and I have to fight all of the dirty, hormonal images away. I like her. And I'm discovering that I like tormenting her as well.

"You're disgusting," she seethes, her pretty white teeth bared, her plump lips parted in a sneer. A few strands of black hair are plastered to her dewy cheeks and temples, her tiny nose so prim and perfect on her pale face. She really is a little

China doll. A fucking gothic one, too, and I'm suddenly a feral golden retriever chasing the neighborhood's stray black cat.

"What?" I grin, resting my hands on my hips as I fight to regain a normal breathing rate. Her eye twitches, but she quickly glances away, resuming our run at a much slower pace. I'm quick to follow. The slap of our feet along the dirt path is as rhythmic as a metronome. "Fine, Cash isn't your type. I don't like sharing anyways, so if you want, I can make you come real quick—"

In her shock at my words, she falters and tumbles over a fallen branch.

"Oof," she grunts, splayed out on the dirt. Snickering, I bend to help her up, snaking an arm around her waist and lifting. She weighs about as much as a sack of flour, her ribs digging into my forearm. Struggling in my grasp to free herself of me, I only cinch down harder until her chest is pressed to mine, her dirt-coated palms resting on my pecs. She blinks up at me, a ray of sunlight slicing across her face and making her strange, violet eyes come to life.

More of that damnable warmth seeps into my veins and leeches into my soul. I've always felt her presence, but feeling her in my arms is another beast entirely. And once my obsession sets in, there's no remedying it. She's about to become my new plaything, and all of the millions of possibilities of what I will do to her rush forth in my brain. Hopefully she can withstand my psychotic ass. If not...I suppose stalking her will suffice, but only for a little bit. There's only so much I can do against myself, constantly at war with my obsessive impulses ever since I let them run free four years ago.

"Let go," she grits out, shoving against me to no avail. I like the way she struggles. Though I've never had a relationship, I know what I like sexually, and I also know it deviates quite sharply from what anyone would consider normal. I've yet to explore the depths of my depravity, but fuck if Eden doesn't make me want to.

We stare at one another for a beat too long, and her cheeks flame to life, our gazes locked as nature comes alive all around us. A cool breeze plays in her hair, robins chirp, and somewhere a squirrel is chittering at its companion. Peace. I fucking feel at peace right now, and it's bliss.

"No," I say softly, my smile tempered for her sake. If I grin as widely as I want to, she'd probably throat punch me.

Her lips twist into a furious sneer, and just before she can knee me in the balls, I catch her thigh with my hand, clamping down so hard onto her flesh and muscle that I wonder if I'll leave bruises. I want to. The purple hue would match her haunting eyes.

Panic floods her gaze, and her cheeks pale when she realizes I'm far stronger than I look.

"Teddy," she breathes, fanning my name across my face at her terrified plea. Fuck. Fuck, fuck, *fuck*. Her sudden strike of anxiety has me getting hard, and I quickly let her go, lest she feel my heat against her stomach. The last thing I need is a sexual harassment claim brought against me. Dick would have a difficult time getting me off the hook for that, and since he teaches here, I have to remain constantly on my toes.

She stumbles backwards, quickly righting herself and smoothing down her deep green gym shirt, her cheeks pinkening again. An awkward silence befalls us, and so I cross my arms and cock my head to the side, prepared to gently interrogate her. I want to figure out where she lives, and Dick has threatened me with everything but death if I hack the school's administration system again. It's more fun this way, anyways. Some good old fashioned stalking wouldn't hurt Eden, right?

But before I can prod her, she takes another step back and hisses, stumbling as she favors her right leg.

"Looks like no more gym for you," I jest. Her eyes snap to mine, irises coated in a layer of fury.

"It's your fault I fell, freak."

Her words are delivered with venom, and it pierces me far more deeply than it should. When she realizes the depths of her anger, her gaze softens, and she shakes her head, turning around to limp down the path in front of me. Stung but not wounded, I follow, a silent sentry, and her a ghost. The asshole in me can't keep silent for long, though, and riling her up is far too easy.

"So, any fun plans for prom?"

Limp. Limp. Silence.

"Yeah, me too. Cash and I want to go together. Maybe spike the punch."

Shuffle. Shuffle. Hiss of pain.

"Y'know, I could carry you. Don't want to damage that ankle any further. Then how would you run away from a murderer?"

That one works. She doesn't stop limping, but she does hiss, "What? Are you saying you're going to murder me?"

My biting grin is quick to flourish, but she doesn't see, too focused on the path now. If only she knew.

"Nah," I say lightly. "You're far too fun to pester."

She must roll her eyes, but it's difficult to see from my vantage point, our height difference remarkable. It reminds me of that Shakespeare line all the girls quote: 'Though she be but little, she is fierce.' None of them actually know the play, though, and none are fierce like Eden. Circumstance has made her hate the world, and I want to know just how deep those wounds go.

"You've never bothered me before now, so quit while you're ahead."

"A mistake I'm greatly regretting at the present."

She glances up at me, intrigue swirling on her confused face for a moment before it vanishes, replaced by stony obstinance.

"Regret it somewhere else."

I smirk.

"And leave you out here all alone, defenseless and wounded? Not very chivalrous of me."

"Don't you know chivalry is dead?" she grits out, her limping becoming more and more prominent with each slow, measured step forward. Calling her metaphorical bluff, I swoop down and scoop her into my arms like a bride, her weight as inconsequential as a feather. Like a wild cat in a burlap sack, she struggles against me.

Our eyes catch, and she stills, anger making her lips purse and her nose crinkle cutely. "Stop fighting me, Eden."

Her brows pucker, and for a fraction of a second, she obeys my command and relaxes in my arms, and those damnable voices rejoice in sick pleasure. Forcing her to do anything would bring me nothing but ecstasy.

She blushes demurely, turning her face away to glare down the path.

"We need to get back before class ends," she mutters, relinquishing. My smile is tempered this time. "You can put me down, though. I'm too heavy."

Now, I roll my eyes. "Don't fish for compliments. It's not classy."

"I'm not!" she barks, elbowing me in the chest as she attempts to roll out of my grasp.

"Goddamn, Eden," I laugh. "It was a fucking joke! Pipe down and enjoy the ride."

"Just hurry back," she says quietly, something awfully close to tears mingling in her tone. Silently, I obey.

Because as much as I desire to control Eden Marie Clemm, I know without a doubt that from today forward, it's really her who will control me. And I'm oddly okay with that.

FOUR
TEDDY

THE OLD BRICK building before me is nothing special. All of the windows are shuttered and opaque with age and grime, the one entrance on the street nothing more than a dented metal door. To the right is an alley, and to the left, the building extends and morphs into other seedy businesses. An adult toy shop. A strip club. A dive bar with a flickering neon sign that says 'Joe's Place.'

I check the address Dick scribbled on a piece of paper again. Elm street. How ironic. It's nearly five in the evening, the bus ride from Prep to this shithole taking that long. It's here I am resigned to whittle my life away for the foreseeable future. Whatever is behind those doors isn't good. Dick is hellbent on punishing me for existing, and so with a heavy sigh, I jog across the empty street and pound my fist against the cool metal.

As sunny as today was, and as warm as holding Eden made me feel, it's all vanquished in the threat of this unknown monster. The only upside I've seen so far is that this would be a prime location to pluck nasty, deserving victims from the streets. It's close to the water, so carving them up and dumping their bloody bits into the Puget Sound would be a breeze.

The door creaks on rusted hinges, depthless darkness greeting me through the crack that slowly widens, revealing a skeletal face devoid of emotion. His eyes are sunken deep into his skull, his cheekbones prominent, his head bald. Ringing those searching, gray eyes is charcoal liner, the older man reminiscent of a washed up rockstar.

"You must be Teddy," he says, voice rough from decades of smoking, a faint London accent nestled there.

Turning to glance over my shoulder, I look back at him with a smirk. "The one and only."

My smile fades when he gives no reaction in return, his expression as still as a corpse, adding to the entire vibe of him.

"I give it six months," he rattles, opening the door another crack wider for me to slip through. I slink into the darkness, the reverberating thud of metal against stone shaking my frame. We stand in that never ending darkness at the top of a set of stairs as my eyes adjust. To the right, a wall, and the left, an empty, dimly lit hallway. Slivers of pale sunlight streak through those grimy windows, millions of dust motes floating past.

"What, my job?" I ask, returning my gaze to his. We stand eye to eye, and something sinister and familiar flickers back at me through that unrelenting stare. After a heavy moment that has all oxygen squeezing from my lungs, he answers me coldly.

"Your humor."

He turns for the hall with an uneven gait, and I follow, unsure of what else to do whilst annoyed I'm here. I should be at Cash's, pestering him to go and find Eden with me.

"Name's Vic," he calls over his protruding shoulder bone. "I'll be your handler, but you need to meet Danny Boy first."

"Joy," I mutter. Anything related to Richard Bird is automatically detestable to me. I'm sure his son will be just as vile, but hopefully not as cunning.

"What's he like?" I ask to his back as we near the end of the hall. Doors line either side, each one sporting a rusted padlock. Although I'm not one to shy away from the dark and macabre, those doors and locks and all they stand for have unease creeping along my spine and sinking its teeth in.

Vic snorts, pausing next to a door on the left. He turns, his eyes now holding within them a keen sort of interest. "See for yourself, kid."

He pushes the door open with a splayed hand, and I peer around the corner into a dank, makeshift office. Old furniture litters the space, along with a dusty desk and a crumbling fireplace. In the middle, two high backed Victorian chairs rest, a chess board nestled between them. Dick occupies one chair, and his spitting image—though twenty years younger—sits in the other.

Glancing at Vic, I salute him solemnly and step inside, eyes catching on the board. Daniel reaches for a knight, and before he even moves the piece, I know he's just lost the game. He glances up, boyish hope flittering in his pale blue eyes as he looks upon his father. Dick's smile is slow to curl on his face.

"That was a shitty move," I say. Daniel's eyes snap to mine, annoyance written all over his features. With a heavy sigh, Dick stands and straightens the lapels of his jacket. Red ink dots his thumb and forefinger. I have to wonder what poor students he's failing now, right at the end of the school year. His eyes find mine from behind aged glasses, and the door sweeps closed, Vic disappearing like a ghost.

"Teddy, the brains I always wanted for my sons."

Daniel stands, jaw slackened in anger. I can't help but to smirk at him. Poor little boy never received all of daddy's love, it seems. I would detest any fond emotions Dick foisted upon me, but seeing his son so disgruntled over that comment is comical to me.

"Keep him on a short leash, or I'll be forced to step in, understood?" Dick says. It's Daniel's turn to smirk at me. I have a feeling I'll be scraping shit off of toilet seats and changing out urinal cakes for the time being. All Dick let me know was that this was some sort of adult entertainment joint. My guess is that it's some sort of strip club...where the dancers give more *private* dances.

If I have to clean jizz from the couches, I'll gouge Daniel's eyes out and force him to eat them.

"Of course, father."

I have to bite my tongue, lest I copy and mimic this childish fucker.

"And Teddy, not a word to Tara, are we clear?"

Tara. Hearing my mother's name on his fetid tongue makes me want to vomit. Swallowing down my nasty retorts, I hold his gaze and nod. "Crystal."

He gives me a lingering look meant to intimidate, and then leaves wordlessly. It's far colder in his absence, and I let my eyes wander around the space, committing it to memory. "What move would you have made?"

My eyes snap back to Daniel's like a rubber band. He's genuinely curious. Tilting my head to the chess board, I say, "Your queen was in position to take that bishop, then he would've been fucked. It was a risk he took because he knew you wouldn't see it."

His eyes trace the board, and he slowly bobs his head as though he understands.

"How old are you?"

Strange question.

"Eighteen," I say, sizing him up in case he likes little boys as much as his father does. He'd be an easy kill, but the ramifications wouldn't be worth it. My mother's life hangs precariously in the balance, always. If it were just me, all of these sick fucks would already be dead. As it stands, I have to be careful with my impulses and reactions.

He nods again, crossing his arms, his suit old but tailored. "You'll do whatever Vic tells you to do. We need a backup circus master, since the fuck is as old as dirt."

And about two steps away from being buried in it.

"Circus master?" I parrot, confused. Where the fuck did my assumptions go wrong? But a slow, snakelike smile forms on his lips as he nods.

"Yes."

My brows raise, relief washing over me.

"So where are the abused elephants and dancing bears?" I ask, motioning around the office.

"No animals of that sort."

My stomach twists.

"Then, what—"

A sharp knock interrupts my question.

"Come in," Daniel calls, eyes still lingering on my face. It's beginning to creep me out, and I'm usually the one doing the creeping out. Following his gaze, I peer over my shoulder, met once again with Vic's somber eyes. He points behind him with his knobby thumb.

"Your prized performer needs to speak with you."

Daniel releases a disgusted sigh. "Send her in."

But when Vic steps away, the unmistakable violet eyes of Eden Clemm clash with mine.

FIVE
EDEN

WHAT IN THE actual *fuck* is Teddy freaking *Poe* doing here?

As our stunned gazes lock, the throbbing of my ankle ceases and my mouth runs dry. He'd carried me today, through the woods and back to the field. No one had remained to witness my downfall other than Miss Peterson and his best friend Cash. I'd spent the remainder of the school day in the nurse's office, icing my tender ankle. By the time I'd hobbled to my bus to make it downtown on time, I had missed it and stood around waiting for the next one, chewing my thumbnail to barely a nub as my brain replayed those moments where he held me on a loop. He'd smelled so good, like juniper and smoke and leather.

The first boy to ever touch me.

For four years, he's never said a word to me. For four years, those strange, teal eyes have skirted beyond me in favor of his friend, Cash. And for four years, I've been relentlessly bullied in front of him, and he's never made a peep.

I hate him just as deeply as I hate everyone else at that school, but after today, my body is betraying my mind.

So now I hate her, too.

He's objectively beautiful. Dark hair, brooding, deep set eyes under expressive brows, hollow cheeks because of his high cheekbones and angular jaw. His lips are full and soft, and when he smiles, he has laugh lines. I still remember the day he came to school with self-inflicted snake bite piercings. A jolt of heat had flared through me when I'd seen them, for it made him beautiful *and* sexy. Which only made me hate him more.

So now that he stands before me sans uniform in a Misfits band tee and dark jeans, I absolutely *loathe* him.

"What's your problem now?" Daniel seethes. Vic tenses, fist clenching at his side. If not for him, Daniel would've raped me a thousand times over by now. For a year, I've been stuck here in literal hell, using my skills as a ballerina to twist my hips for disgusting, lecherous men. For a year, I've gone to school and come straight here nearly every night, paying down an ever-growing debt. It keeps me fed and housed and clothed, the money I never see. And it keeps my father comfortable as he waits to die.

My eyes flit disbelievingly between Teddy and Daniel, wondering at the connection—if Teddy is affiliated for sinister reasons or not. That little girl in me that has a crush on him really hopes that's not the case. Swallowing down my fear, I say, "Umm...I hurt my...ankle. Sprained it today. I can't... work..."

Work. A tactful way to say I've been hundreds of men's wet dreams for a year, Vic following more than half of them to their cars and pressing his knife to their throats, promising to slit them if they ever touched me. Vic is here because, like everyone else, he has to be, but I know he'd rather die than see anything bad happen to me. He's become something of a loving uncle since I've been here.

Daniel wipes at his jaw and rolls his eyes, ever the dramatic drunkard. Gesturing to the door with an angry pointing of his fingers, he dismisses me. "I'll find something for you to do later. Go get ready."

Teddy's gaze burns a hole in my face, but I turn without giving him my eyes, making my way slowly down the hall to the imposing set of stairs. Vic is hot on my trail, slow as I am.

"I don't need a lecture on being more careful. I know," I mutter, pressing a hand to the wall as I ease down the steps, pain lacing up my leg with every minute movement.

"No lecture," he rasps, attempting to whisper. He clears his throat, his accent thickening in his need for quiet. I glance at him, paused on the steps, the question on my lips. His eyes are narrow as he scrutinizes me. "You know that boy. Or he knows you."

My cheeks flame to life at his accusatory tone, but Vic will find out the truth one way or another.

"We...uh, go to school together."

"Well fuck me, then."

"What?" I hiss, taking another step downward. Vic follows, ignoring my slow pace.

"That's the teacher's step son."

I miss the next step and nearly fall to my death. Vic catches me, awfully spry for something that looks like a living corpse. Gasping, I press my shoulders against the wall, and his brows raise in question, his hold on my bicep firm.

"I...didn't know that."

"Now ya do, sweetie, and I'd be cautious if I were you."

We make it to the bottom, an aisle between the risers leading into the circus ring. It isn't lit currently, but music still plays softly in the dusky space, a few of the other girls warming up and chatting. I'm the youngest one here by a mile.

"What's he doing here?" I ask, Vic still supporting me as we make our way around the ring, to the back dressing room hallway. Above us, the red and white striped canopy top gently flutters in a breeze from the vents. After spending a year here, I know the ins and outs of this building like the back of my hand. Of course, I owe some of the credit to the dead, always.

They're great tour guides when they want to be.

"Not sure. Daniel wants me training him. Going to off me, I s'pose."

"But I perform with *you*," I mutter, confused and disgruntled. It begins to settle in that Teddy is here, that he saw me, that he knows a really fucking big secret about me. Not even my father knows where the money is coming from.

I lied and told him it was compensation from the state for... how they handled our *situation* years ago.

Vic chuckles, giving my shoulders a gentle squeeze.

"I am getting old, dearie."

"He's not throwing fucking knives at me." I level him with a serious glare, my stomach twisting at the thought. I barely trust Vic to perform that little stunt with me. All the other girls sob the entire time and ruin the performance. But me...I think some deep, dark part of me is begging for the bite of a knife to sink into muscle and viscera.

It would end the pain of this world, that's for sure.

"Never. You're my favorite, remember?"

Flashing him a small grin, I nod. He doesn't have favorites, not really, but I also know that he does, and it's me.

With a sigh, he drops me at the girl's dressing room door, and I waddle inside, closing the door behind me and slumping against it. Thank fuck it's empty right now. I smack the back of my head against the cool metal a few times, fighting terrified and angry tears.

Because if Teddy Poe is here, it can't be good.

If he knows my secret, it could ruin everything.

SIX
TEDDY

CASH IS SAYING SOMETHING, but I don't hear him. I've stared at Eden, waiting patiently like a lion in the grass for her to look my way just once, for *days* now.

It's been three days (which is a lifetime to me), and she refuses to acknowledge me. She's stubborn, I'll give her that. It's kind of a turn on. I've done nothing but fantasize about all the ways I'd like to fuck her, and it isn't helping my obsession that I'm truly holding back for once in my life. If I allowed those voices to control me in this situation, I'd have already made her mine in every way that counts. Each time her eyes skirt past me, my obsession grows, snarling like a caged bear.

"Are you even listening?"

"No," I grumble, dropping my glare to my tuna sandwich. Mom knows I hate tuna but forced it upon me this morning anyways as I ran out the door to catch the bus, saying I needed more protein in my diet. Would be convenient if Dick would drive me so I'd have more time to eat breakfast, but the one time she'd asked, he'd refused, saying the bus builds character.

"God, you dick, I said we need dates for prom. I refuse to go stag or with you. You've been all mopey lately. Go kill someone."

I'd love to, starting with Dick. She's there because of him, I know it. He has something on her, and she's working to pay him off. It's how he operates. But after Monday, she never came back. She also hasn't been in gym class, so I can peg her absence on her ankle. Every night I get to that stupid fucking circus, every word Vic yammers goes in one ear and out the other, my mind forever searching for Eden.

"Eden's dad. What more did you find out?" I ask, glancing at Cash for what feels like the first time in a week. He rolls his eyes, but I can tell he is trying to help me. If anyone understands my crazy ass, it's him.

"Nothing. No next of kin. Nothing about a previous wife. They've lived here for four years, moved up from some small town in Oregon."

"And for sure terminal?"

He nods solemnly. Although I was banned from telling my mom about Dick's extra sources of income, he never told me I couldn't say anything to Cash. Naturally, he is up to speed about everything, and just as confused as I am. Dick's son's business is shady as fuck, but I've yet to determine just how shady.

"Maybe she's paying for treatment?" he suggests with a shrug.

I shake my head. "No, he refused it, remember?"

He shrugs again, standing and clearing his tray as well as mine. I follow suit, still lost in a clouded daze, my mind focused solely on the puzzle that is Eden as I throw away my half eaten sandwich. Our next class is gym, so I know I won't have a chance to corner her there. Then I have AP World Literature, and last, art. All three with her, but not many opportunities to chat.

My head has been stuck in this storm cloud for days now, and it's all her fault, the little temptress. By the time I catch the bus downtown, my fingers are twitching, my leg bouncing, the bloodlust potent on my tongue. I haven't hunted in weeks, and I need to satiate the urge before I storm up to Eden and demand she spill her secrets. There wouldn't be much fun in that, which is what annoys me further.

"No, no, no," Vic rasps, exasperated. Gritting my teeth, I turn to glance at him over my shoulder, motioning to the circular board with a weathered red bullseye in the center. Splinters of aged wood fleck off and fall silently to the floor, three of my knives residing quite snugly in that crimson center.

"How is that wrong?"

Arms crossed, lips pursed in his British annoyance, he tips his bald head to the board. "Too much deviation. One slip, and it's death."

I still haven't quite figured Vic out, but his ghostly presence isn't vile. Not like Dick or Daniel. And he's decent to the girls—a little crotchety, but kind. He doesn't leer and salivate in their direction like every other fucker here. Aside from Eden, there are four other women, all older, all eyeing me with suspicion and a touch of lust. The standard must be in hell if they find me attractive, because I know it has something to do with the fact that I'm kind, and polite, and would never hurt them unnecessarily.

I toss a knife in the air, flipping it from blade to handle and catching it ceaselessly, a nervous habit. He nods to my little display. "You're good with the blade, but your mind is too busy. Clear it, or you'll kill someone."

I can't help the biting grin that paints my lips, and Vic's eyes simmer in the darkness. I think he knows, or at the very least suspects that I am not what I appear to be; some emo high schooler who hates the world. I mean, that is true, but there's definitely more. He takes a few measured steps forward, lowering his voice and driving his eyes into mine when he speaks.

"You would never forgive yourself if you harmed an innocent."

My heart gives a heavy thump, but I smile, brushing off his comment as though he didn't just acknowledge I'm a voracious serial killer.

"Is anyone truly innocent?" I quip, keeping our eyes locked as I flip the knife through the air, grinning all the wider as I hear it sink deeply into the wood. His eyes never leave mine.

"That's not for you nor I to judge, Teddy Poe."

A noise at the top of the stairs snags both of our attention, and we glance up the darkened ascent. Daniel and Dick are making their way down, chattering quietly about something. Behind them, a dark haired little beauty silently follows, her eyes refusing to rise and meet mine. Potent rage pumps through my veins like magma, and I grit my teeth so hard a headache blooms in my temples.

They get to the bottom and disappear behind the risers, and Vic moves to rip my knives from the wood.

"How long has she been here?" I ask, the question leaving my lips unbidden. When he doesn't answer right away, I tear my eyes from where I could last see her and glare at his skeletal figure. Gripping the knives, he uses his thumb to wipe one of the blades clean, not meeting my gaze or acknowledging my question.

"Hello?" I prod with annoyance.

His gray, lifeless eyes flick to mine, filled to the brim with a type of ferocious protectiveness I feel in my soul.

"You'll leave that one alone, understood?" he seethes, pointing a shiny knife tip at me. I know, in my bones, that he's killed before and would do so again. I recognize that look. I've seen it in the mirror on nights when I hunt for child predators and frat boy rapists.

So I also know I need to approach Vic with caution, or he won't be willing to share anything of substance with me. Shoulder rising in a shrug, I feign nonchalance, swiping my water bottle from the floor and taking a long pull before I speak, his predatory eyes watching my every move. "We go to school together. She twisted her ankle because of me. Just feel bad I guess."

He doesn't seem fully convinced of my motives, for she's the only one I've shown any interest in since I started a few days ago. The same can't be said for the women towards me. They're all older, strikingly and objectively beautiful, but nowhere near Eden. Her allure sings to my soul like a siren. I'd happily drown at her hands, if that's what she wanted.

She's just as filled with darkness as I am, I just have yet to figure out what kind.

"Been here a year. My best performer. Only one that isn't afraid of my knives."

Fuck, she's perfect. Why hadn't I been able to see it sooner? Why was I such a selfish dick throughout high school? It could've been her and I and Cash for four years, a band of misfits amongst nepo-babies. Although I am mentally kicking myself, I also know that I was far too distracted, trying to find a way out for my mother and me, trying to get my impulses under control and failing miserably, begging the voices to give me an ounce of reprieve so I could be normal.

I just don't care to control myself anymore, and that's fucking dangerous.

"Is it because of her dad?" I press, a shot in the dark. His eyes narrow in suspicion.

"You'll have to speak with her yourself, laddie. Everyone in here is entitled to their secrets, no?" He cocks a weathered brow at me, the suggestion hidden in between his words.

I frown, glancing at the stairwell again, aching for another glimpse of that little sprite.

"Yeah," I mutter. I'll figure hers out the hard way, I guess.

Whether she likes it or not.

SEVEN
EDEN

WEEKENDS at the circus are hell. Friday and Saturday nights are packed, and there's always some sort of disaster waiting to happen. We practice all week just to perform with no breaks, and none of us will ever see the money these rich, nasty assholes throw our way. I suppose I need to be somewhat thankful; I've never had to give a private dance. Those happen on weeknights as well as weekends, and the girls drone on and on about their despicable clientele as they douse their faces in powder and prepare to paint on fake smiles.

"Eden, where the fuck is my—oh, nevermind," Chastity grunts, triumphantly holding up her tube of signature ruby red lipstick. I don't bother with that shade, too pale for most of those colors to look decent on me anyways. I never had a mother who could teach me how to do makeup.

With my ankle still smarting, Daniel had threatened to double my debt if I didn't get my ass to work tonight. It's no secret I'm the best dancer, a tantalizing prize that the patrons aren't ever allowed to touch. It's not because Dick and Daniel are kind by any means, either. It's all a business scheme. Show them the best, and give them something mediocre so they keep coming back begging for a chance at more.

If my father wasn't on his deathbed, and if Dick hadn't discovered my other deplorable secret, I wouldn't be here. I can blame and hate myself for what I did, but I cannot ever bring myself to hate my father for succumbing to his disease. He saved me, saved us, and now it's my turn to save him by giving him peace in his last days on this earth.

Reminding myself of that makes being here a little more bearable.

"Don't you have prom soon, girly?" Jess asks, swiping blush on her cheeks as she puckers her lips in the mirror. I run a brush through my long hair until it's pin straight, eyeing myself in the mirror surrounded by bare lightbulbs. Chastity snorts.

"Eden wouldn't get invited."

My teeth gnash together.

"Wow, rude," Jess retorts.

"What?" Chastity says, pulling her lipstick away from her mouth and dabbing at the corners until the color sits just right. She's always been a bitch to me, ever since my first performance when Daniel booted her from the main act and replaced her with me. All those years spent ruining my toes because I had girlish dreams of dancing my way to New York weren't technically wasted, then. But the worst of it is knowing I've always been nothing more than a puppet on a string, controlled by vile creatures. Just when I thought life was turning around, I landed myself here.

As hopeful as I'm still able to be, something deep within me knows it's going to get worse before it gets better. Just how much worse, I don't really care to ponder at the present.

Jess pats my shoulder, ever the sweet, older sister type.

"Break a leg tonight, Eden. Heard Vic was letting the new guy have a go at you with the knives."

My stomach nearly falls out of my ass, and the brush I'm holding clatters to the floor. Whirling around in shock, my eyes catch Jess's. All the other girls stare, some with pity in their gazes, others with fear. I've proven I'm the only one capable of performing that stunt with Vic, because I'm not terrified of pain, or death. I trust Vic with my life.

It's Teddy I can't trust.

Jess bites her bottom lip, and the beaded bodysuit I'm wearing is suddenly a thousand degrees. "Sorry, I thought you knew."

"He...he doesn't..." I sputter pathetically. Chastity rolls her eyes.

"For fuck's sake, Eden, wouldn't you rather have some hot guy try to kill you over that old fart?"

It's easy to ignore her, my gaze stuck on Jess.

"He's pretty good, Edie. I've watched him. All week he's never missed, not once."

Her words do nothing to console me. Teddy being here, working here, is a thorn in my side I can't ignore. I think it's safe to assume he's somehow being forced into this, but the way he breezes about the place so nonchalantly is unsettling.

As though he is one with the darkness of this world.

Everyone simmers down into frightened silence the moment Daniel's frame fills the open doorway, but they shouldn't fear; his eyes are on me alone. And draped over his arm is a new outfit, black and sparkly and as skimpy as a string. A sick smile curls his lips.

"Come, Eden. We need to have a little chat."

DO THIS, *or you're fired.*

49

Daniel's harsh words rattle around in my skull like a pinball in a machine. It's the only discernible thought I have right now, standing here at the end of the hall, wearing a robe, heels, a thong...and nothing else.

We have very high paying clientele tonight.

My stomach writhes and twists like worms in the grass after a downpour.

We needed to clean the main act up, make it more...sellable.

I attempt to swallow, but my tongue is stuck to the roof of my mouth. My palms are clammy, my hands clenched so tightly my fingers ache. Vic opens the door, his face blurring into view, blotting out the ring behind him. In his eyes are resignation, and sorrow.

I'm...I'm still in high school.

I'd pleaded, but the reminder of my father dying alone on the streets while I rot away for attempted manslaughter had me stripping out of my sequined bodysuit and into a single strip of fabric.

Vic holds out his hand, and I slip mine into his, needing to feel anchored to this world right now. Not only will my life be in Teddy Poe's hands...

He's going to see me nearly naked.

I suppose everyone is, but for some reason, it hurts knowing he's about to witness my downfall. Being bullied over the years made me withdraw into myself until only a hard shell remained. Whenever I'd be getting kicked, I'd peek out, praying someone would intervene for once. Every time, I'd fall into those twin teal pools, and every time, they'd look away. He's just as much my bully as the worst of them.

The thought of him seeing me this vulnerable makes me want to vomit.

Vic's hand is warm and calloused against mine. He gives my fingers a gentle squeeze, a silent reminder that he's still here, still on my side. There's just not much anyone can do once they make a deal with those two devils.

The lights circulating the ring become blinding as I step onto the springboard. Vic releases me, my heart pumping so hard I fear I may faint for the first time ever during this stunt, and not because I'm afraid of the knives, or pain, but because this feels too intimate to be witnessed by so many salivating patrons.

And it feels far too intimate to be sharing this moment with Teddy.

He stands alone in the ring, tall and broad shouldered in an ebony suit that matches my g-string and heels. A top hat rests on his head, an addition that makes him appear somehow more sinister than ever before. Like some dark, evil version of the Mad Hatter. Those familiar eyes dance with glee and a touch of mischief, never straying from mine as I take my measured steps forward in time with my heavy heartbeats, the music thudding all around us and drowning out the whispers from the risers.

He holds out his hand, the daunting slab of wood an omnipresent force behind him. My skin crawls in an unfamiliar way, knowing he is the one who will be strapping me down this time. I try to swallow again, only to find my tongue somehow even drier, and place my hand in his, our skin barely touching. Eyes still locked, his fingers cinch down on mine, and he pulls me closer, so close our noses almost touch, and his scent swirls around us. It's calming, those notes of juniper and leather and smoke, and as his impish gaze rakes over my face, my cheeks flame to life.

"I've always wanted to throw knives at a pretty girl," he says, voice cutting just a notch above the rumbling music, so deep and rich and velvety smooth right now. It's sinister, and should be illegal how sexy he looks like this, and I curse myself for finding him attractive at all, but especially right now. Baring my teeth as my last defense, I yank my hand from his.

"If you're going to miss, Teddy Poe, be sure to fucking kill me."

When his grin blooms, his canine teeth appear, longer than normal and vampiric in nature. Another thing about him I find sinfully attractive. He chuckles, the sound dark and foreboding.

"Not today, Eden Clemm. I'm just getting started with you."

And for once in my life, I'm glad those knives never sink into my skin.

EIGHT
TEDDY

"THEODORE ALEXANDER."

"Fuck."

I cough a cloud of putrid, skunky smoke, dispelling it with a wave of my hand and quickly ashing my joint on the concrete that surrounds the pool. She's the only person in this world capable of sneaking up on me. Another trait she passed down to me.

In the light of the moon, the water glows, throwing various shapes across the back of the darkened house. I got home an hour ago. Dick still downtown greedily counting his earnings from our little performance.

And now, I smoke a joint, a pathetic attempt to rid my mind of Eden so I don't storm into her house, pin her down, and carve her bloody before I fuck her into oblivion. Discovering where she lived was all too easy for a man like myself, and I didn't even have to hack the school system. The idiot left a piece of mail addressed from the school in the women's dressing room at the circus.

My mom rounds the corner, arms crossed against the dewy

chill of the night, her slippers shushing against the ground as she comes to a halt and glares up at me.

"What?"

"You know what. No drugs."

I grin, knowing she isn't truly upset with me. She never is. We're all one another has, and she understands my need for escape better than most. I hold up the cooling blunt for her to see.

"It's a plant, mom. And it's going to be legalized soon anyways." Reaching into my pocket, I produce a lighter and relight it, sucking in a substantial amount before releasing an opaque cloud into the night. When I'm done, I hold it out to her.

Lips mashed together, her glare deepens. "You know I don't do that stuff."

"Yeah, but I wish you would. It'd help you sleep."

The corners of her eyes crinkle, a soft smile tugging at her lips. I take another hit, warmth flowing through me, the weed washing my memories of Eden away for the time being. All I'd wanted to do was be a typical, hormonal teenage boy and stare at her tits, but I knew she'd hate me even more than she already does if I slipped and did that. Now, my mind circulates on a loop, poking at all the defenses Dick has put in place, searching endlessly for a way out—for me, my mother, and now Eden.

What kind of sick fucks parade around a barely-legal girl to perverted men like that? The other girls are at least a few years older, are there willingly from what I gather. Eden wouldn't be there unless she had to be, and so I need to figure out a way to get us all out before it snowballs into something far worse.

"Where were you tonight?" she asks, her soft voice pulling me from my dark thoughts. She knows better than to ask it, but she does every time, her eyes always searching me to ensure I'm intact. But I roll my eyes all the same, because I am her son, and she is my mom, and as much as I love her, she still has the capacity to annoy the shit out of me.

"Not murdering anyone, if that makes you feel better."

"Teddy Poe," she gasps, swatting at me. I chuckle, bringing the joint back to my lips, the rough paper moist, the taste potent on my tongue. She releases a heavy sigh, turning her attention to the pool we never use. It's all for show, this house, the cars, the landscaping. Dick gives us nothing in return. A measly allowance once a month for my mother and I to split. We've lived off rice and beans and canned tuna for years now. Whenever I do end up killing someone, it's always a nice surprise to find cash on them. A little bonus for all my hard work, ridding the world of pedophiles and psychopaths. "What kind of life did I force you into?"

Her muttered words are a question not meant to be answered, but they sting, an arrow to my heart.

"You didn't force me into anything," I growl, flicking my ashes into the pool. She says nothing about my surliness, but her eyes—the exact shade of mine—waver with thousands of emotions, most centering around sorrow and guilt. My frown deepens. "Mom...I would've done it eventually. I always...knew I was...different," I say, searching for the right words to remain tactful yet honest.

She hugs herself tighter, her frame far too skinny to be healthy, her hair growing more gray by the day. I'm losing her, slowly and painfully, and once she's gone, I worry I really will devolve into that monster everyone fears. She's the only thing standing between me and my voices.

"You were different, even as a baby," she reminisces, and I smile, watching the side of her face as she comes alive in the moonlight. "Never cried unless you were mad. Or unless...he held you."

He, meaning my piece of shit dead father.

"I'm just a good judge of character," I growl. She snorts, shaking her head.

"I wish I had been, but then I never would've had you. I will never regret a single thing. You are my pride and joy."

Her voice wobbles with unshed tears, and she keeps her gaze on the water. Her hand begins to tremble, and she hides it beneath her bicep. Worry is unfamiliar to me, but lately it gnaws at my stomach like a dog chewing a bone. If she has something wrong with her, I have no idea where to even begin to fix it. So to distract myself, I continue on the same path our conversation is naturally taking.

"What's it like, having a kid?"

She barks out a laugh, covering her mouth quickly when the neighbor's cat hisses and sprints from behind the bushes. I grin lopsidedly at her.

"Oh, honey. You'll understand someday."

My eyes search hers as my smile fades.

"Tell me."

Her lips thin, and she arches a brow at me. "Do you have something to tell *me*?"

It's my turn to snort. "Nah, don't need to worry about that yet. Just curious. I don't know...I just don't understand it. It's hard to envision having that type of connection."

Her cold fingers smooth over my bare arm, my band tee still smelling like smoke and musk from the circus. That soft smile has returned, a knowing glint in her wise gaze. "It's not something you have to work for. It just...exists. The moment you lock eyes. You'd...endure anything to protect them. You'd burn the world for them without a second of hesitation. It's the purest love there is."

She swallows hard, eyes glassy, and grips my arm.

"Despite whatever you think you are, Teddy, you are *good*," she emphasizes, patting my chest above my heart. "You are good and pure, and I wish everyday things could be different for us. I pray that someday you'll find your peace. Maybe it will be when you look into *your* child's eyes."

My nose wrinkles. Kids. I'm way too fucking young to think about that right now, and I don't know that I'd be a good parent. Definitely not a normal one. And my spawn would definitely have a dark, murderous streak in them. My father did, and he used it for evil. He passed it to me, and I righted his wrongs. What if my kids end up killing me?

"You'd give them the life you never had, Teddy, and I think there's something...tragically beautiful about that."

She pats my chest again, turning to leave with tears in her eyes. I let her go, my mind returning to Eden. I'd want that, with someone like her, I think. She'd be sweet and caring but tough when necessary, and I could care for all of us in the way I desire. Maybe they'd have her eyes, beautiful gemstones that haunt the hell out of me.

"Fuck me," I growl, shoving the remainder of my joint into my pocket. The voices begin to reawaken and rejoice as I slink across the yard to the alley behind the house, each footfall bringing me closer and closer to my obsession.

NINE
EDEN

Be here at five, or we cancel our little deal.

MY EYES SKIM the message for the thousandth time today. Usually Sundays are free to me and everyone else at the circus, so why Dick is texting me has anxiety bubbling up in my stomach like rancid food. As if performing with Teddy last night wasn't punishment enough, I'm sure they have concocted some other idea to keep raking in the dough. Vic let slip that last night was their highest grossing evening so far, and the two imbeciles have pegged it on that stunt. I hadn't been afraid of Teddy killing me, and he never once let his eyes slip to my bare chest, but the thought of seeing him again on Monday at school is enough to make me toy with the idea of feigning sickness.

A small cough snatches my attention, and I fumble to stow my phone in my hoodie pocket, bringing my knees up closer to my chest as I sit perched on his windowsill. My father's dusky blue eyes are staring at me from across his hospice room, a frown painting his lips. The tube of oxygen attached to the wall runs to his nose, the only bit of medical attention he allows.

It's so he can chat without running out of breath.

Last week, we were informed the cancer had spread to his lungs. The doctor had hesitated to share the news with me, because now it's simply a race of which necessary organ will fail first, succumbing to the cancer like a knight overrun on a battlefield.

I used to think my dad was a knight in shining armor, the way he saved me from my mother and her insanity. But now I'm grown up, and knights don't exist anymore. The world is cruel and cold, and hope—however small—is damnable.

"You're quiet for once."

His voice is raspy, his body frail and decaying from the inside out. His salt and pepper hair thins more each day, and the bags under his eyes grow. He's worried about me. He knows I want to hate him for not fighting anymore, but that's a battle I lost in order to win the war.

"Work was...tough last night," I mutter, picking at a piece of lint on my jeans. He frowns, giving me a knowing look. I swipe my sweaty palms on my thighs, always nervous when the topic of work is broached.

"They need to give you a break, kiddo. You're about to graduate. School comes first."

It's the same fatherly spiel every time, and so I smile blandly and agree, unwilling to rock the boat and raise his blood pressure further.

"Need me to talk to 'em?"

"What? No!" I say quickly, terrified at the prospect that he may discover my secret. He's under the impression I work at a bar and restaurant on Bainbridge Island. The commute would suck, and the hours would therefore be long and arduous. The perfect cover for the real hellhole I'm stuck in.

His frown deepens, the stubble across his cheeks and chin matching the hue of his hair. At least he kept his hair this time, although it grew back even more gray than last time he went through chemo. I'm not disillusioned enough to think life should be fair, but a man like my father dying slowly after just getting me back feels like a fucking slap to the face.

"Eden Marie," he threatens, and his tone still has the capacity to make me want to crawl into a hole and hide. I grin to disguise my nerves and fish for something to distract him.

"Are you still going to come to graduation?"

His eyes soften, and so does his smile.

"Of course, lovebug. Wouldn't miss it for the world. As long as you're still valedictorian?"

I roll my eyes, resting my chin on my knees, disgruntled but returning his smile. He's filled with pride at my accomplishments, no matter how small I deem them. I was never the athlete he'd hoped, dance being my chosen route and one I put aside years ago. I threw myself into my studies and took every AP class I could wriggle my way into in the hopes that when he died, I'd have scholarships to pave my way to college and a better future.

Now, I'll be at the circus until the debt of his death and dying is paid.

"Duh. But I told them I'm not making a speech."

He glares.

"Why not?"

"Because," I grumble, slipping my hands into the sleeves of my hoodie. "I don't need anyone throwing rotten vegetables at me and booing."

His eyes dance.

"They wouldn't."

"They would. They're all assholes."

"Because they're too selfish to realize what a smart, beautiful young lady you are."

"You have to say that. You're my father. It's like, dad code."

He chuckles, covering his mouth with his fist as it turns into a pitiful cough. Straightening out my legs, I swing them over the side and plant my feet on the ground, prepared to grab him a glass of water. Before I'm able to, his favorite nurse waltzes in with his next round of pain meds and a tray of food.

He waves me away with his handkerchief, bright blood dotting the white linen, and my heart sinks at the sight.

"What do you have for me today, Betsy? More gruel?"

She chuckles, sliding his tray onto his table and handing him the little clear cup of pills. "Funny. My son says the same thing at dinner every night."

My dad downs the meds with a swig of water, nodding in my direction as he swallows. Betsy fiddles with his oxygen mask, her scrubs dotted with daisies. I've always liked her, and I'm thankful I found a place like this for him. Somewhere peaceful that he could go to die with whatever dignity remained.

"Eden, do you know her son? Cash? Just found out you two go to the same school."

My heart, on the floor a moment ago, gives an angry thump, and I do my best to hide my shock as I smile wanly at Betsy.

"Umm, yeah, yeah I do. He's nice."

She smiles, and it's then I see their resemblance. They have the same mouth and nose and kind brown eyes.

"He'd better be. I'll take his precious Mustang to the junk-yard if he isn't. That boy has put more miles on that car than should be legal."

"Eden isn't too fond of the students at Prep. Says they bully her."

"Dad," I hiss, indignant, my cheeks flaming to life as I smile again at Betsy. She laughs, hand on her hip as she holds my gaze.

"Oh, honey. Cash hates it there, too. We wanted him in a

good school, but you're right. The kids are...harsh. I'm just thankful he met Teddy. Those two...peas in a pod. Can't ever separate them."

My dad lifts the lid on his tray, sniffing at whatever steaming pile of food is on his plate. Distractedly, he asks, "You know him, lovebug? Teddy?"

Teeth grinding and heart clenching so hard it aches, I feign nonchalance and fool no one.

"Yup."

Betsy and my dad quickly share a knowing look before he glances at me coyly.

"Anything I need to know, Eden? If he's wanting to court you, he'd better be a gentleman and come meet me."

"Dad!" I yelp, slapping a hand to my face to cover my eyes. If only the floor would swallow me whole. It would fix an innumerable amount of problems. Betsy lets out a generous laugh.

"He's quite the gentleman, Rob, I assure you. Still calls me Mrs. Johnson after all these years. Are you two going to prom together?" she asks, eyes dancing.

"Ugh! No! No, there's nothing going on between him and me. The only thing we have in common is that we're freaks."

Silence befalls the room, and I freeze, my tongue plastered to the roof of my mouth. Betsy looks away as the awkwardness grows, and my father...he looks wounded. As if he's in more pain because of what I just said than any pain his cancer could cause.

"You're not a freak, Eden, do you understand me?"

His voice has gone cold and quiet, and tears suddenly brim my eyes. He worked so fucking hard to get me back, to make me feel whole again after what my mother did. I was a freak in her world, and she made sure everyone knew it, even as they continued to exploit me. And once I was free, I became a freak in this world, too.

Betsy leaves silently, and a chill befalls the room. His stare is unwavering and potent, his militaristic background pushing to the forefront in this moment. He's always been hard on me because of how he was raised, and because of his job. As much as I used to hate it, I appreciate it now that I'm about to go it alone in this fucked up world.

"I...I have to go...have to catch the ferry. I have a work meeting," I lie easily. After a moment, he shakes his head, releasing me in his disappointment. Every time I leave, I have to wonder if it will be the last time I see him. I'll replay every minute interaction in my mind on a loop, praying I hadn't said something I'd regret. It's the worst form of torture I could ever imagine, the not knowing, the slow decay of life before your eyes. If I could give my life for his, I would do so a thousand times over.

"I love you, Eden," he says, reaching across the bed for my hand. I grasp his fingers tightly, and he tries to hold me back, his strength waning more each day. The lump in my throat burns. His eyes flick between mine, aged beyond their years. There's a sort of melancholy to his gaze now. He knows his time is soon, and knows he can't keep fighting it anymore. I can't imagine it, knowing your death is coming, just not knowing when or how badly it will hurt to get there.

"I love you more," I say, my tears slipping loose and trailing down my cheeks.

TEN
EDEN

MORE OFTEN THAN NOT, I wish my cover of working at a fancy restaurant was real, and that I didn't have to watch my back every other step the moment I get off the bus and descend into the hell of the circus. It feels sacreligious, being here on a Sunday, the emptiness of the place eerie and foreboding. Seattle has its dark side of history, a city built upon another city, leaving tunnels and dank spaces for evil to breed. This building is reminiscent of that history.

Seated before Dick, I twiddle my thumbs nervously, fighting the urge to bite my lip to shreds. Daniel stands behind his father, arms crossed, smug little smirk plastered to his face. Dick scrawls something on an envelope and shoves it aside, capping his pen and finally glancing at me. Thank fuck I only ever had to take one of his math classes. Feeling his beady eyes on me at school is hard enough to bear.

"You did well last night, as did...Teddy," he says, forcing out his step son's name. It's sickening to think they're related, that they all saw my bare breasts last night. My cheeks heat at the reminder.

"Th-thank you," I mutter quietly. He clasps his papery hands together, staring at me over the brim of his glasses. Daniel shifts from foot to foot behind him, as excitable as a puppy. And Daniel being excited is never a good thing, I've learned.

"We would like to extend you an offer. One of our patrons rather enjoyed...you. We would be willing to cut down your debt to one year instead of five if you agree to this..."

Already, I want to bite at the chance to say yes, hope flaring to life in my chest. I rock forward, shoving my hands under my thighs so I don't jump across the desk and agree without hearing the terms.

"What...what will I have to...to do?"

A private dance? The thought is sickening, but shaving four years off my sentence would be a dream come true. I could force myself to dance on someone for that. I'd be able to go to college if I only had one year left here.

Dick smirks, glancing behind him at his son for a moment. When his eyes settle back on mine, a cold, heavy chill settles in my stomach.

"We know your mother is...quite the religious zealot," he begins, and my confusion turns to watery fear at the mention of her. How he discovered that bitch, I don't care to know, but I want her and all of her mindless drones to stay as far away from me as fucking possible. "Therefore, it's safe to assume you're still a virgin, yes?"

My eyes go so wide they water, and I glance between father and son so quickly I give myself a headache. Daniel chuckles, smirking at me like I'm his favorite meal he's about to devour. Dick continues.

"Our most illustrious client is willing to pay...well, what I think is an egregious amount," he says, and I feel as though I am strapped into a guillotine, face up, waiting for the blade to fall and slice my head from my body, severing the connection to life forever. "For your innocence. Should you refuse him and this offer, then our deal is null and void. I will withdraw payments immediately."

A strange, insanely loud buzzing fills my ears as he continues to speak, his lips moving but no words discernable. He's joking, right? He wants me to sleep with someone to cut down my debt, but if I refuse, then he's taking away my father's peaceful and painless death?

I am a virgin, that much is true, but it's not because my mother is a religious zealot. She was grooming me to be a child bride before my father won that custody battle. No, I'm still a virgin because I'm a freak and no one wants me, but I also don't want *them*. I don't want attachment, despise the thought of being that vulnerable with anyone. Last night was the closest I ever came to being intimate, and I was having knives thrown at me, for fuck's sake.

"Think on it quickly," Daniel snarls. "This client is... important."

"Wh-When...when would I..." I stumble breathlessly. The world tilts and spins, as though I'm on that vomit-inducing fair ride.

"He's away on business for two weeks. But upon his return," Dick answers smoothly, as though he's talking about the exchange rate between the US and Canadian dollar and not the exchanging of my innocence for cold hard cash. A bitter part of me wants to ask how much this fucker is willing to pay to sleep with a *teenager*—a girl who just turned eighteen in March—but I bite my tongue and swallow my pride, my father's eyes forever in my mind. I can't let him die on the streets, not like that...

"Your little prank from last year will be...advertised as well, Eden, if you don't comply."

71

Another punch straight to the gut. This isn't a fucking deal they are offering; they're just twisting the knife of blackmail until I scream and relent. If they let spill that I stole Cadence Smith's windshield wipers the day of that storm, I will go to jail, no questions. Her father is the county prosecutor. It was all over the news when it happened, how he threatened to find whoever played that prank and nearly killed his baby girl.

Wasn't technically my fault that Cadence is dumb as a box of rocks and chose to drive knowing full well she had no way to see through the rain. She wrapped her pretty little BMW around a tree that night, and Dick, of all people, had seen me steal the wipers and shove them in the trash near the fieldhouse.

To be fair, that was the day she'd rounded up a week's worth of used tampons and strung them up in my locker. Did she get in trouble? Was there ever an investigation to see who had bullied *me*?

Mind racing a thousand miles an hour, Daniel chuckles. "Tick, tock, Eden. Way I see it, your choice is already made."

Bile rises up my throat, threatening to spew forth all over the desk. Dick would probably faint at the sight.

I can't do this, I can't, I can't, I chant in my mind. *But I have to, I have to, think of dad, think of him suffering, think of him finding out that the money from the VA ran out, think of him discovering your secrets.* That alone would kill him. He would miss my graduation, which is the only thing keeping him going right now.

I have to see you graduate, lovebug, he'd told me when he found out the cancer had returned and was in his pancreas. *I have to see my baby girl cross that stage.*

I can't take that from him. Virginity is a social construct anyways, right? *Right?*

Heart thumping, time slowing to a crawl as I come to the

harrowing decision that I know I have no choice in, I swallow my fear, raise my eyes, and nod once. "Fine. One year, though."

Dick nods, satisfied, pulling another piece of paper in front of him as though we weren't just discussing prostitution. Daniel grins like a giddy child, smoothing his hands together.

"Keep your cunt to yourself between now and then, got it?" he growls.

As if I'd want to share it with more people before? At least I'd have a choice in my partner, though...

At least I'd have a choice in who shares that moment with me.

Standing quickly, all of my blood rushes to my feet, and I wobble unsteadily, needing to flee home to our quaint trailer so I can shower away the last twenty four hours.

And muster my courage to do something more terrifying than anything I've ever dreamed of doing before.

I'm going to ask Teddy Poe to fuck me. Because if I'm being forced to give up my virginity, it's going to be on my own terms, and something tells me he, of all people, will say yes.

ELEVEN
TEDDY

IT'S PISSING RAIN TODAY, and all I've managed to do since I first spotted Eden at 7:58 sharp is stare at her and try to recreate Saturday night. Just...with my own little fantastical, imaginative flair is all. I was a gentleman through and through, forcing the voices into submission and prolonging my own torture. Someday, I'll see her breasts. Hopefully someday soon, because if we have to perform again on Saturday, I don't think I'll be able to hide how I feel about her.

She's turned me into a prepubescent boy without even trying.

It's currently our shared class after gym, AP Literature. Mrs. Simons is droning on about *Dracula*, and most of the students are fast asleep, the atmosphere calm, the lighting dusky from the storm rolling through. Elbow grinding into the top of my desk, cheek resting angrily against my fist, I stare rather pointedly at Eden, who is staring out the window to her left.

I'd warred with myself on Saturday night, paced up and down the street, tempted to hop on a bus and go knock on her door, but on the chance she would react poorly, I decided to stay put. Better to ensnare someone like her, slowly and calmly, so she doesn't have time to realize that's what I'm doing.

Lost in my musings of how exactly I'd like to trap her, I almost miss the flick of her eyes in my direction. Thinking it was nothing more than a trick the voices are playing on me, I tune back in, sitting straighter, raking my hair from my eyes and tugging on the ends. After a few more moments, my patience is rewarded, and those violets clash with my gaze. Her eyes widen briefly, a flare of surprise at being caught, and her cheeks bleed.

Outside, the rain and wind picks up, pelting the window hard enough to drown out our teacher's voice. And inside, deep in my soul, a different storm rages, one that brings with it a hurricane of unfamiliar emotions and leaves a path of wreckage and destruction in its wake.

Composing my features, I wink at her the next time she glances my way, which has her brows pulling low over her eyes and into a glare. It had been impossible not to see Eden on Saturday, as discreet as I'd tried to be. When you're concentrating on *not* murdering someone for once, it's a little difficult. Her body had been pale and pliant, soft in all the right places, her ribs heaving with every measured breath to ensure she kept still. But the way her pupils had flared to life every time my knife sank into the wood mere millimeters from her precious skin is something I cannot scrub from my mind no matter how hard I try.

It's like the voices all pitched in and created the perfect human for me, plucked her from my skull, and set her before me, a gift for feeding their bloodlust so thoroughly and viciously.

The bell blares through the classroom, more than a few students jolting awake, Brant one of them. Forced to sit in the front row because he's failing, he raises his head and blinks away the sleep, drool on his cheek.

Eden flees, and I gather my books, hot on her trail. The slamming of lockers and yammering voices of students is easy to drown out with how focused I am on her, and when she pauses at her locker and spins the dial, I lean against the neighboring one, composing my features as best I can. Slow and steady has been my mantra for a week. A week for me is an eternity when I want something.

She slams her locker closed, having traded her tattered copy of Bram Stoker's most famed work for her sketchbook. We're drawing in art currently, and I've seen her skill. Brilliant, as would be expected. She jumps when she sees me, closing her eyes and clenching her fist before skirting around me, heading for the basement where all the art rooms reside. I follow, fighting my smile, enjoying the way her ass moves beneath her pleated skirt.

I've always loathed these uniforms, but now the thought of her pretending to be a naughty school girl while I spank her ass with a ruler makes me hotter than I care to admit.

"Why were you staring at me, Eden?"

She scoffs, but refuses to look at me.

"Excuse me? You're the one who can't keep his eyes to himself," she growls, shoving her way past a throng of people who give her no notice. No one notices her, and I used to be one of them. I hate myself for it, but vow to make it up to her now. She has my undying attention whether she wants it or not. I've wriggled myself beneath her skin like a parasite, and I'm not going anywhere.

"I was trying to assess the storm, don't flatter yourself."

She pauses at the top of the stairs, hand on the worn wooden railing, and glances up at me. Her hair is wavy today, framing her face like black curtains in a funeral home, her eyes a deeper shade of violet thanks to the stormy weather. As though she's come alive with the rain. I can't help the way my smile grows as our eyes flick between one another's, the world passing us by noiselessly because we are in our own, and I never want this feeling to go away.

This feeling like I'm home for the first time in my life, my soul safe and warm as long as it's next to hers.

Jutting her pointed chin up, she says, "Then next time, pick a different window."

I snort, descending with her into the chilly darkness.

"Wanna ride the bus together tonight?"

"What? Fuck...no, Teddy," she says, exasperated as we round the corner. The noise from above dies down as everyone settles into their prospective classrooms, the bell about to ring. The only shitty thing about art class is that our batty old teacher, Miss Whitman, doesn't allow us to talk. By the end of the school day, she's usually so hungover she can barely function, and being holed up down here, no one aside from myself knows her little secret.

"Why not? We're going to the same place," I argue, and we pause outside the door. Chewing her lip, she blinks up at me again, her brow slowly beginning to crinkle, as though she has something she wants to say but isn't. I quirk my brow, leaning over her, an intimidation tactic that has her pupils dilating.

The bell rings. My heart hammers in my chest, waiting anxiously for her to part those pretty lips and whisper anything to me. I'll take her hate, and her ire—I'll gladly take anything this girl gives me. She finally releases a shaky breath and says, "Meet me in the library in thirty minutes."

LEAVING ART WAS SURPRISINGLY A BREEZE. All I had to do was hold my stomach and groan a few times, letting Miss Whitman overhear me whispering about that damn tuna fish sandwich. She slipped a hall pass onto my desk and told me to just stay gone until tomorrow. I'd winked at Eden as I breezed by, and now I'm alone in the library, eyes skating over dusty tomes as wan, gray light filters in from the high windows.

Seattle Preparatory School sucks ass for a lot of reasons, but the one redeeming quality is the architecture. It's dark academia at its finest, gothic and melancholy and macabre. The library is as massive as one would be at a university, with a second level overlooking all of the work desks below. The rows and rows of shelves jut high into the air, the ceiling a cathedral, the gray stone walls cold. With the deep green carpet and trimmings, along with dark oak wood accents, it's cozy and foreboding all at once.

My eyes skim the empty space, the old librarian Mrs. Spencer snoozing behind her desk, her aged computer lifeless. She refuses to use it, the luddite, and a few times she's accused me of not returning books because her check-out system is trash. Frowning, I glance around again, searching for that little ghost, my stomach twisting. For once in my life, I'm on edge, unable to predict what she could possibly want to speak with me about in such a secretive manner.

Something to do with the circus, most likely. Maybe to tell me to fuck right off and never look at her again, but the way she'd held my gaze at the top of the stairs not long ago tells me that's not the case.

It's frustrating, the not knowing, and I wonder if this is how normal people feel daily. If so, fuck it, I don't want it. But if it means getting closer to Eden...I'll swallow that challenge whole.

A flash of black and ivory peeks around a bookshelf, and the predatory side of me jolts awake, a slow grin curling on my lips as I prowl toward her, to the back of the library where it's smothered in inky darkness and the scent of old books. She's chewing her lip as I draw near, and she backs away between the shelves, her shoulders hitting the stone wall behind her when I finally relent my forward momentum, leaning a shoulder casually against the spines and smirking down at her. Those big round eyes blink up at me, a deep, luxurious purple, and I nearly salivate, tempted beyond what I can bear. How did I never *really* see her before? Probably because I was so wrapped up in my own turmoil, and I'm kicking myself for being such a selfish prick.

"You don't seem too keen on me, so forgive my confusion as to why we're all alone where no one can see or hear us."

She pales a few shades at my subtle threat, throat bobbing as she swallows. My teeth grind together, desire waging a war in my body, the voices screaming and clawing inside my skull, begging for me to sink my teeth into her flesh and draw that precious crimson. At the same time, though, they calm in her presence, a sort of controlled burn simmering through my veins at our proximity.

"It's not...not like that...umm..." she stutters, fumbling for the words she clearly doesn't want to say. Cocking my head to the side, I study her, crossing my arms and fighting a grin. It's adorable, how hesitant she is for whatever reason. When she doesn't continue but just stares up at me, I quirk my brow, encouraging a more thorough response that I know I won't get. She's nervous, and for once in my life, I'm nervous, too.

"Is this about the circus...?" I hedge, and she wags her dainty little hands quickly, her mouth popping open.

"What? No...I mean...just..."

God, she's cute when she's flustered. I've only slept with a handful of people, none of them wanting a relationship, which suited me just fine. But the thought of making Eden mine, of exploring all of these dirty fantasies I have with *her*...I doubt I'd ever grow bored. The possibilities with her are somehow endless. I'm not sure how I know, but I just *do*, and I want her so badly my heart aches.

"Eden. Just spit it out. I threw knives at you while you were in a fucking g-string—"

Her cold fingers press against my lips, her eyes wide and darting beyond my shoulder to ensure no one heard me. I smile against her frigid skin, warmth curling pleasantly in my stomach like a cat in the sun. I wish she'd slip those fingers past my lips.

Those eyes return to mine, and she yanks her hand away, as if just realizing she willingly touched me. Arms still crossed, my hands curl into fists at my sides as I fight back the urge to touch her in return, to feel her smooth skin, to warm the chill of her ancient soul.

"Okay," she breathes, shoulders raising comically, her hands twisting together again as she glares at my chest. "Okay... we graduate soon..."

She hesitates, eyes still pinned to my loosened tie.

"Astute observation," I encourage with sarcasm. Her eyes flit to mine and away just as quickly, like a little minnow darting to and fro in a murky lake, unaware that a bigger fish is watching, waiting.

Ignoring me, she continues.

"And...high school sucked for me, Teddy." Her eyes find mine with determination this time, round and beautiful and overflowing with an innocent type of vulnerability that has my hackles raising and my brows knitting together. Is this where she asks me why I never stood up for her? Because...fuck, I don't have an answer for that, and she deserves one. Guilt is an unfamiliar emotion to me, but I feel it now, so potent that it physically hurts. I hate it, but I deserve it. "I just...before we graduate...I want to have a normal...teenage experience."

Well, that took a sharp turn in a direction I never saw coming. I think I understand what she's hinting at, but the moment I open my lips to ask, she rushes out a full explanation, and my heart stops beating as those damning words sink in.

"I...will you...will you sleep with me?"

TWELVE
EDEN

HE DOESN'T SAY ANYTHING, doesn't even move, and the tears burning a hole in my throat threaten to burst forth. If he doesn't say yes, then I'm out of options, because who else would willingly sleep with me? Who else will help me lose my virginity on my own terms before some sick fuck tries to rip it from me? I know I'm desperate, but I also know that if I can do this with him, if my first time is filled with decent memories instead of horrible ones, then I'll be able to muster the courage to keep going.

There's no way he's a virgin, too. I've overheard him and Cash making jokes, and I feel confident that at least Teddy will know what he's doing, because I sure as fuck won't. Sex and anything to do with it was a banned topic growing up. I was the homeschooled religious freak, locked away inside, wearing nothing but dresses or skirts. I never even knew periods existed until I had one, and my mother rejoiced, saying I was a woman.

I'd been thirteen, and the next week, she introduced me to my *husband*, a man affiliated with the church she would die for.

He was forty.

I'd written it in a letter to my father while he was away overseas, and the ensuing custody battle was wrought with pain, but he got me out of the cult that raised me, and ever since I've been forced to learn the real world on my own.

Peeking up at Teddy from beneath my lashes, I bite my lip and cross my arms, shaking as a sudden chill befalls us. It's dark back here, and the storm outside rages, rain pelting the panes of stained glass so hard it sounds like marbles being thrown at it. Thankfully, it must drown out the rampant beating of my heart. His teal eyes blaze down at me, his expression stony and unreadable. He's tall, so tall, crowding my space with his presence alone. But his scent, now familiar to me, is a comfort, and if he says yes, then I'll close my eyes when we do it and just breathe him in so I don't panic.

"Eden," he says finally, a small smile on his full lips. He's so beautiful it hurts, and I hate that for four years, he's held every ounce of my attention, while I gained nothing in return. I must look like a desperate fool, and I'm about to run away. With a shake of my head, I move to push past him, but his arm strikes out far too quickly to be normal, his hand gripping the shelf on the other side, effectively caging me in with his lithe body. Stunned into stillness, ice creeps into my veins as his smile grows, that sinister glint entering his eyes. "Say it. Say you want me to fuck you."

Now would be an excellent time for Mrs. Spencer to catch us. I'd gladly take detention in exchange for being removed from this situation I created. My cheeks flush so hotly I begin to break out in a cold sweat, but I bury my embarrassment and glare at him.

"No."

His brow quirks, and he's suddenly an impish, playful schoolboy.

"No? Shame."

He's being coy, because he knows I'll say it, because the fucker can read me like a book and must see how desperate I am. Grinding my molars, I take a steadying breath and deepen my glare.

"I..." I croak, clearing my throat. *Nice, Eden, you try to be intimidating but you're just a weird little freak.* "I want you to... to...fuck me," I say, breathing the last part so it's barely a whisper.

His smile flourishes, but it isn't good-natured, or kind. It's... terrifying. Dark. *Ominous.* His eyes are worse, though, his pupils expanding and pushing out the blue in the span of time it takes me to say those words. Even his hand, still gripping the shelf to my left, clenches so tightly his knuckles turn bone white.

"How do you want me to fuck you, Eden?"

Oh my God.

Fire burns through me, casting out the chill I'd felt a moment ago, but it settles at the apex of my thighs, an ache blooming there that is familiar, but one that has never been so potent. My heart races so hard it drowns out the pounding of the rain. He's smirking at me, and if I didn't know him better, I'd think he was being cocky with that statement. But I feel like I do know him, somehow, and I seem to understand that it isn't arrogance painting his tone, but raw desire. Desire I can't fathom, but desire so overwhelming and powerful that it's consuming him whole.

I shake my head, jittery and nervous again, because I don't know. I mean, obviously...*gently*, right? Do I have to answer him this time? Because the second I open my mouth, he's going to realize how out of bounds I am. "I...I don't know."

His eyes simmer, the fire banked for now, and the intensity he was just exuding cools off, but only just.

"Why do you want this?" he asks, motioning between us. A question I expected him to have, and rightly so. My lie is well-rehearsed, thank fuck.

"Because...when I'm done...working," I say, lest Dick round the corner and catch us. "...then I'm going to college, and I want to...be normal, for once. I want to be somewhat...experienced." It takes effort to choke out that lie, and I doubt he buys it, but he nods all the same, playing along for my sake.

Teddy is far too cunning to believe me wholeheartedly. But if I can keep him guessing until the deed is done, then I'll have succeeded in my endeavor.

"Fair enough," he muses, eyes tracing every pore on my face. His attention lately has been unyielding, and intense, and I don't get it. I want to be angry, lash out and demand to know why he chose now, right before we graduate, to show any interest in me. On the flip side, I don't want to push him away now that I know how it makes me feel.

Warm. Seen. Safe. Things I only ever dreamed of, but the real thing is far more devastating.

"If I say yes," he says, eyes flicking quickly between mine. "Then I have conditions you'd have to agree to."

Somehow, I expected this as well, because Teddy Poe would never make this easy on me. He seems to like watching me squirm, and that thought has more heat centering between my thighs. I rub them together beneath my skirt absentmindedly, and wetness begins to pool in my underwear. His eyes flick downward, catching me in the act, and when they find mine again, they are positively feral.

Attempting to distract him, I nod quickly. "O-of course, what are they?"

He grits his teeth so hard his temples flare along with his squared jaw, but he smirks, still playing at nonchalance when we both know there's something transpiring between the two of us right now. Something formidable. Something intrinsic.

"One," he says, holding up a finger, "you tell me the real reason you want me to fuck you. Two, we ride the bus together every night until we make good on this deal, and three..."

Heart in my throat as his smile blossoms, he finishes his demands with a flourish. "You go to prom with me. If you want the high school experience, then we're going all out."

Jaw clenched, I fight the word *No* as it dances on the tip of my tongue. Go to *prom?* Be paraded around and made fun of more than I already am? And, despite how I feel about Teddy, despite the fact I find him utterly and devastatingly beautiful, we're the freaks. Everyone would have a hay day, seeing us together. "I don't have a dress."

He smirks.

"Simple fix."

My lips press together in annoyance.

"I *did* tell you the real reason."

His smirk grows, playfulness dancing in his eyes.

"No, you didn't."

"Everyone is entitled to their own...secrets," I hiss. "I never asked you why you're at the circus, but we both know it has to do with blackmail."

His gaze darkens to shades unknown, and I recoil slightly in fear. Just as quickly, it vanishes, and he seems annoyed but resigned. "Fine. I'll earn your secrets then, Eden Clemm. That's a threat *and* a promise."

Ones I know he will eventually make good on, but my desperation is currently winning, so I don't care.

"Great," I say. "So I'll ride the bus with you."

"And go to prom with me."

"No."

"Then my dick isn't going anywhere near what I am sure is a very pristine pussy."

My jaw falls to the floor, and I gape at him in shock. He laughs, the sound so beautiful and rich that I don't have it in me to tell him to be quiet. I seem to know that he doesn't truly laugh like this very often, and I suddenly feel lucky to be witnessing it, his head tilting back, exposing the sturdy column of his throat, his Adam's apple bobbing with the force of it.

"God, fine, okay! I'll go to...prom with you."

Eyes still twinkling in mischief, he grins at me. "Great. Don't worry about a dress. I'll be over on Saturday at three."

"We work," I hiss.

"No, we don't. I'll take care of that. You just pick where you'd like to have sex. Let me know so I can plan."

My brow crinkles for a few different reasons, and I rub my forehead. How the fuck did I end up here, discussing this with Teddy?

"Plan? Plan what? And you don't even know where I live."

The bell rings, startling both of us, but the library remains quiet. After a beat, he returns his eyes to mine, all of my problems vanquished under his potent stare.

"Eden, if I'm going to take your virginity, then I'm going to make it memorable for you," he says, a softness creeping into the corners of his eyes. In that instant, I melt, because there's a sorrow hidden deep within him, a sorrow that makes him unfailingly kind, but one he hides behind his wit.

"Oh...umm...okay."

"Are you on the pill?"

"What pill?"

His smile fades.

"Birth control?"

"Oh," I blurt. "Umm...no."

He nods while I flounder in a pool of clammy sweat. The

doors to the library slam open, and voices waft to us, boisterous ones of students thankful the day is done. There are a few clubs that meet here, and we have to get to work soon. Teddy smiles gently at me.

"Let's catch our bus."

And for some reason, the thought of him next to me as we both descend into hell makes it a little easier to bear.

THIRTEEN
TEDDY

"FIGURE OUT who you're taking to prom yet?" I ask, frowning into the black depths of my locker, shuffling aside a few books as I search for my AP Chemistry tome.

Cash slams his locker closed, acoustic guitar in its case slung over his shoulder. With the morning rush through the halls, a few wily freshmen bump into us. He shakes his head. "Nah. That was a stupid suggestion. We're too mature for prom."

I halt in the middle of the hall, more people running into me and hissing "Freak," as they pass by. Once Cash realizes I'm no longer next to him, he turns and gives me a quizzical look.

"What?"

"You fucker."

His smirk is broad. "Who'd you ask?"

I simply press my lips together, and his grin falters, his shoulders drooping and the strap of the case slipping down his bicep.

"Eden? C'mon, Teddy, we talked about this!" he whines.

Resuming my strides, I catch up to him, and we pick up our pace to our first period classes.

"I was under the impression you were serious about wanting to get dates for prom." I growl. I'm not taking it back now, not after I was able to...well, sort of force her into it. Our bus ride was bliss yesterday after school, me pestering her and her ignoring me. Then we practiced together under the watchful eye of Vic, and she even let me walk her to the bus that would take her home.

Threatened to stab me in the jugular if I boarded it, though, so I had to wait for the next one and follow, unbeknownst to her. I'd sat up all night, until dawn crested Rainier, painting it in watercolor hues of pink and purple. I'd kept her safe through that darkness, pondering every possibility of why she would ask me to sleep with her.

She isn't one for nostalgia, and she doesn't strike me as the type to check things off a metaphorical bucket list, so her bland reason for wanting to lose her virginity to me because it's some rite of passage isn't the truth. The obvious direction I need to search is the circus. It makes me physically sick to my stomach for a few different reasons, but that sickness is always quickly replaced by fury.

I'll still fuck her regardless, because now that she's offered herself up to me on a silver platter, the voices demand that virginal sacrifice, or I'll claw my own fucking eyes out and devolve into madness. I'll tame myself for her benefit, but hiding who I really am from her won't last long. She'll know every facet of me, just as I'll know all the darkness in her. My soul feels alive at the prospect.

"Yeah, you said we needed to go, so I asked her, and she said yes," I grunt. We pause at a branch in the hallways, Cash needing to go to the music wing, and me to the science building. He's mad, but he'll get over it.

"Fine, whatever."

The warning bell rings through the halls, and a few stragglers begin to run. Cash turns on his heel and marches away. With a sigh, I turn to leave as well, prepared to reminisce more on our conversations last night. The breath stills in my lungs as I do, my eyes clashing with muddy hazel ones, a sickening spark in her gaze.

Miss Goss, the guidance counselor.

"Teddy," she says, beaming, her teeth and mouth theatrically large, her body slender but curvy in all the right places. With her thick mane of light brown hair and the way she dresses—professional, but tight—she's every boy here's wet dream.

Except for mine.

"Hey," I say, dodging around her before the late bell rings. Her claws dig into my arm as I attempt to pass, and I pause, sucking in a deep breath through my nose to calm the voices in my head that beg for her death.

She blinks up at me, then nods her head back toward the front office.

"We have a meeting scheduled. I already emailed Mr. Anderson."

My teeth grit, and my stomach writhes, Eden's eyes flashing in my mind. The way she'd looked up at me in the library yesterday, so timid but determined, so trusting, so innocent—it made my bones *ache* to hear that note of desperation in her voice. Of everyone here, she entrusted her innocence to *me*.

I wish that could be something we shared together, the exchanging of our virginity.

I blink again, and Miss Goss' eyes come back into view. I have to fight the urge to vomit. This fucking cunt is the reason I can't share that with Eden.

The bubbly counselor turns and clacks her heels back down the hall, and I have no choice but to follow.

Sophomore year, Brant's old buddy Jeremy filled my locker with cod, and when I'd opened it, the slimy fish had ruined the new shoes my mom had bought me. Still young, still finding it hard to control the voices, I'd beat him in the hallway within an inch of his life. Fearing I'd end up in prison, I'd been awaiting the wrath of Dick.

But Miss Goss had gotten to me first.

At sixteen years old, I'd lost my innocence in her office on a chair hundreds of other students occupy daily. And for the rest of my time here at Prep, I've had meetings with her once a week, her finger always on the metaphorical trigger. *I'll tell everyone you raped me, I'll file a police report about your aggravated assault on Jeremy, I'll bury you, you're eighteen now, what does it matter?*

That last one was said to my face two short weeks ago. It fucking matters, and it matters even more now that I want no one in this life but Eden. As I follow Miss Goss into the office, I can't help but to shake the feeling I'm about to betray the girl I'm falling hard for. Rage so overwhelming that it blinds me seeps into my veins, and the voices begin to seethe.

Kill her. Strangle her until her eyes pop out. Slit her throat with the scissors on her desk. Make her watch you take the life from her in that mirror on the back of her door.

All grand ideas, and it fills me with a sense of peace as I allow them to speak, each voice distinct and forceful. They know her time is soon, and so being patient and enduring this is the smallest bit easier.

The office doors shut quietly behind us, phones ringing and a printer whirring while the thick scent of black coffee permeates the air. Through the glass windows, a few late students slink by in the hallway, but Mrs. Smite is quick to catch them.

"You have mail, Megan!" one of the office ladies quips to Miss Goss.

"I'll get it after my appointment. Thank you, Dotty," she says, voice sickly sweet. We continue down a back hallway to her office at the very end. A dank, cramped space I'm sure she detested until she figured out she could rape me and get away with it. I'm no stranger to enduring hellish circumstances, I just have to wonder (with what little hope in me remains) when they'll end. When will my life just be...peaceful? And by that time, will I even be able to enjoy it, as fucked up as this journey has been so far?

She allows me in before she follows, shutting and locking the thick oak door. The chair—the seat and back of plush leather, the arms of sturdy wood—jumps out at me, so stark and filled with such detestable memories. Even the scent in here— some sort of vanilla lotion with hints of sugar—makes me sick.

Slipping my book and binder onto her desk, I sit dejectedly, praying like every time that I've somehow developed erectile dysfunction. I was so angry at myself the first time, so furious with my body for betraying my soul in such a way. Now, I'm just resigned.

She giggles behind me, giddy at having me all to herself in her lair. Like every time, she kicks off her heels, pulls up her too-tight skirt, and straddles me. Reaching her hand down between us, she cups me, rubbing me until I begin to harden. I look anywhere but her face, my fingers gripping the arms of the chair so hard I hope they break.

"Relax," she breathes, voice fanning over my face, her curtain of hair obscuring my view of anything but her. When our eyes catch, I see nothing but hedonistic desire and raw lust in hers, along with a predatory glint. Her jaw clenches, a flicker of anger behind her eyes. She always threatens me, uses her power to manipulate and control me. *Not much longer, I* promise the voices. Maybe I'll cut her up into little pieces but keep her alive so she can watch as maggots devour them. That wouldn't make up for the three years of molestation, but it would at least quell that particular festering wound.

Her fingers fumble with my zipper, but she eventually frees me, coaxing me until I'm hard enough. My eyes slip closed. I refuse to make a single noise as she sinks down onto me, instead biting my tongue until I taste blood. She moans quietly in her sickening ecstasy, and every muscle in my body tenses as I fight the urge to pin her by the throat against the wall and choke the life out of her.

"God, you're so...big...so good," she breathes, bouncing on my lap, simply using me to masturbate. Bile rushes up my throat, bringing with it the plain, stale bagel I'd grabbed from the counter this morning before I rushed to catch the bus. I focus on that, on my morning, how I raced home at the crack of dawn to shower and eat and change after I ensured Eden was safe. It annoyed me, not being able to watch her get on the bus to school, but seeing her in the hall running to class soothed that worry away.

"Fuck, fuck, fuck."

She bounces harder, faster, and for the first time in three years, when she climaxes, I don't. Shivering as she comes down from her stolen high, our eyes meet. Instantly, I go soft inside her, and her brow crinkles, fear rippling across her forehead.

I sneer, hand lashing out, fingers curling one by one around her throat as I lift her off of me and stand. She tries to gasp, her eyes bulging, her legs kicking and hands clawing at my arm as she sways by her neck, my hand the noose. My vicious smile grows, her skin turning pink, then red, then as purple as Eden's eyes.

My Eden.

"Someday, I'm going to kill you," I swear, a newfound

strength residing in my bones, a new reason for me to fight, to stay alive.

Eden. Mine.

Miss Goss' mouth gapes as she struggles to remain conscious. I know I'll leave bruises, but I don't give a fuck anymore. I see it in her eyes, know she believes my threat, especially as she dangles in the air.

Slowly, I bring her back to earth, and she wrenches away from me, clutching her desk and gasping in heaping lungfuls of oxygen.

"You...you're...done," she rasps, a pathetic attempt to threaten me. So quickly she doesn't fight it, I lash out and grip her hair, pinning her with my body to her desk, smashing her face into the wood.

Her terrified eyes find mine.

"I have bigger problems than you now," I hiss. "You're going to die at my hands. And not even the Devil himself will be able to stop me."

FOURTEEN
EDEN

THE DAY FLIES by in a blur, with not many chances to speak with Teddy. So as I stand in the drizzly Seattle spring, hood pulled up, I don't notice the dark figure next to me right away. When he speaks, I jump, clutching at my racing heart, glaring at him.

"Decide on a place yet?"

His smirk broadens at my fear-stricken face. Exhaling slowly to calm myself down, I say, "No...well, maybe."

He quirks a brow, and over my shoulder, I can hear the bus approaching as it splashes through the puddles. My raincoat traps the heat my body is suddenly exuding in his presence, and my skin becomes clammy. Those eyes of his are dangerous, not just because they're beautiful, but because they see everything you don't want them to see. He's kind of a genius, and that's scary, too. His classes are all AP, and he's nipping at my heels for valedictorian. It's only because he failed gym freshman year that he hasn't surpassed me.

"That sounds like a yes. Your place?"

The reality of what we're about to do soon settles in my

stomach like a rock. My cheeks heat further, but I quickly shake my head. Our bus pulls to a stop, and I board it without hesitation. Teddy follows silently, a cocky smirk still plastered to his lips. Lips that will probably kiss me, right?

God, I've never even been kissed before. *Way to jump right off into the deep end, Eden, asking someone like Teddy Poe to fuck you.* Something tells me he wants to devour me whole, and I don't know whether to be frightened or...turned on?

Sinking into the hard plastic seat in the very back, Teddy follows and traps me against the window, pinning me with his dark presence. I keep my hood up, avoiding his prying questions, disgruntled that I have to answer them in the first place but acknowledging that I dug this grave myself.

Sort of.

Dick and Daniel handed me the shovel.

"Eden," comes his sultry voice, a hint of humor winding around the syllables of my name. I like the way it sounds, coming from deep in his chest and out through his perfect lips, and my cheeks flame to life anew.

Reaching down into my bag, I produce a notebook and a pencil, flipping it open to a blank page, scrawling down a set of coordinates I have memorized, and ripping the sheet from the metal rings. Folding it a few times, I glance around before handing it to him. Daniel's threat about remaining a virgin until I'm forced to give it to some shady fucker is a constant warning bell in my head. I can't take any chances. Asking Teddy to do this puts us both at risk, but I'm selfish enough to go through with it despite all of the unknowns.

His long, deft fingers pluck the paper from my hand, and he snorts as he unfolds it, glancing at the numbers and degree symbols. Brow furrowing in annoyance, I glare at him. Those stunning eyes of his dance, his black hair damp and pushed back, long on the top and shorter on the sides.

He holds up the paper between his fingers, smirk growing. "What are we, Seal Team Six?"

Crossing my arms, I sink down in my seat and deepen my glare, the bus bumping along the pothole filled streets of Seattle.

"There's no address for it," I hiss, feeling surly. He tucks the paper away in his own bag, leaning back.

"Fine. I like a challenge, anyways."

Biting my lip, I keep my eyes on the window, watching droplets of rain streak down the panes, my heart fluttering constantly, my emotions at war with the logical side of my brain. What we're doing could get us both a one way ticket to a lifetime membership at the circus. It could end my father's life before I graduate. It could land me in jail. I'm not sure what dirt they have on Teddy, if any, but guilt gnaws at the frayed edges of my heart for dragging him down into this with me.

We both stew in silence for longer than normal. Teddy usually can't go thirty seconds without pushing my buttons, and after a while, I glance at him, unfamiliar concern swirling in the depths of my empty stomach.

His arms are crossed, his jaw clenched, and he glares straight ahead, something...something really, really dark lingering in that unyielding gaze. It's sort of frightening, the magnitude of it, and I'm not sure why, or who it's directed at, but my anxiety forces the words past my lips unbidden.

"I'm sorry," I whisper.

His eyes slice to mine so quickly it stuns me into stoney stillness. My heart stops, blood cooling in my veins. His brows pull lower over his eyes as he studies my face. After a moment, he shakes his head, dispelling some of that hellish darkness from a moment before.

"For what, Eden? You have nothing to be sorry for."

Fiddling with my hands, I shrug, holding his gaze. "I...kind of forced you into this, and it was stupid, and I'm sorry—"

I'm cut off, his hand lashing out quickly, fingers pinching my cheeks and palm resting over my lips, halting my words. He continues to stare deeply into my eyes, his grip tightening more each second, and heat flares through me, my heart restarting and forcing that congealed blood through my veins.

"No," he says, the word delivered quietly but forcefully, his teeth clenched. Before I realize what I'm doing, I nod against his grip, acquiescing to his undeniable power. A slow, sinuous smirk crawls onto his lips, and he releases me. "I'm sorry. Today was just...a little shitty, but it's better now."

"Oh," I mutter, relief flooding me.

He crosses his arms, holding my gaze with a bemused expression on his face. "Cash is mad I asked you to prom."

"*Oh*," I say again, this time with a shocked raise of my brows. After my interaction with Cash's mom, I find it surprising that he's upset, but the longer I stare at Teddy, the more it begins to sink in, and my brows raise even further.

"Oh...is he...was he wanting to go with...you?" I ask, the suggestion there. Being queer in Seattle is quite accepted, but Seattle Prep is a different story. Teddy chuckles, shaking his head and raking his hand through his hair.

"Not in that sense, no. He's just...protective of our friendship. It's been us two for a long time, and he's thinking about leaving in the fall for boot camp."

"You know," I hedge, smoothing down the pleats of my itchy wool skirt. His eyes follow the motion like a cat hunting a mouse. If he had a tail, I'm sure the end would be flicking, his instinct to pounce overwhelming. I don't understand his newfound interest in me, and maybe it's because of the circus, or maybe it really is because we're both freaks, but I'm starting to like the way he looks at me. I like the way he notices the little things, and I need to stop liking it now before it festers in my soul and grows into something more. "We don't have to go to prom."

He rolls his eyes, casually throwing his arm around my shoulders. Warmth seeps from him through my rain jacket, and I shiver, enjoying this closeness and his intoxicating scent far too much. I shrug him off with a glare, but he's still grinning, unperturbed by my obstinance.

"Yeah, we do. Rite of passage, and part of our little deal."

"I told you, I don't have a dress."

He sighs in annoyance and rolls his eyes again. "Do you have amnesia? I told *you*, I'll take care of everything."

"How are you going to convince Dick and Daniel to let us have Saturday off?" I fire back, looking for any way out of this part of the deal. I'd almost rather spill the real reason I asked him to fuck me, if it means not being paraded around in front of my bullies, more fodder for their fires.

He taps the tip of my nose coyly, so flirtatious now it makes my head spin and my heart race.

"That's for me to know, and you to find out."

FIFTEEN
TEDDY

"SWEETHEART, I know you're eighteen and what I'm about to say will likely fall on deaf ears, but you've got to stop staying out until the crack of dawn," my mom chastises, cupping my face and smoothing her thumb over the growing bags under my eyes. Steaming cup of pitch black coffee grasped in my hands, I flash her a grin meant to appease her, but her frown just deepens, and her thumb trembles against my cheek.

She knows—I feel it, her smile as well as my own fading. Clearing my throat, I nod to the steaming plate of scrambled eggs she just whipped up.

"I don't think the passengers are going to appreciate eggs, mom."

She smirks, spatula in hand as she piles a heaping scoop onto my plate, adding two slices of buttered toast and pushing it toward me. "Dick—I mean, Richard, is letting me take the car to the grocery store today. Figured I could give you a ride. Unless you're too cool to be seen with your old mother?"

I roll my eyes, pulling the plate toward me and spearing the fluffy yellow eggs, shoveling them into my mouth. I'm always starving, my metabolism insanely difficult to keep up with, but I'll never tell her that. She fights for every morsel we put into our mouths, and I'm not about to stress her out more than she already is.

"Mom," I say, swallowing down my second forkful. She waits, fist on hip, smiling gently at me. "I could never be too cool for you."

Her eyes shine.

"My sweet boy," she says gently, and I know she's seeing me as I was when I was little. She comments on it often, how quickly time flies, how I morphed into a man in the blink of an eye. She's terrified to lose me, no matter how many times I tell her I'm not fucking going anywhere.

It's not her fault that every man in her life was a fucking disappointment aside from me.

Before things get too heavy, I grin at her. "I need a dress for prom."

Slowly, confusion creeps onto her face, and her brows pull together. "Honey...no offense, but I don't think a dress will look good on your frame. I'm sure I can make you something, though, if you really want it."

I burst out laughing, that feeling of lightness bubbling up in my chest, and she grins as well, relieved that she hasn't hurt my feelings. "Thank you for always supporting my queerness, but no, it's not for me."

"Oh?" she asks, coy smirk on her lips as she leans on the counter across from me, abandoning her spatula for her own mug of coffee. Normally, I'd be sprinting to catch the bus by now, but if I'm able to hitch a ride with her, I have plenty of time. I know I need to broach the subject of Eden with her at some point, because the plans I have for that girl...well, my mom will likely be seeing a lot of her.

"My...friend, Eden, she needs a dress. She won't go unless she has one, but she's refusing to get one."

"She's nervous, sweetie."

"I know," I say, taking a bite out of my toast and chewing quickly. "So I figure if we can make her something she likes, she won't back out at the last minute."

My mom's eyes are melting, pure and radiant joy etched into every fine line on her face. I know this is what she wants for me, some semblance of normalcy, and I know once she meets Eden, she'll be even happier. Plus, my mom is excellent at sewing, so it shouldn't be too difficult, what I have in mind.

"Well, I'll need her measurements, and you will have to help me."

"Perfect. Can we have it by Saturday?"

She drops her head with a chuckle and shakes it.

"My son, ever the worst procrastinator," she mumbles. But when she glances back up at me, I see it, hidden there in the eyes that match mine.

Sorrow, and relief.

Sorrow, because no matter what, we're still stuck here with Dick, me more so than ever before. But relief, because for the first time in my life, I'm doing something *normal*.

My fingers tap my mug, the ceramic cooling as the liquid does. Our mutual smiles fade at the same time, and I glance down into the inky coffee. "I'm sorry for worrying you. I've... been following her. Eden."

When I glance back up, she's staring at me, a guarded look to her eyes now. She knows about my...extracurricular activities, but she's never once tried to stop me, or asked any questions regarding my murderous streak. She seems to intrinsically know it's something I can't stop, but something I control by only taking out the worst of them.

With a heavy sigh, she reaches for the pot of coffee and

pours herself another steaming cup, leaning back over the counter and clutching it with both hands this time, leveling me with that lips-pressed-thin look that means I'm about to get a lecture. Leaning back and crossing my arms, I brace myself.

"How would she feel if she knew that, Theodore?"

Not the full name, but still bad enough. I smirk, knowing precisely what Eden would say, and also knowing the exact shade of red her cheeks would turn. "She'd threaten to murder me, but she'd secretly like it."

The corners or her mouth quirk upward, but she fights it, nodding sagely.

"What makes you think anyone would like to be stalked?"

I can't keep the biting grin from my lips. When it unfolds, my mother doesn't react like anyone else. She's completely unfazed by it. Others—even Cash—have fear deep in their eyes when I smile like this, when the voices are whispering detestable things in my ear. But she knows me better than anyone ever will, and I don't scare her in the slightest.

"It's Eden. You'll understand when you meet her."

"And what will her family think of you?"

My grin broadens.

"Her dad will love me, obviously. But...uh...well, he's sick," I say, frowning at the end. Her eyes soften.

"Sick?"

"Terminal cancer."

The early morning light filtering in through the kitchen window above the sink is bright and orange, painting my mom's face the shade of a tangerine, and bathing everything else in a warm glow. Robins chirp. The rumble of the garbage truck down the road grows closer. Everything is still in this moment, and for some reason, I feel the need to commit it to memory, my mom's hand trembling on her mug as her eyes glass over.

"She's lucky to have you then, sweetheart."

And it's then that I know in my soul, I'm going to lose my mom, too.

I just pray I can give her the freedom she deserves before then.

SIXTEEN
TEDDY

"SO...I need to borrow your car. Today. Preferably the beginning of lunch."

Cash raises an eyebrow, leaning his shoulders against the locker next to mine. Per usual, I've already spotted Eden, and can relax slightly now that I know she's safe.

"Where are we going?"

I grimace at him, trying and failing to appease his growing glare. "We are not going anywhere. *I* am going somewhere...I just don't technically know where it is, yet."

We turn, walking down the hall again, same as yesterday. Today is already off to a much better start. Miss Goss' car was missing from the lot this morning. She's either taking me at my word and is terrified, or she's ruminating on all the ways she'll try and fail to ruin my life while the bruises on her neck heal. Either way, I'm decided and set in my decision, and the voices chitter excitedly in the background of my brain; a constant noise but one I don't think I could live without at this point.

"Is this a Teddy thing, or an Eden thing?" he asks, annoyance hindering his tone near the end. I glare at the side of his face but remain truthful.

"It has to do with Eden, yes."

His head whips in my direction, and though he's still glaring, his eyes are melting. At a glacial speed, but melting all the same.

"So you're taking her to prom...she works at this shithole adult club with you...her dad is dying...what haven't you been telling me?" he growls, knowing there's more. There's always more to the story with me, and he's learned that. I don't want to embarrass Eden by telling Cash, but who is he going to tell?

We pause, about to separate for the morning, and I sigh. "Look, she asked me to do something...private, with her, and my stipulation was that she go to prom with me first. Don't pry, asshole. I think this has to do with those two fucks."

He's frowning at me, but I can see it in his eyes, the hurt he feels for her. Cash has always been empathetic, something I fail at. He grins suddenly, elbowing me.

"Not one to pass up the chance, huh?"

My lips press together, and he sobers. "She's...*mine*, now. So if she has to deal with me and my...impulses...then I'll be damned if I don't treat her like a queen."

He shakes his head but his smile remains, a touch of sadness and resignation in his eyes.

"Fine, weirdo. We're a package deal anyways, so she better be cool to me."

I grin.

"Don't worry. She still hates my guts."

Just hopefully not after Saturday.

THE DRIVE to wherever the fuck Eden is sending me is long, the highway mountainous and winding, each side of the road ensconced by massive pines and evergreens. I'd searched the coordinates on a school laptop during chemistry this morning, printing out a map to follow as though I'm a pioneer on the Oregon fucking Trail.

Cash's Mustang rumbles smoothly through all the hairpin turns, and I have to grip the steering wheel and grit my teeth to prevent my toe from pressing down harder and harder on the gas pedal, the temptation to let it fly making my skin itch. I'd never take advantage of Cash like that, though—risk wrecking his baby. Plus, I need it on nights when my hunting takes us out of city bounds, Cash always happy to get stoned and wait for me to kill whoever the voices have deemed worthy of death by my knives.

As I round the next bend, a small, quaint village comes into view, and a light drizzle patters against the windshield. *Hangman Hollow, Population 328*, the worn wooden sign reads, the white paint delineating the amount of people that reside here chipped and flaking away in the Olympic weather.

A small, warm smile creeps onto my face.

Wherever Eden is leading me, it has her soul written all over it. The perfect amount of mystery and darkened peace.

Once I'm through the town, it's another five miles until my turn. The road grows more and more narrow, the elevation climbing enough that fog begins to cling to the trunks of trees, the sun hiding its face from whatever is lurking in these haunted woods. The silver clouds above roil with heavy, impending rains.

Eyes skirting to the map on the passenger seat again, I nearly miss the turn, no sign pointing me in the right direction, just a light break in the trees. Slamming on the brakes, I skid across the wet pavement, tires squealing. Alone in the desolate woods, I stare down the bumpy, rocky dirt road and wince, praying the suspension in his 'Stang can withstand this leg of the journey. The trees and undergrowth are so thick that no light permeates the canopy to paint the forest floor below. A sinister warning crawls its hundred legs down my spine as my eyes adjust to that darkness, a flicker of something ghostly white a ways down the road dissipating into thin air.

Shaking myself loose, I grin. It's just the fog. But I wouldn't be scared if it were something more, and neither would Eden.

Just another reason she is meant for me. No other girl would give me coordinates and make me work for something she is offering up. No other girl would play into my predatory side and send me on a scavenger hunt to make our tryst perfect. How she discovered this place, so far out from the city, is a question I need answered. I want to crawl inside her mind with her, harbor all her darkest secrets and twisted fantasies. And if she doesn't have any, then I'll share mine with her.

Slowly, I turn the wheel, edging the nose of the Mustang off the highway and onto the foreboding path before me. The map shows a red dot about four miles down the snaking road, and I take it slow, splashing through puddles of mud, cursing to myself because I know Cash is going to make me wash his prized possession.

At some point, it grows so dark beneath the thick trees that I have to flick on the headlights. Their glow bounces off the dewy ferns and moss-coated tree trunks. I'm met with more gauzy fog, but no other hints of phantoms. It feels as though the forest is holding its breath, everything pulling back with hisses as I willingly wander nearer their macabre home. By the time I have half a mile to go, I *feel* their eyes on me, the pitiless eyes of hundreds of souls. Some are curious, others bat shit crazy, and the worst are like mine; evil.

My chest feels as though a stone tablet has been laid upon it. It's so heavy here, and the closer I get to this unknown location, the harder it becomes to breathe. As though all those lost souls are pushing against me, begging me to turn around before it's too late. Some, however, entice me, lure me in because they want me to join their legion of the dead. But then, the trees thin, some semblance of humanity still awaiting nature's brutal reclaiming. A long, wrought iron fence materializes out of the darkness, and my toe presses down a little harder on the gas pedal as sick excitement builds in my chest, fighting against that heaviness.

And there it is, a massive break in the trees and the gate to an abandoned insane asylum.

My heart positively soars, the gray, cloudy day casting eerie shadows in the empty, gaping windows. I roll to a stop in front of the gate, stone pillars keeping the wrought iron upright on either side. Spires pierce the sky above, and dead ivy winds between the bars. It's absolutely huge, this place, so derelict and sorrowful and terrifying all at once.

But I am Teddy Poe, and ghosts never scared me.

SEVENTEEN
TEDDY

MY BOOTS CRUNCH over broken glass and all manner of debris as I cross the threshold of the asylum and stand in the foyer. Hands in my pockets, I grin, tilting my head back to take in the high ceiling above me. Goosebumps litter my skin, the chill in here enough to make my breath cloud in front of my face.

So we will need a few sleeping bags. *Check.*

Like a giddy kid in a candy store, I explore every nook and cranny of this place for hours. I won't make the bus ride to the circus with Eden, but I trust Cash will keep an eye on her, per our agreement. If I'm not back, he takes her downtown. That peace of mind gives me the freedom to conjure up some truly horrifying ideas of what I'd like to do to this space, were it to ever become mine.

Certain rooms are calm, others childlike, and some downright vile. At one point, the patter of little running feet can be heard above me. Though it is unnerving, the sound is innocent. Just a little ghost excited for a friend. There's a permanent smile stuck on my face, my heart racing and alive for the first time in so many years. Ironic, to feel this way amongst the dead, but I never claimed to be normal.

Eventually, I settle on the perfect room. Three floors up, facing the front gate, the windows busted out, which creates the perfect view of the mountains in the distance. Watching a sunrise from that vantage point?

Well, someone's getting morning sex, that's for damn sure.

I'll have to have Cash help me bring up a mattress or some shit. And candles. Lots of candlelight to set the mood. Mind lost as I put together what I think will be a really fucking good night with Eden, I meander downstairs, aiming for the basement. Jogging down the ancient steps with the small beam of my flashlight flicking left and right, I see him at the last second, a grizzled man dressed in rags, his blue eyes pale, surprised. I should've known there'd be squatters here. I'll have to clear the building on prom night, but Eden won't have to worry; she's far safer in this phantasmic building with me than anywhere else in the world.

"Fuck, sorry, man," I say, skidding to a halt so I don't smash into him.

But for the first time in my life, my heart stops from unrelenting fear alone. In the time it takes me to blink, the man is gone.

Somewhere upstairs, a woman screams.

I make it downtown with minutes to spare, grinning as I pull up to the sidewalk, Cash and Eden standing outside the door that leads into the circus. When Cash sees his car, his eyes widen, and his hands spear his hair, fingers tugging on the ends. Killing the engine, I get out and grin, winking at him as I toss him the keys. He purposely misses, letting them crash to the sidewalk with a metallic *clank*. Shoving my hands in my pockets, I rest my ass against the cherry red hood.

"You're washing it," he growls.

"I know," I say, winking, unable to keep my eyes from assessing Eden. She stands in her uniform, her hair down and playing in the wind, arms crossed and cheeks pink. Her glare could melt the ice caps, and I have to wonder what they were chatting about as I pulled up. Quirking my brow at her, I say, "Yes, dear?"

"Where were you?" she demands icily. Her ire warms my cold heart, and I catch Cash's coy smirk. She can play at being mad all she wants, but we both know she was concerned. I'd made sure Cash knew not to divulge my whereabouts.

"Were you worried about me, baby?"

Her eye twitches, and her alabaster cheeks turn as red as Cash's Mustang. I have to bite my lip to prevent my smile from growing.

"I told her not to worry, but she wouldn't leave me the fuck alone," Cash jests, forgetting his muddy car for the time being. She glances between the two of us, stewing in her annoyance, that long, silky hair so shiny beneath the clouds. Imagining her exploring that place—St. Ignatius, I'd discovered—is fucking sexy as hell. To have no fear of the dead, to seek out refuge in what was once a place of nightmares? She's damn near perfect.

"You asshole. I just asked where he was one time."

Cash smirks at her, arms crossed. "Once every five minutes."

She makes a disgusted sound, throwing her hands up and attempting to stomp past us, but my hand juts out, and I catch her bicep, spinning her toward me as I stand to my full height. Those alluring violet eyes clash with mine, and I melt beneath her enraged stare.

"Let go, asshole," she growls through clenched teeth, a little black kitten ensnared by her wolf.

"Admit you were worried."

She attempts to shake herself loose, a touch of worry

appearing in the corners of her eyes when she realizes yet again how strong I am. In the wind, her scent wafts to me, something akin to lavender and rosemary and rain. Earthy. *Witchy.*

"Not worried. Annoyed you had Cash following me everywhere. He threw me over his shoulder and forced me to get on the bus with him," she seethes, reddening even more in her embarrassment at the memory. Cash laughs, the sound deep and rich, and I catch his playful eyes over the top of her head.

"Thanks, man," I say. He nods with a proud grin.

"Of course. Sorry about the whole skirt thing, Edie."

She stamps her foot and tries to twist away from me again, to no avail. When my eyes catch hers, she's fuming. "Everyone saw my ass when he tossed me around like a damn rag doll, and now he thinks it's okay to call me *Edie.*"

"Duh. You're Teddy's. Which, by proxy, means I'm your new big brother."

Warmth floods me. I knew Cash would relent once he spent a few minutes with her. But my eyes search hers, resignation swimming in the depths of those amethysts, her body relaxing in my grip.

"I'm not Teddy's," she says, with far less ire and conviction in her tone this time. Cash snorts, swiping his keys from the dirty concrete.

"Yeah," he says, striding by us to the driver's side door, casting a long glance at Eden. "Good luck with that, Edie. When he wants something..." he trails off, and her eyes flick between mine and my best friend's.

"Then I get it," I whisper, her body trembling at my words.

"Fine. Whatever. Can we go now?"

"Only if you promise to be my pickleball partner again tomorrow," Cash quips. I snort.

"Damn. Bummed I missed that."

She rolls her eyes, and my fingers begrudgingly loosen their grip on her skinny arm. I keep my hand there all the same, for feeling the warmth beneath her jacket after seeing that fucking ghost is helping to calm me. I'm not one to shy away from the dead, obviously, but...I've never experienced anything like that before. It's chilling and confusing but also super fucking cool all at once. If we could ditch the circus tonight and go back out there, I would in a heartbeat.

Fuck, if we could *live* out there? My mind floods with the endless possibilities. I'd hunt her through those haunting halls, chase her through those wistful woods. The thought of catching her, both of us breathless as I forcefully take what's mine, holding my knife to her slender throat as I fuck her—

"See you two lovebirds tomorrow."

Cash's voice rips me from my dark fantasies, and Eden's cheeks and neck pinken anew, her eyes narrowed as she searches my face.

As though she can read my mind and see all the dirty, kinky fantasies residing there.

"We're not lovebirds," she growls, finally wrenching herself free of me in my distracted state, my cock growing harder by the second. And in these atrocious khaki slacks we're forced to wear, she will definitely notice my dick print if I don't calm down. I'm allowed to be arrogant in that realm, at the very least.

I know I have a nice cock.

One that is now Eden's alone.

She storms away, yanking open the metal door and disappearing into the void that is attempting to suck our lives dry like a vampire. I glance at Cash, and he must see the happiness morphing into fury on my face. His brows pull together, his lips pressed into a thin line.

"Where did those coordinates lead?" he asks, an attempt to distract me from my darkening thoughts.

My biting grin flourishes like the brandishing of a quill.

"To our future home," I say with conviction. He grins.

"You've got it bad, Tedster."

My smile fades, because he's right. I do have it bad. I've never been obsessed with someone like this before. It's entirely new and dangerous territory. I have no idea what I'm truly capable of, but I know in my bones I'd do fucking heinous things for her. *To* her.

I just hope that when this all ends, she'll still be holding my hand amidst the flames of our lives.

Not a ghost haunting those halls and my soul for eternity.

EIGHTEEN
EDEN

TEDDY FLIPS his knife into the air, catching it by the blade with utter precision before he flips it again, and again, and *again*. We're waiting for Vic in the ring, always practicing under his watchful eye. I stand with arms crossed near the back wall watching Teddy, my soul festering, annoyed at the lack of an explanation for his disappearance today. I know *why* I'm annoyed, but I'm not ready to broach that topic with myself yet.

I'd rather hate him just a little bit longer before I sink into the temptation he presents, before our lives become inexplicably intertwined.

"I loved it," he says finally, his voice velvety smooth and deep, and I catch his eyes through the dusky light, the teal seeming to glow at me.

"Loved what?" I grumble, shifting from foot to foot, anxious to have any of our conversations overheard. Dick and Daniel are holed up in their office, probably plotting my demise. A few of the girls pace around the ring, Chastity casting me a glare every chance she gets now. She's made it clear she's attracted to Teddy, and the lack of attention he gives her makes her even more venomous towards me. I can't help it; it's not like I asked for him to sink into some weird obsession with me.

Cash confirmed it today, though, during our pickleball match against Brant and his partner. Said something about Teddy being protective of me. When I'd asked why, Cash had stood straight, paddle dangling from his hand, confusion on his pretty face. *"Because he's fucking obsessed with you?"* He'd said, as though I were clearly missing out on something and very stupid because of it. We hadn't spoken about it again, because in his distracted state, Brant had directed a hit right to Cash's temple.

Thankfully, the hole-ridden plastic ball hadn't done much damage. I'm still annoyed with him for picking me up like a sack of potatoes and flashing my plain white underwear to everyone in the vicinity of the bus stop, though. It's strange, having two people—I *think*—I can now consider friends. I've been alone for so long, just me and my sick dad. The day the courts sided in his favor, he'd taken me home, and I'd watched a movie with him for the first time in well over five years.

But at the end of it, he'd held my hands in his and told me about the cancer, promising to fight it to the bitter end.

Teddy saunters toward me, his eyes alight with mischief, and the look digs its claws into my soul. He belongs here. Not at the circus, per se, but in all the darkened corners of the world, on the very fringes of society where evil and good meet, brushing against each other in the moonlight. I've always found comfort in darkness.

Maybe that's why I find comfort in him.

He leans a shoulder against the wall, eyes tracing my face as his smile slowly unfurls. "Your coordinates."

A jolt of heat hits my heart and fans out, centering between my thighs. The days draw ever-closer to Saturday, to prom and our agreement, and every day, I grow a little more terrified and a lot more...turned on.

"Did you...what did you think? Will it work?"

His canine teeth appear, his smile growing.

"Oh, it will work alright."

I can't help my own smile, feeling assuaged at his response. It may have been a bit of a test, one I had a feeling he would pass. I don't think I'll ever share my secret with him, how often I find myself there, going from room to room, speaking with the dead.

I still remember being punished as a five year old, shoved into a dark closet, my mother locking the door and barring it. She'd expected me to be afraid, to cry and scream and beg to be let out. But I'd sat down and listened, and my world became something entirely new. The voice at our old house on that farmland in Oregon had been soft and quiet and sweet, a little old lady who hated my mother and would always do things to frighten her.

Flicker the lights. Scoot glasses off the counters. Open the cupboards. Being so small, she knew it wasn't me, and I watched with smug satisfaction as my favorite ghostly friend drove her mad.

I'd sobbed the day we moved, and my life has been hell ever since.

"Not too...strange?" I ask nervously, though I sense I shouldn't be. Teddy seems to like the same things I do. When I thought of losing my virginity to him, I knew I didn't want it at my home, or his, or some random hotel. I wanted it to be in a place where I'm at peace.

He shakes his head.

"No. It's perfect. How'd you find it? I couldn't find any records."

My smile slips from my face, and I flounder for an explanation that will make sense and satisfy his genius. Gaping like a fish, I jump as Vic approaches me from behind. I whirl, thankful for his interruption.

Because how would I explain to Teddy that the reason I found that asylum was because a ghost visited me?

"Alright kids," Vic rasps. Teddy's eyes simmer in annoyance at the interruption, but I spin toward Vic, beaming to hide my strike of fear. I've never told anyone about the ghosts, not even my father. People think mediums and clairvoyants are insane. Which, maybe it's good I'm willingly putting myself in an asylum, but that's besides the point. "Today, boxes."

My shoulders drop and I whine, "No, Vic, c'mon!"

Teddy glances between us, arms loosely crossed.

"Boxes?"

Vic grins, a skeleton with prominent teeth and terrifying eyes. "Aye, boxes. Miss Clemm will be theatrically chopped in half by you."

Teddy's smile is sinister and sexy all at once, and I glare at him.

"Sweet. Hop in, Edie."

"Stop calling me that," I hiss, indignant. Cash can get away with it, but I don't need Teddy thinking we're going to become closer than we already are. Even if that's what I undeniably and annoyingly want, I know it's something I can't have. I need to lock that desire away in my heart until I'm free of this hell.

Vic chuckles, brandishing a saber, and I stride away from them and toward the boxes. I hate being stuffed in them while Vic practices, but he's usually quick. Teddy being new to this will take longer, and I have to wonder if I'll suffocate.

But the moment my foot graces the step that will lift me into the box, the wretched voice of Dick calls down the stairs, stilling the breath in my lungs. "Teddy...Eden, upstairs, please. *Now.*"

TEDDY'S SHADOW BLANKETS ME, and in the chill of the office, I shelter myself beneath it, feeling cocooned and safe in his presence as he stares down Dick and Daniel. Peeking up at him, I watch in fascination as his jaw flexes, his gaze brooding and dark, his brows pulled low. I can feel it, the way he leans slightly toward me, as though poised to strike out at the threat with one hand and shove me behind him with the other.

For the first time ever, I'm fighting a smile instead of tears in this room.

Dick clears his phlegmy throat, bringing me back to reality. Daniel, standing dutifully behind his disgusting father, plays on his phone. Whatever Dick is about to say, it can't be too bad if he's not involving himself.

"Tara let slip you were going to prom this weekend. With someone named *Eden*."

My heart becomes encased in ice and ceases beating. Before a panic attack sets in, Teddy speaks with grace and fluidity and a touch of that threatening darkness.

"Yes. We are. I wanted to go and figured you would like me to take Eden."

Every eye in the room is on Teddy, and confusion muddles my thoughts. What the fuck is he doing? Dick chuckles and shakes his head.

"Why in the hell would you think I'd want that?"

"Because you're not taking that experience away from us, and I figured you'd want someone to keep an eye on her. She's about to bring in a pretty penny, isn't she?"

Daniel's arms slither loose and fall to his sides, and Dick

goes pale before an angry, mottled red creeps up his wrinkly neck.

"You insolent little freak," Daniel seethes, turning his glare to his father. Dick holds up his hand, his eyes studying Teddy.

"I should've known," he hisses. Teddy's smirk is arrogant as hell. "What else did you find?"

Teddy brings his hand up, flipping his palm over to study his cuticles nonchalantly. "Not sure. But I wouldn't chance it by making me mad and not letting us go."

Dick is about to turn purple and spew like a volcano, and the beginnings of a panic attack have my hands trembling. What is Teddy doing, playing with fire of this magnitude?

"You've exiled me to a school that can't accept men liking men. I *want* to go with Cash. Eden is my cover, and I'll make sure she doesn't do anything...untoward. Feel like it's a win-win, right, Edie?" Teddy says, glancing down at me, mirth hidden in his gaze that only I can see.

Slowly, giving him my trust in this moment, I begin to nod.

"Yeah...Yeah," I say, clearing my squeaking voice, looking at Dick. "My dad kept...pestering me about going. I couldn't tell him about...working here, so..."

Dick grits his teeth.

"Fine," he seethes, pointing a gnarled finger at Teddy's chest. "But I'm warning you now, if anything funny is going on, then it's *her* I will be punishing, not you."

Rage rolls off Teddy in that instant, so potent it's tangible, an entity of its own. My body recoils in fear instinctively. I know Dick doesn't mean me, but the person he is referencing is unknown.

Whoever it is, they must mean the world to Teddy, and my anxiety only grows. After a long moment of the two staring each other down, Teddy speaks, his voice low and rumbling like thunder across the Puget Sound. "Careful who you threaten, Dick. Because once she's gone, so are you."

He turns on his heel and strides out, leaving us all in the wake of his unrelenting fury.

I may have my secrets about speaking with phantoms, but something tells me he has his own secrets...

And I think it *also* involves the dead.

NINETEEN
EDEN

I'M awoken by a warm palm slipping over my thigh, fingers curling inward and gripping me possessively, his sultry voice in my ear as his lips brush against my skin. I shiver at the intimate touch, and as I fully wake, the screeching of brakes disrupts the peaceful slumber I just found myself in.

"It's your stop, Eden."

Swallowing back my drool, I lift my heavy head from none other than Teddy's shoulder, a wet spot left behind on his soft, dark gray hoodie. Immediately, my cheeks flame, and my eyes zero in on his hand that's still gripping my thigh. Through his pale skin, tendons and veins snake along the back and wind their way to his wrist before disappearing up his sleeve. I wonder his thoughts on tattoos, because he'd be even more beautiful inked and covered in the darkness that he seems at one with.

Wiping my lips free of drool with the back of my hand—my heart still hammering—I move to stand, but he keeps his hand on my thigh. When my eyes clash with his, they're positively murderous. "I'm walking you inside tonight. Don't argue with me."

In that instant, I become a frightened little girl again, needing her dad to chase away the monsters under her bed. I've been alone in that double-wide for a year, and sure, some nights I get scared, but I'm an adult now. Except for when Teddy looks at me like this, demanding my obedience. My body gives it to him before my mind can keep up, and I nod dumbly. He doesn't smile, or acknowledge my lack of fight, but instead stands and extends his hand to mine. Again, without a thought in my brain, I slip my hand into his, and he laces his fingers through mine, warmth seeping from him to me.

We exit the bus, my mind still in a fog from being so soundly asleep and awoken in such an...*erotic* sort of way. We walk slowly and in silence down the street, turning sharply onto the abandoned dirt road that leads to my home. Teddy seems to know the path even in the darkness, and I realize he's probably followed me a few times. Why that makes my underwear unbearably wet, I'm not sure, but it does, and I begin to tremble. I lie to myself and peg it on the chilly, damp air.

No lights guide our way, this part of Seattle beyond rundown. Empty homes weep at us as we walk by, their inhabitants the ghosts I'm fond of or addicts passed out for the night. The silence between us grows thick, as though he wants to say a lot but is instead biting his tongue. It makes me nervous for a few different reasons, especially after that meeting in the office.

The white picket fence surrounding our quaint home comes into view amidst sweeping pine boughs, the grass within wildly overgrown. I never learned how to use the lawnmower before my dad got sick, and I've done my best to keep this place up all on my own, but it's exhausting when there's so many other things I have to do.

We pause outside the gate, and I glance up at the side of his face, chewing my lip. His eyes narrow on the house, but he's not scrutinizing the broken screen door, or the siding that needs a powerwash. His eyes are on the front window, and he's as rigid as a German shepherd poised to lunge. Something flickers in his gaze, his eyes widening slightly, and he pushes me behind him. In the next breath, the glint of a long, deadly knife strikes my eyes, and my breath catches in my throat.

"Keep your eyes down and only walk where I walk," he whispers, and raw fear courses through me.

"Wh-what?" I breathe, glancing around his tall frame, but he shoves me gently behind him, stern and forceful but still soft enough not to hurt or scare me.

"Eden," he warns, voice taking on an authoritative edge. That's all it takes, that tone, so deep from within his chest. Hearing my name spoken in such a manner has my spine stiffening. "Grab my sweatshirt and keep your eyes down."

My trembling hands obey, fingers curling into the fabric as I breathe in his scent. He takes a step forward, and I can barely see our feet through the darkness, clouds scuttling in front of the moon and blotting out our only source of light. He takes another step, each one so carefully measured that he makes no sound. Is he even *breathing*?

The silence he is capable of is unnerving. Before I know it, we're on the small stoop, and the asshole is slipping my key from its hidden spot beneath the fourth piece of siding to the right of the door. Despite the fact there may be some murderous lunatic in my house, I pinch the skin of his back through his hoodie, a reprimand for him clearly stalking me and knowing how to enter my home. I suppose I am partially to blame for not being more alert about my surroundings and discreet about where I keep my key, but still.

He makes no show of pain, and the door swings open slowly, the blackness of night pouring out and spilling onto our feet. I do listen and keep my eyes down, now, because I may not be afraid of the ghosts who haunt my home, but I have always been afraid of people.

When he takes a step forward this time, I hesitate to follow, the dark gray fabric stretching out between us. But then the thought of being left out here alone forces me to follow, for I'd much rather be safe next to Teddy than a sitting duck, and then it sinks in; he's having me follow him for a reason.

In every horror movie, the boyfriend tells the girlfriend to stay put and he will go be chivalrous and take out the bad guy. And nine times out of ten, the monster is already there, ready to strike once she's alone. Teddy forcing me to come with him, to keep my eyes down...he trusts himself against whatever could be in here, trusts that in a fight, he will win, so he'd never risk me by leaving me outside.

Teddy is prepared to kill to ensure that, and then his prowess with knives sinks in. I mull over these thoughts as a distraction from my fear. I can acknowledge that I am afraid right now, but that I'm also sort of just...numb. Because the most frightening person in here is the one wielding a knife, the one who went to an abandoned asylum alone and said he *loved* it.

I'm beginning to hate how perfect he feels to me, as though I am a puzzle missing an integral piece, and he is it. As my heart begins to race for new reasons, we clear each room of the house until we eventually stand in my small kitchen. He flicks on the light above the sink and slides his knife onto the counter, the sound grating after so much quiet.

I release him, stepping back and blinking away the harsh light. When he comes into view, his jaw is still set, but his eyes are...haunted.

"I saw someone through the window," he all but whispers, holding my gaze so tightly it feels like a rope anchoring a ship in a storm. Dread fills me, and then awe, because if he can see things, too, then he really *is* perfect for me.

"No one's here," I hedge. "I live alone."

"I know."

My brows drop over my eyes in a deep glare, and I cross my arms.

"*How* do you know that?"

He waves his hand dismissively in my face before pulling at the ends of his hair. "Not important right now. I *saw* someone, Eden. A figure. In your house."

I chew my lip, feeling as though he's accusing me of something. I'm not sure what, though.

"Maybe you're seeing things? We're tired—"

His eyes slit in my direction, awfully accusatory, and I hug myself tighter.

"Why would you suggest that?"

Shit.

"Umm...because we're tired, and it's been proven that people see things when they're tired—"

He snaps his fingers at me, his teal eyes burning. It's like I can see the synapses firing in his brain. It makes my head hurt, but it's also fascinating, watching him figure things out, skipping the thousands of other steps normal people have to take to finally make it to the right conclusion. He is a genius, and that is terrifying.

"But, see, I wasn't tired at the asylum and I still saw *him.*"

"Him?" I parrot, now utterly lost. Maybe he hadn't figured me out...

"The ghost, Eden," he says flatly, his unwavering stare pinning me to this spot, as though my feet are encased in blocks of concrete. My eyes begin to water, my heart thumping a little harder the longer we stare one another down.

"There's no such thing as ghosts," I say, jutting my chin up, feeling insolent. The way his grin flashes immediately, his eyes taunting me, makes me petrified. All of my bravado slips to the floor, along with my erratically pounding heart.

"Filthy little liar," he hisses, towering above me, his presence suddenly as consuming as night itself. I take a step back, fear coursing through me. He follows, his step heavy and meant to be heard this time. "Why do you like it there, Eden?"

I shake my head, about to part my lips and spill a lie, but he shakes his head, and takes another step forward. Backing away, I hit the cupboards behind me, trapped.

"I just do."

"That's not normal," he says, cocking his head at me in his scrutiny. He's playing with me, because he already knows these answers. He just wants to make me admit it, wants to wield his power over me to force my darkest secrets from my lips. The genius in me admires him for it, but I won't make it easy for him.

"Normal is subjective."

"Stop denying it."

"Denying what—"

"That you can see them. The dead."

Ice becomes my veins. He's sadistic, the way he enjoys jerking my emotions around like this. Like a cat bouncing a befuddled little mouse between his paws.

"Teddy–"

"I saw *him*," he says again, eyes ignited. "And then he disappeared. *Poof.* Gone."

"*Who?*" I yell, dropping my fists to my sides in anger. Lips twisting, he reaches behind my right shoulder, plucking a magnet from the fridge. Shoving it into my line of sight, the faces in the photo register. Me, grinning outside the courthouse the day I was given to my father. And my dad, hugging me back, proudly beaming.

"And I just saw him, here, now."

My fingers are numb with cold, but I reach up, clutching the popsicle stick frame, taking it from his hand. Rubbing my thumb over my father's face, tears well in my eyes. How in the fuck can Teddy see someone who hasn't died yet, but someone who is close to death?

"Eden?"

My eyes bounce to his, and I smile softly, so confused, yet so amazed at the same time.

"He's my dad. But he's not dead."

TWENTY
EDEN

MY FINGERS ARE WRAPPED TIGHTLY around the steaming mug of chamomile tea, my feet tucked up under me as I sit in my nest of pillows on my bed. I'd pushed the small twin sized mattress into the corner of my room, right beneath the window, so I could watch the wind play in the trees, and so during Christmas, I could see the lights my father used to string up around the outside of the house. In the dimness of night, my eyes sweep across my quaint, clean room, to my open door and the hallway beyond. Light seeps out beneath the bathroom door, the sink running.

I don't know how it makes me feel, having another man here besides my dad. I've never had friends to bring over, let alone a boyfriend. It feels a little taboo, wrong. My dad would be furious if he knew I had one here now. But considering how Teddy comforted me after everything?

He had reached behind me and plucked my chipped mug from the cupboard and set about making me my favorite night time tea. I'd pestered him, demanding him to admit he's been watching me, but he'd only smirked and told me to go shower.

Hair still damp, I curl further in on myself, nestled in the corner of my bed, my back against plush pillows held up by the joining of my familiar walls.

The light in the bathroom shuts off. Through the impending darkness, Teddy appears in my doorway, still wearing his hoodie and black jeans, his sleeves pushed up to reveal the sinuous muscles of his forearms. When our eyes clash, he smirks and strides into my room, pulling out the chair from my desk, spinning it around, and plopping down onto it, resting his arms along the curved back. His eyes dance and shine as they hold mine; if he were a dog, his tail would be wagging, his tongue lolling.

He's far too happy after what he just witnessed, but I think it has to do with the fact that he's here in my room and I'm not throwing shit at him and screaming for him to leave.

"Sleep, Eden."

My brows furrow in consternation at being told what to do, and resistance claws its way up my throat.

"No."

"We have school tomorrow. I'll stay up."

"What? Why?"

He cocks his head, smile fading. "To keep you safe."

"From what?" I growl. He rolls his eyes, tearing his gaze from mine and searching my room. Cautiously, I sip my tea when he isn't paying attention, disgruntled that he made it just right. It had been sinfully sexy, watching those deft fingers rip open a tea bag, coil the string around the handle of my mug, pour the steaming water from the kettle into it. He makes everything physical look so easy and graceful.

"From monsters," he quips, eyes returning to mine, smile snaking onto his lips. I'm exhausted, but I'm too keyed up, having a boy in my room for the first time. He seems so out of place, but also...not. Maybe he appreciates the My Chemical

Romance posters, or the *Nightmare Before Christmas* snow globe on my desk that dad bought for me.

"Admit you've been stalking me," I grumble with much less ire than I was hoping to infuse into my tone. Two can play his little game. But he flashes me a grin, unperturbed in the slightest.

"I have been, yes. Promise I haven't seen you naked. Scout's Honor," he says, holding up his three middle fingers to his forehead. My cheeks positively flame, and my oversized band tee becomes a tent, trapping in my body heat. He shrugs. "I'll see you naked on Saturday anyways, though."

My teeth grind.

"Says who? Maybe I want to keep my...my shirt on..." I say, trying and failing to be as obstinate as him.

I know, deep in my soul, there could never be another Teddy Poe.

He laughs, those lines around his perfect lips forming, throat bobbing. In my exhausted state, I can't help but smile with him, albeit timidly.

"You're more than welcome to. I hope you know I'm not going to force anything..." he trails off, eyes searching mine. A drop of adrenaline sinks into my belly, moving lower and lower until I'm subconsciously rubbing my thighs together beneath the stifling blankets.

"I know," I mutter hotly.

"You're still nervous, though."

"Of course I'm nervous," I snap. His eyes continue to hold mine, and my hands begin to tremble. I grip the mug tighter, attempting to hide my anxiety and arousal. It's so confusing, to feel so many things in the presence of one person. The fact that Teddy can make me feel anything besides fear or loathing is a testament to who he is as a person, and of all the people I could've chosen to lose my innocence to, I'm thankful it was him.

"What are you most nervous about?"

Dropping my eyes to the murky tea water, I shrug, fiddling with the papery tab at the end of the string.

"Pain?" he suggests. I peek up at him, gnaw my lip, and shrug. I'm not about to admit that to him. Not about to journey along the road of my upbringing in a fucking cult and the sick man who hurt me. I know there are ways to pleasure myself...but every time I've tried, I get too nervous and wrapped up in my own head and I stop. When you're constantly told that sins of the flesh are especially immoral, you begin to think yourself dirty. For years, I knew I was destined for Hell because of those five hour long sermons we attended.

Now, I know I'm heading straight there...but Teddy will be right beside me.

"I won't ever hurt you, Eden. Not like that."

His voice is soft, his eyes swimming with desire and lust and a protectiveness I don't understand, but one that makes me feel warm all the same.

"I know," I whisper back.

"Will you tell me the truth?"

A lump settles in my throat, and I shake my head. I don't want to think about that right now. I'll face it after prom, after we have sex. But right now, I just want to be a teenager for once. He doesn't push for more, and I'm thankful.

"Will you tell me about your dad?"

That lump grows, and I say, "Like you don't know. Cash's mom is his nurse. One of them."

He smiles blandly.

"I'd rather hear it from you. I want to meet him."

My brows rise in shock. "Wh-what? You what?"

He smirks. "I want to meet him. Preferably on Saturday. You'll meet my mom."

Curiosity piqued, I nod slowly. "Isn't she married to...to..."

His frown is filled with barely contained rage. "She is, but not by choice."

So Dick has his claws in everyone, it seems.

"I'm sorry," I whisper. I can't imagine how...hard life must be for him, having his mom be married to that piece of shit, now having to be at the circus with me. I can only wonder when Dick will force Teddy into a situation like mine, selling his body to greedy patrons. It strikes me, then, like lightning. No wonder Teddy never really stepped in when I was being bullied. He had a lot going on behind the scenes, and a lot he couldn't do because his filthy step dad teaches at our school. I don't forgive him, not yet, but it makes the last four years of his absence a little more understandable.

He stands lithely, gently pushing my chair back under the desk, eyes lingering on my books and trinkets there. A tattered copy of *Dracula*, a weathered piece of driftwood from Seaside, Oregon, and another book close to falling apart. It's that one his fingers brush over, the black cover with a single swirl of white cigarette smoke comforting and familiar to me.

"You read this a lot before bed."

I should be annoyed—disgusted, even—but being seen by someone for the first time—*really* seen—is addictive, and warmth pools in my lower belly. His eyes skirt to mine, and he grins softly. "What's it about?"

I shrug, taking a gulp of cooling tea.

"*Looking for Alaska*. The girl's name is Alaska. She's...kind of a misfit, but she's friends with other misfits, and they go to a boarding school."

He grins, plucking it from my desk and flipping it over. As soon as I was free from the hell my mother put me in, my dad took me to the bookstore and let me buy anything I wanted. I'd never read anything like it, and the emotions it unearthed within me are nostalgic now.

Gently, he sets it down and glances at me. "Are you Alaska?"

I smile, shaking my head. "Why don't you read it and tell me?"

He nods. I don't have the heart to tell him how it ends, but there's something so beautiful about that level of tragedy. How one moment, life is flowing through your veins...

And the next, you're one of the ghosts that haunt me. I'm thankful he hasn't pushed that topic any further tonight, but I know it's coming, a conversation I can't avoid.

Distracted by my thoughts, I don't notice that he's standing at the edge of my bed, that he's reached behind his head to grip his sweatshirt and pull it over his frame. My mouth runs dry, eyes zeroing in on his abs, his shoulders much more broad than I initially thought. In a few years, I can see how those muscles will grow and fill out, a young man fully entering and embracing his masculinity.

"Scoot over."

"What? N-no!" I hiss, glancing behind him to my open door, worried for my father to walk through, something that I know is impossible. He snorts.

"God, Eden, I'm tired, too."

He plucks the mug from my hand and sets it on my desk, returning to me, fists pressing into the mattress as he cages me in. With our faces mere inches apart, I have a striking view of those eyes. They're even more devastating up close. My heart is hammering, pulsing in my ears and...down lower. A ball of fire is centered in my chest, burning straight through me, his teal eyes dancing and playful.

"We're sharing a bed on Saturday. Practice makes perfect and all that shit, right?" he teases.

"But...but..." I flounder. He chuckles, climbing in and enveloping me in his sturdy embrace, pulling me down until we're facing one another, my head resting on his bicep, one of his legs thrown over both of mine. His back is to the door, his body shielding me, and I sink into this moment, suddenly exhausted because I feel safe for the first time in so long.

For once, I'm not alone.

"See? Not so bad, right?"

I stare at his chest, inhaling his scent straight from the source, my head woozy, my skin sweltering. Ever since he agreed to sleep with me, it's like my body knows what's coming, and I've had to change my underwear multiple times a day just from thinking about him, or being near him. If his presence alone makes me wet...then what the fuck is Saturday going to be like?

Gently, he brings his hand up and cups my head, pulling me closer until I'm tucked under his chin, my fingers splayed over the warm, smooth skin of his chest. My eyes flutter closed as those deft fingers play in my hair, and I beam, thankful he can't see how much I am enjoying this, how much I've missed physical contact.

Goosebumps litter my body, the devastation of his touch a beautiful storm I am willingly trapped in. Slowly, our measured breaths sync up, and I begin to fall asleep, nuzzling closer to his protection in my dreamy state. The last thing I remember before I slip into peace is the soft rumbling of his deep voice, lulling me into slumber.

"Sleep, Eden. I've got ya."

TWENTY-ONE
TEDDY

Saturday.

"FUCK," Cash hisses, breathless as we drop the queen sized mattress to the floor. It thuds resoundingly through the empty, desolate asylum, a cloud of dust probably filled with mites and asbestos rising from the floor. Sweat dots both our foreheads, and with his hands on his hips, he flashes me a cocky grin. "Okay, fine, you win. She's cool. Wish I would've snagged her before you."

Crouching to push the mattress (one we stole from Cash's parents' guest bedroom) kitty-corner, I smirk up at him. "Snooze ya lose."

He grins, eyeing the room I chose to take her virginity in. Tonight. *Soon.* Just hours away. I've had a raging boner all fucking day, but at least carting this mattress up three flights of rickety stairs has exhausted me somewhat.

Falling back onto my ass, I reach for the plastic bag with the grocery store's logo emblazoned on the front, dragging it across the ancient wooden floors and fishing out the candles we bought down in Hangman Hollow. The cashier—an elderly woman a step away from death—had eyed us with knowing suspicion, as though selling a bunch of unscented candles of varying heights and widths was actually a common occurrence. I'm sure the town is used to teens and freaks using the asylum to attempt to perform seances, but I know none of them have succeeded.

Only Eden can speak with the dead, that I am damn sure of, and quite fucking attracted to as well.

"What time am I picking you two up?"

"Early," I mutter, standing with a candle in each hand, eyeing the space like an artist before a blank canvas. Who ever would have thought that I, Teddy Poe, would be stressed about candle placement, but here I am. I need this to be perfect for her. "We gotta get back soon. I still have to help my mom with the dress...and convince her to buy us strawberry wine."

Cash, sticking his head out the window and looking down, pulls himself back in and gives me a queer look. "Why the fuck would you wanna drink that sugary paint thinner?"

Nestling a few candles in one corner, I scrutinize my work, satisfied enough for now. Stalking past him, I grab a few more and place them on the left side of the windowsill. "Because. I read her favorite book, and the girl buries strawberry wine around their boarding school at the beginning of the year. Brilliant, I might add. We should've buried some flower by the fieldhouse."

Jaw slackened, he stares at me and nods slowly. "Dammit! That would've been so fucking convenient. Why did you ever try to talk me out of being friends with her?"

His grin is shit-eating, and I smirk, brushing back past him to fill the other corner of the room with candles.

"Asshole," I mutter.

Above us, the creak of footsteps echoes, starting off slow before pounding down the hall and then stopping just as suddenly. Cash's eyes widen until the whites are all I can see, and he slowly tilts his head back, gazing at the ceiling in horror. I snort.

"What did you expect? It's a fucking asylum."

"How...how did she find this place?" he whispers, morphing into a frightened little boy. I shrug, standing tall and using my toe to scoot the candles closer together. Good enough for now.

"No clue. She won't tell me."

"You sure that isn't a squatter?"

I grin, patting his shoulder and gripping it as I pass by. "Trust me. I was fucking thorough the other day."

On cue, the faint giggling of a child drifts to us from down the hall, and I smile, not scared in the slightest. She's playing with us, I think, or at least that's the vibe I'm feeling. A little girl stuck wavering between this world and the next, happy to have new friends.

"Fuck this shit," Cash hisses, grabbing his keys and all but running away. But I stay for a moment, closing my eyes, breathing in the scent of rot and decay and misery. On the breeze through the open window, the tang of the ocean is potent on my tongue. We're near an inlet, I think. I'll have to ask Eden, because I'm sure she's found a path to it, probably knows more about this place than the people who worked here a century ago.

Because I know that little shit can talk to ghosts, she's just too scared of me judging her to tell me.

Slowly, I take a deep breath in, allowing the oxygen to

expand my lungs as I open my eyes. I'm met with nothing but an empty doorway, early morning sunlight streaking in through the busted out windows. Disappointment deflates me, and my shoulders drop. Ever since seeing the ghostly visage of her father, I've been keen to see more. She at least explained he was alive, but wouldn't give me much more information that next morning on our bus ride to school.

I'll meet him today anyways, something I'm actually nervous for. If he's about to leave this world, to leave Eden behind, I need him to know that I'll take care of her.

So with a sigh, I gather the empty bags and make my way out after Cash. The rumble of his Mustang reverberates through the cavernous building. Shaking my head, I snort and start down the hall, a chill fanning across the back of my neck. When I turn and glance down into the dark, gaping emptiness, I see nothing.

But when I glance down to the floor, a set of tiny, bare footprints are etched in the dust.

"TADA!" My mom says, stepping aside to reveal the dress she's been slaving over for days now. She holds her hands clasped near her mouth, nervous for my reaction, but she has no reason to worry. My brows shoot up, my eyes widen, and a beam splits my cheeks.

"Fuck," I breathe, reaching out to run my fingers over the fabric. Hues of crimson and black jump out at me. The top is fitted, akin to a corset, and from the hips, gauzy tulle flares out, the crimson peaking through. Around the top of the bust is more tulle, adding flare to the chest but also shielding bare skin. I know Eden doesn't want to be flashy in that sense.

So naturally I had to have my mom make her the dress from the *Helena* music video, only it's somehow better than the real thing. I hadn't bothered asking Eden her measurements, because one, she wouldn't know them, and two, she wouldn't tell me if she did. I'd simply...rifled through her room sometime last week after we made our deal. Someday, I'm going to buy her underwear and bras that actually look comfortable and aren't purchased at the same time as buying your groceries.

"Fuck, it's perfect," I say, grinning at my mom. She beams back, relieved and excited.

"Oh, good! I can't wait to meet her, honey."

Reaching for her, I pull my mom into a hug, resting my chin on her head. She squeezes me back, patting my shoulder.

"She's...important, mom."

"I can tell," she says against me, voice muffled by my shirt. When we part, her eyes are glassy with pride. "Which is why I have one more surprise for you."

Brows furrowing as she turns and rummages through a bag, a bittersweet sort of melancholy forms in my chest when she produces a black and red corsage and matching boutonniere.

"Mom," I chastise, taking them from her. "That's way too expensive."

The rose is ebony, the lace and ribbon bloody, and it will look stunning on Eden's pale, slender wrist.

"You get to go to prom senior year one time, sweetheart. Let me spoil you a little."

I don't bother telling her the extra money I had lying around was from a recent kill.

Grinning sheepishly now, I hedge, "On that note...I need you to buy us alcohol."

I say it with surety and conviction, and she immediately frowns, hands fisted on her hips. I gently set aside the flowers and grip her shoulders, driving my eyes into hers. "Just one bottle. Just some strawberry wine. I promise not to spike the punch," I say, holding up my pinky finger. She swats it away.

"Theodore," she says, a warning note to her tone.

"Please?" I beg. "I'll find a way to get it no matter what, so you may as well just make it easier for me. It's...a special surprise for her."

Now, she quirks her brow and crosses her arms.

"What does her father think of this?"

"Stop being a parent just for tonight," I plead.

"You don't just quit being a parent, Teddy. You...you two... ugh," she growls, cheeks reddening.

Oh, god.

My mom and I are pretty open with one another, but that whole sex talk? No fucking thank you. I had to make Cash buy me condoms today, too, and he'd argued with me for forty-five minutes, saying there was no way I needed Magnums. I'd eventually threatened to show him my dick, to which he raised his brows at enticingly, but he'd finally relented.

"I promise not to drink and drive or get anyone pregnant, so can you just buy the wine and stop torturing me?"

Burying her face in her hands, she shakes her head and laughs.

"My God, Teddy, who made you so blunt?"

You did, because you never fucking speak your mind or stand up for yourself.

But I don't say that, because I've said it many times and it only ever hurts her feelings. Sighing, she purses her lips and glares up at me. "You won't be home tonight then, I'm assuming?"

"No..." I mutter. Her lips thin.

"I'm never doing this for you again, understood?"

Biting my bottom lip, I grin and yank her into another hug. "Understood. You're the best."

She squeezes me harder this time.

"Just treat her right, no matter the circumstance."

My eyes slip closed, and I hug her to me even tighter, knowing where she's drifted off to in her mind.

"I promise, mom."

And I mean it.

TWENTY-TWO
EDEN

"THANKS FOR THE...RIDE..." I mutter, distracted as Teddy's house comes into view. Cash rolls to a stop at the curb.

"Don't mention it," he says. "But do mention to that fucker that the amount of miles I'm putting on Giselle for his sake is getting a little out of hand."

I have to rip my eyes from the beautiful home, all brick and white trim, the landscaping immaculate. Cash is grinning goofily at me, the big brother I never had or wanted. I hate admitting I've fallen for his charm, too, and I can see why him and Teddy are so close. Reaching over, I pat his arm and smile softly.

"Trust me, I'll make sure he repays you tenfold."

He winks at me. "Knew I liked you. I'll be back at five."

Anxiety curdles the toast and coffee in my stomach, but I broaden my smile and nod, popping the handle and jumping out. He's quick to drive away, tires squealing on the wet pavement, and I'm left alone on the curb, so nervous I could puke. Nervous, because the clock is ticking away the hours until I have sex with Teddy. Scared, because I'm about to meet his

mom, and he speaks so highly of her, I know she's super important to him.

And terrified, because when Cash picks us back up, our
first stop isn't the gymnasium of Seattle Prep. It's the hospice
center where my dad is slowly dying, and I'm about to introduce a guy I really fucking like to him.

So taking a deep breath, I step off the curb and into the
grass, striding across the lawn in a beeline to the front door, my
finger punching the bell before I can talk myself out of this.
Bouncing on my heels, praying Teddy answers, the door
unlocks and slowly pulls open. Why does time always seem to
stand still in these anticipatory moments?

I'm met with his eyes set in a beautiful woman's face, her
hair as inky as his but beginning to gray. She beams at me,
ushering me in with a wave of her hand. "Eden, come in, come
in, sweetie. Teddy is just showering. Not sure what that boy
gets up to, but he was covered in dust this morning."

I follow her in, my heart racing so quickly I might actually
faint, and the moment my feet grace the pristine white tile, I toe
off my shoes with haste.

"S-sorry, sorry," I say, bending to pick them up, cradling
them to my chest like they're my child.

She laughs gently, giving my arm a squeeze before she rubs
her hand gently up and down in a calming manner. She really
is stunning, an age old, classic type of beauty, like Audrey
Hepburn. I can see where Teddy gets his looks, and my cheeks
flame to life at the thought. I feel grimy, wearing my oversized
band hoodie and holey skinny jeans, my hair thrown into a
sloppy bun atop my head.

"Come on in. Would you like anything to drink, eat?"

I'm starving, but I'm just going to pretend I'm not.

"Umm...no...no thank you," I say, obediently following her

to the massive kitchen. Everything is so clean, so neat and tidy. I wonder if Teddy's room is the same.

Pausing awkwardly at the end of the counter, I wait and watch while his mom goes to the fridge and produces a jug of lemonade and a tray of crackers, cheese, meat, and fruit. My stomach grumbles, and I hug my shoes tighter to my torso in the hopes that it muffles the sound. She slides the tray onto the counter next to a plate of fresh chocolate chip cookies, and my eyes begin to water.

It's...overwhelming, being around someone I've never met, but someone who is being so kind to me.

"I remember being nervous before my prom, too, and I made the mistake of not eating," she says, pulling the plastic wrap off the top of the meats and cheeses. "I fainted during the photos and ripped my dress. Don't make my mistake."

She pours me a glass of lemonade and holds it out expectantly. Chewing my lip, I bend and slowly place my shoes on the ground, taking the cool glass from her and having a sip. Sweet tartness paints my tongue and zaps through me.

"Thank you, Mrs. Poe," I say softly. She grins.

"Call me Tara, honey. The way my son plans to woo you, you may as well start calling me mom."

My eyes nearly bulge out of my skull, and I cough, stunned when I shouldn't be. Teddy had to learn his behavior from someone, and as Tara laughs, I know who it was.

"Mom, stop scaring Eden away."

I turn toward his voice sharply, my subconscious reaching out for him like a frightened child seeking their parent after a night terror. He ascends the stairs from the basement, toweling off his hair, wearing gray sweats and a band tee. My mouth runs dry, my eyes dipping to the bulge below his waistband before I can stop myself. It's...big. And I am just now wondering how the hell it's supposed to fit inside me.

Why did I even bother to wear panties if I knew they were just going to be ruined the second I laid eyes on him?

"I am not," Tara chastises, piling food onto a small plate for her son. "Eden, sweetie, is there anything you don't prefer? Teddy is about to steal you from me."

She points to the tray as my cheeks flame so hotly I begin to sweat, and I shake my head. She smiles, casting Teddy a coy look, and makes me a plate as well, only by the time she's done, mine is *heaping*.

Teddy takes both the plates, nodding his head toward the basement. "Don't worry, she's going to come bother us sooner rather than later anyways."

Eyes wide, I glance at his mom, wondering how she will react to his sarcasm. She just rolls her eyes, plucking a cookie from the tray and taking a bite. "I can still ground you, Theodore."

"I'd like to see you try!" he trills as he jogs down the steps, me sheepishly following. The basement is cool and dark, and he leads me down a short hall, taking a left into his room. Soft music spills from speakers that seem to surround the perimeter of his walls, the paint a deep, navy blue. His bed is larger than mine, an oak frame supporting it, a soft plaid duvet tucked neatly into the wood. To the wall directly across from his door is a desk, devoid of anything except for a lamp and a stack of weathered books. Posters and string lights cover patches of the walls, some bands I recognize, others I don't.

But the best, most comforting part is the scent. It's him amplified by a thousand, and I wish I could just crawl into his bed and sleep until all the dark and gory parts of my life pass me by.

I've never slept so soundly before the night he held me. Of all the things to look forward to on this day, you wouldn't think sleep would be a priority, but it is. To end such a momentous night in his arms in a place that brings me peace and comfort? I could think of nothing better, and for the first time in a long time, I feel content.

He slips our plates of food onto his desk and tosses his towel in a hamper near another door from which golden light and steam spills. He turns to face me, hands gripping the edges of his desk behind him, a sinuous smirk playing at his lips. "She likes you. A lot."

Swallowing hard, I cross my arms and nod. "Well...obviously. I'm sure the other girls you brought home were vapid and annoying."

His eyes dance like the blue flames at the bottom of a fire.

"You're the only girl I've ever introduced to my mother, and the only one I plan to. So no need for jealousy, baby."

Oh, god.

A tremble begins to take root in my core and flare out through all of my limbs. Why does he have to look at me like that? And say such things? Especially because...he can't really mean them, right? Bristling, I snap at him. "Don't lie to me."

He strides across the room, eating the distance between us in two steps, a voracious sneer on his lips that ignites something deadly in his eyes. Before I can even gasp, his long fingers have curled rather gently over my throat, and he walks us back until my shoulders hit the wall. Blinking up at him in utter shock, that mad glint in his eye slowly fades, hiding behind simmering annoyance. As though I just provoked the Antichrist, but something about *me* made him back down.

"I'll never lie to you, Eden. So remember that when I earn your secrets."

Gulping against his palm, I can do nothing more than nod quickly. When he gets like this, the only thought in me is to obey. In my past, I would have done so out of fear, but with Teddy...I do it out of trust. After what happened the other night, where he protected me, where I knew he was willing to kill to keep me safe, it's easy to trust him.

I'm free to fall, because he won't let anything happen to me.

He smirks, eyes flicking between mine, the storm clouds departing in his gaze and the sun shining through. "I'd love to keep you pinned here all fucking night, until you begged for me to stop, but we're on a tight schedule, little ghost. C'mon."

Head positively spinning as he turns away and walks nonchalantly into his bathroom, it takes my body a minute to react to those wanton words. My tongue feels thick, unable to move, my legs are trembling, and my nipples are as hard as they've ever been. The electricity that precedes a devastating storm crackles through my veins, and I follow without a second thought, addicted to this man in a way that I seem to know stretches even the most subjective view of normal.

TWENTY-THREE
EDEN

TEDDY STANDS between my dangling legs as I sit upon his bathroom counter. An array of makeup litters the clear spot on the other side of the sink, palettes of eyeshadow, all manner of tubes and sticks and brushes—all of which I never learned to use. Painted faces were for whores, my mother used to say. But she was so ugly, not even the most expensive shit would ever make her look better.

He pinches my hoodie, tugging it away from my body, and I glance down at it.

"What?"

"Do you have something easier to take off?"

My cheeks flame, and a strike of fear jolts my veins. He... wants to do this...*now*? He grins and chuckles. "No, goofball. Not like that. I just meant something that won't mess up my masterpiece when I'm done."

Even more confused, my brows pull together. "You...you're doing my makeup?"

He smirks. "What? Don't trust me?"

"No...just...surprised, I guess," I mutter, slipping my arms through the sleeves.

"I helped make your dress, too, if you were wondering."

I tug the hood over my head and peel my sweatshirt off, shivering on his counter in a plain black tank top. His eyes dance, but they never leave mine. Nervous, I fill the heavy silence. "Seems there's a lot to learn about you."

"Same goes to you," he says with a raise of his brows, reaching over to sort through the different brushes, fingers deftly plucking skin-tinted moisturizer and a sponge from the surface.

"I...I was thinking...since tonight is going to be pretty, umm, intimate...maybe we should ask each other questions," I suggest. I feel like we are doing this all backwards, having sex before we even know what the other person's favorite color is. I'm hoping this helps stem some of my nerves regarding tonight.

Maybe it will make him seem less godlike, and more human, and therefore less intimidating.

He smiles gently. "Deal. I'll even let you go first."

"Favorite color?"

He rolls his eyes with a chuckle, but brushes the tendrils of loose hair off my cheek with the back of his knuckles. My eyes flutter, heart racing in ecstasy, and I have to force myself to focus on his answer. "Black, obviously. You?"

"Blue."

He nods, blotting my cheek with the damp sponge. "Favorite flavor of ice cream?"

I smile, slowly kicking my feet to the beat of the metal music playing in the background. "Birthday cake. You?"

His smile is permanent, his eyes focused on his task, his breath minty as it fans across my face. "Coconut."

"Weirdo," I giggle. He laughs, pulling the sponge away.

"What? How the fuck is that weird?"

"Who picks coconut? It's so...obscure."

He brushes the hair from my other cheek. "Eden, it's ice cream. Stop psychoanalyzing me."

"Fine," I mutter. "Hmm...what books are on your desk right now?"

He pulls away slightly, dimples appearing near his laugh lines. "*The Art of War, Dracula, Looking for Alaska, A Midsummer Night's Dream,* and *The Turn of the Screw.* I only allow my favorites to be on the desk. You?"

My smile fades.

"You...you read that book? Alaska?"

"That's two in a row, but yes, I did. I see why it's one of your favorites."

My heart aches in happiness, something I didn't know was possible. "It's my *favorite*, favorite."

There's a heavy pause before he answers, our eyes locked on one another so tightly it feels as though if that invisible string were to snap, the world would end.

"How do you think we'll escape the labyrinth?" he asks softly. Sadness and deep melancholy transpires between us. He means the circus in our situation. I wish I had a better answer for him.

"I don't know," I say just as quietly.

"Do you trust me?"

His second question catches me off guard, but I nod silently.

"Will you tell me why you want this? Why you asked this of me?"

Ice pushes out all the lava that had just been flowing through my veins, and I shake my head, mouth opening and closing as I search for the answer. He deserves the truth, because it feels wrong to do this without telling him why. But if I tell him before, will he still go through with it?

I can't afford for him not to at this point. Dick scheduled my meeting with the man this upcoming Tuesday night. If I want any control over this situation, then tonight *has* to work.

"After," I whisper. "And that's four."

He cocks his brow and smirks, dismissing my rejection with ease and brevity, something I am thankful for.

"God, I guess I'll brace myself," he teases.

For the remainder of the process, I keep my line of questioning lighthearted, and he does the same. The amount of rich laughter that bounces between us makes my chest ache with how full my heart is. We have more in common than it seems either of us thought, and each time we answer a question the same, our laughter doubles.

"This is seriously you and Cash?" I ask, pointing in the direction I hear the music emanating.

"Yes. Why is that so surprising?"

"It's more...I don't know. Annoying," I mutter, trying not to move my face too much.

"How?" he asks, aghast.

"Because you're good at everything. You guys should seriously start a band," I say, being sincere. It shouldn't surprise me that his singing voice is even more devastating than his speaking voice. He dabs at my bottom lip with the pad of his thumb, stealing my breath with the intimate gesture. Our eyes lock again, but before I can get sucked into the black hole that is his gaze, he grins.

"Mom's coming."

On cue, Tara knocks on the door frame to the bathroom, a garment bag draped over one arm, a bright and kind smile on her lips. Her eyes widen when she takes me in. I haven't been allowed one glance in the mirror since he started, so I have no clue if he painted me to look like a damn clown or not.

"Oh, *beautiful*, Eden! Just like the photo of that dancer Teddy showed me!"

Brows furrowing, I glare at Teddy, who just smirks satisfactorily, smug with his work apparently.

"What did you do? What dancer?" I hiss.

"It will make more sense *after* you put this on." He reaches for the garment bag, but his mom pulls away slightly, a reprimand in her matching eyes.

"Nah ah. Out."

He smirks like the Devil himself.

"Mom," he says, gripping both her shoulders and giving her a gentle shake for emphasis. "I'm going to see Eden buck ass naked in like, eight hours, tops. There's no need for arbitrary discretion anymore."

"Oh my god, Teddy!" I squeak at the same moment his mom swats him.

"Theodore Alexander Poe, I did *not* raise you like that!"

His laughter follows him out of the bathroom, and his mother and I stare at one another with red cheeks and wide eyes.

"That boy," she mutters, hanging the bag on the back of the door and unzipping it to distract herself. Clasping my clammy hands together, I remain on the counter, unsure of what to do. The dresses I was raised in felt like wearing a burlap sack. I highly doubt whatever Teddy helped make for me is anything close to that.

Through the slit in the bag, black and crimson appear, tulle and silks and ribbons all unfurling out of the cover like a gothic waterfall. My breath stops in my throat as she fully releases it and steps to the side, revealing what must have taken hours—*days*—to complete. I only asked this of Teddy a week or so ago. He must've started on this that very night, meaning he knew precisely what I would want, what I would feel comfortable in.

Maybe he has seen me all these years. Maybe he was just stuck in his own hell.

"It's...beautiful," I whisper. She bites her bottom lip to hide her grin, though it is as wide as Teddy's, the two so much alike that I find it comforting.

"Hop down, let's make sure it fits," she says excitedly. For some reason, undressing in the same room as her isn't as awkward as I thought it would be, and I need her help zipping it, anyways.

I never had a mom who would be so kind to me, one who would teach me how to be feminine, one who would chastise me gently instead of beating me with a broom handle before locking me in the hall closet.

Once the dress is settled on my frame, she backs away and stares at her finished work, eyes overflowing with pride. Holding my arms out, I peek at her from under my new, long lashes.

"So perfect. Teddy knows you well, dear, look, look," she encourages, hands gently grasping my shoulders to spin me to the mirror on the back of the door.

And the moment my brain registers that the gothic, punk princess in the mirror is *me*, I begin to cry.

TWENTY-FOUR
EDEN

"YOU LOOK STUNNING," Teddy says for the fiftieth time, slipping his palm over my thigh and giving me a squeeze. The corsage on my wrist is heavy but exquisite, matching my dress perfectly. Peeking up at him, I smile softly, the sunset playing with his eyes, setting that teal ablaze. In the front seat of Cash's Mustang, Tara rides, the two chattering about the weather while my world tilts, shifts, and becomes inexplicably entwined with Teddy's in the backseat.

"Helena?" I ask softly, smiling. His fingers give another squeeze, and butterflies erupt in my stomach.

"Duh. May have been a little bit of a fantasy on my end."

My cheeks heat, and I turn away, staring out the window. His soft chuckle rumbles to me. But as we draw nearer the hospice center, the thicker the silence grows.

By the time Cash parks, my hands are trembling.

"We'll meet you two inside," Teddy says, and Cash salutes him, striding away with Tara, so debonair in his tuxedo.

Teddy, though.

When I glance at him in confusion, my mind becomes

befuddled all over again. He's sinfully handsome, sporting an all black suit and tie, the only red accent his boutonniere. His hair is slicked back, his keen eyes dancing at me through the sunset.

He turns, scooting a knee onto the tough leather seat, facing me as fully as the lack of space will allow. "Nervous?"

I shrug, stuffing down my emotions like hoping to fit your socks into an already overflowing drawer. No matter how hard I try, different feelings are going to escape and roll across the floor. "It's just...a lot, all at once. I'm not used to...having friends."

His eyes darken a few shades, and all traces of humor that normally surrounds that smart mouth of his are gone. At that moment, the sun descends behind Mt. Rainier, bathing us both in violet twilight. He clears his throat, reaching for my hand, his nails sporting a new coat of black polish. Boys aren't allowed to do anything deemed effeminate at our school, so this little 'fuck you' at the end of our senior year feels appropriate, somehow.

I wish he had put his snakebites back in.

"Eden...I know you're too sweet to hold me accountable for how I treated you these last four years," he begins, and my cheeks start to heat. "I'll never forgive myself for watching you suffer. There's no excuse good enough, other than I was self-absorbed and busy hating the world. I'll spend the rest of this lifetime, and every lifetime after, trying to make it up to you. And I hope you know that I expect you to keep me in line."

He flashes me a grin, and I answer it softly, my heart aching and tears clogging my throat. I'm going to ruin the striking masterpiece he created on my face earlier, smoky eyes and dark red lips to match my dress. But I tease him back with brevity, choosing to think happy thoughts until later, when ruining my makeup won't matter.

"I don't think I could keep you in line," I laugh, shaking my head. His eyes dance, never leaving mine.

"I think you're the only person alive who stands a chance."

My smile fades like the waning sunset, and something foreboding grips at my chest, sinking into my stomach. I feel like he's trying to tell me something, but whatever it is, I don't know. Not yet. But I think I will learn, and soon. This road we're heading down is fraught with peril and sorrow...I just hope there's an end in sight, and I hope that it's happy for the two of us.

"I'll do that," I say with a nod. "But..."

I chew my lip, ready to spill my own truth to him, no matter how much I think it will hurt him. "I don't forgive you. I'm...I'm not there, not yet."

He grins lopsidedly, his reaction unexpected but forceful.

"Good. You shouldn't. I was an asshole, and so was Cash, so be sure to make him apologize, too."

I snort, rolling my eyes.

"He tried during pickleball. Tied Brant's shoelaces together when he called me a freak."

Teddy bursts forth with more of that rich laughter I'm growing to love, and I smile back. He grips my fingers in his, giving them a squeeze.

"Will you do me the honor of introducing me to your dad?"

Feeling a little lighter, I nod.

"WOW...LOVEBUG, YOU LOOK..."

I shake my head with a light laugh, standing beside my father's bed, gaze forever searching his face. His eyes have sunken another degree, his cheeks paler and his hair longer, shaggier. But he beams with pride, tears pooling in his eyes.

Teddy and the rest are waiting outside the room, giving me a few minutes alone with him. I didn't think I'd need it, but I do, and I grip my father's weak fingers, sinking down onto the edge of his lumpy bed. "Is it too much?"

He smiles, reaching up to brush a strand of hair from my cheek. Tara and Teddy attacked my messy bun, curling my long locks before pinning them up, referencing the photo of Helena to get the look just right. "No, Eden. You're beautiful. And you're happy. I haven't seen you smile like this in...in a long time."

Again, I have to fight against the incoming tears that threaten to consume me.

"Yeah," I whisper, clearing my throat of the emotions lodged there. "Yeah I...I am happy. Why does that feel so wrong right now?"

He smiles at me, but there's sorrow in his eyes, as deep as any physical wound would go. "You feel the need to be sad for me, lovebug, but that's not what I want for you. I'm beyond happy, Eden. I've been so blessed to watch you become the kind, brilliant woman you are, and I can leave this life knowing that you'll be okay."

Tears cascade down my cheeks like a waterfall after a monsoon, and I can't respond. He squeezes my hand as tight as he's able, emphasizing his next words. "Eden, I want you to be happy. You deserve every good thing in this world after all you've gone through. And if that boy out there makes you happy, then that's all I could ever ask for."

"He does," I croak, smiling wanly through my tears before I laugh. That feeling of joy juxtaposed with so much despair is hard to swallow down. "He does make me happy. I think... you'll like him."

He rubs his thumb across the back of my hand.

"Let me scare him a little. I'll like him even more, then."

"Dad!" I laugh, dabbing at my wet cheeks. He grins, pressing the nurse button on his bedside remote. The line crackles.

"Nurse's station, what can we help you with?"

"Can you send in Betsy with that surprise, please?"

My brows furrow, and my stomach winds up like a frightened snake.

"Surprise?" I hiss.

He ignores me with a smile, but moments later, the door bursts open, and in marches Cash, proudly carrying three boxes of pizza. Behind him, his mom brings in a liter of soda and a polaroid camera.

And behind him, Teddy and his mom linger, Teddy holding something behind his back. Shocked, I stand, body trembling as my nerves short-circuit. When he crosses the threshold into the room, he brings forth a handmade poster board sign, the hues—black and red—matching the theme of the night with perfection. Glittery words jump out at me, along with two side profile faces of a girl and a boy—just like the album cover of my favorite band.

I'm not okay if you don't go to prom with me, the sign reads, and he holds it for me to see, grinning boyishly but proudly.

"Let's eat before I get shitfaced!" Cash laughs, sliding the pizzas onto a table and flipping open the lid. "Nice to meet you, Edie's dad!"

"You are *not* drinking tonight, Cash Michael Johnson, and if I find out you do, you can kiss that car goodbye," Betsy seethes in warning while her son just chuckles and stuffs his face. My dad laughs, *loudly*. Raw and radiant joy sparks in his eyes. He's never had so many visitors before.

"Kids will be kids," Tara says, glaring at the side of Teddy's face. He continues to hold my gaze, waiting for my answer. Heart near to bursting, I nod, stepping away from my dad's bed to lace our fingers together and pull him close.

"Dad," I say, voice wavering with nerves. "Dad, this is Teddy."

My dad grins softly up at him, sticking out his hand. They shake, and Teddy holds his gaze like a gentleman. "I promise to take care of her tonight, Sir. And every night hereafter, even if she doesn't want me to. I've learned she's quite the obstinate little shit."

"Teddy, my God," Tara hisses, shaking her head and hiding her face in her hands.

I bite my lip, unsure of how Teddy's...well, Teddy-ish ways will seem to my militaristic father. Everyone is silent for a heavy beat, and then his raspy chuckle shakes his thinning frame, and I breathe a silent sigh of relief.

"Good to hear, son. She's been alone for too long. And she is a little shit, but she's a...special girl."

Teddy beams, snaking his arm around my waist and pulling me into his warm side. It feels so good, his body next to mine, his scent strong in my nose, those sinuous muscles making me feel safe. My dad grins at us, eyes misting over. I reach for his hand, holding us all together as flowers bloom from the cracks in my heart.

TWENTY-FIVE
TEDDY

EVER SINCE I WAS A KID, I never longed for the past. For those glorious *good old days*. When I think of my past, I think of watching my mom go through fucking hell every single day. She taught me how to do makeup, because I used to help her cover her bruises. I didn't understand what they were from until I was a little older, but once I did, I stopped aiding her. Told her to leave that piece of shit sperm donor. But she never would, and I'll never understand, just as I'll never blame her for staying.

Nostalgia is a decrepit liar, painting the past in wide brush-strokes, muddying your view until you see the good and the bad becomes murky.

The theme of this year's prom is "Time of Your Life," like that Green Day song. And for the first time since I came into existence, I want to cement this night into my memory, want something to feel nostalgic towards when life becomes too heavy again, because I know it will.

It always does.

So as I pull Eden over the threshold and into the main gym,

silver, glinting streamers swaying in the breeze as innumerable bodies dance to popular music, I grin. And with each shocked face that turns our way, my smile grows all the wider. Eden's hand becomes sweaty in mine, but I give her a squeeze and glance down at her.

"They're going to love ruining our lives on Monday," she whispers, voice timid and just barely rising above the noise from the speakers. She glances up at me.

"So let's fucking ruin theirs tonight."

She beams, ethereal and radiant, more alive than I've ever seen her before. Cash sidles up to us, effectively ruining the moment as he tugs on his lapels.

"I'll see you two at..." he checks his watch theatrically. "Eleven sharp. We have a long ride ahead of us, and I need to go find Brant's girlfriend. She owes me a BJ."

"Juniper?" Eden hisses. Cash just winks and strides off, and Eden turns her shocked and questioning stare up to me. I'm thankful this has distracted her from not wanting to be anywhere near these assholes. I only feel a little bad making her go to prom, but I couldn't pass up the opportunity to show everyone the girl who is *mine*.

"Hmm?" I ask, quirking my brow at her. She swats me.

"Teddy, you know. Tell me."

"Didn't think you were one for gossip, Miss Clemm."

"That's...this is not..."

I watch her flounder, my smile growing, the voices gnashing their teeth in preparation for tonight. I haven't stroked my dick once since she asked me to fuck her. I'll do my best to hold back tonight, but I doubt I'll be able to completely.

She'll just have to be a little sore tomorrow morning. And the next morning. I'll lick it better, though, and bottle the tears she cries.

She stamps her foot in annoyance, bringing me back to reality, all of my fantasies evaporating, and I wink at her.

"Cash will share when he's ready. But he is smart, and he may have...blackmailed her."

Her pretty little mouth pops open in shock. Before she can pester me for more answers I'm unwilling to give, Brant strides up to us, shock on his face before he full-on belly laughs, everyone in our vicinity pausing to look. Again.

"Look, everyone! The freaks made it!"

No one truly reacts to his antics, other than to whisper or give us glances of disgust. He turns back to us, still laughing. "Shouldn't you two be jumping off a bridge or something right about now?"

"Nah," I say, squeezing Eden's hand and pulling her past his taunting face. "But if you're not nice, Branty boy, I'm sure karma will be pushing *you* off one."

He stares after us in confusion, one too many hits taken to his poor brain. Dragging Eden to the punch table to help soothe more of her nerves before I ask her to dance, the eyes of all the chaperones lining the wall now stare at us in surprise. Dick's beady little pupils glint with annoyance as they catch sight of us, but he bought my lie about being into Cash easily. Heard him discussing it with Daniel, saying how despicable being homosexual was.

Funny, that he hates what he is.

"Punch?" I ask, but Eden is staring out at the dance floor, her body tense. She's terrified of their judgment, their jokes, their pranks. I can't blame her. Fuck, I even blame myself, but now she has me in her corner. Now, we're almost out of here, and she won't ever have to worry about petty shit like this again.

I'm not sure if that's a good thing or a bad thing yet though.

She glances at me and nods, biting her lip. Fuck, she's so

stunning, even better than the image the voices made for me when I fantasized about this night. The dress hugs her petite frame, her makeup accentuating those violet eyes until they shine like gems, her hair pinned back but curling around her slender face and cascading over her pale, bare shoulders. I'm about to tell her again how beautiful she looks, but my eyes snag on Miss Goss.

"Teddy," she says, eyes terror-stricken, decorative scarf encircling her throat. *Good.* Seems my threats didn't fall on deaf ears. The smile that paints my lips is evil in nature, as vile as the snake that seduced Eve.

"Miss Goss. Do we have another meeting next week?"

She trembles visibly, her wide eyes flicking between Eden and I. Deep, sick satisfaction pools in my gut, and the voices pace like obedient soldiers, patient now that they know I've set a date for her death. It will be bloody, and beautiful, what I have planned for her. She'll be alive for most of it.

Unless her heart gives out.

"N-no, no, we're done with our...meetings."

I smirk.

"Shame. I hope you enjoy your summer, then," I say, choking back a laugh as she sputters and reels at my subtle threat. I love toying with my victims beforehand, if I'm ever able. She just nods shakily, eyeing Eden again before she rushes off. When we're alone, I can feel my little ghost's eyes on me.

Ladling punch into two clear plastic cups, I hand one to her and avoid her gaze. Her tone is deep and slightly accusatory when she speaks. "What the hell was that about, Teddy?"

Taking a sip of the punch, I raise my brows.

"What was what about?" I tease. This girl will learn all of my darkest, most vile secrets. The voices ache for the day she watches me hunt and kill. To fuck her over a cooling corpse? To satiate my bloodlust with killing *and* fucking? It has to happen. She's not afraid of abandoned buildings, or ghosts.

So I doubt she'd be afraid of watching me kill for her. I know her secrets run as deeply and darkly as mine, and therefore know that before this lifetime with her is over, I will kill in her honor. The voices can't wait to give her such a gift.

"Teddy," she growls again. Reaching up, I press my thumb between her furrowed brows and smooth the worry lines away.

"Eden, if I have to earn your secrets, then you have to earn mine."

Her shoulders deflate. She's resigned, but she isn't happy about it.

"Fine," she grumbles.

"Now," I say, holding her gaze. "Let's dance and pretend we're normal for a little while longer, deal?"

Smiling with a shake of her head, she says, "Deal."

WE ROLL to a stop just outside the wrought iron gates of St. Ignatius. In the bluish light of the full moon, the stone edifice looms into view. At night, the asylum takes on an even more eerie edge, as though in the darkness, evil is given a chance to seep forward.

Cash drums his fingers on the steering wheel incessantly, his fear palpable.

"I don't think I can drive back through those woods alone," he whispers, because whispering just feels right in the shadow of this building. Eden leans forward from the backseat, grinning between us, unperturbed in the slightest. I think I love her.

"It's only scary if you let it be, Cash."

He glares at her through the rearview mirror.

"Says the little witchy freak," he grumbles. With a chuckle, I grab my duffel bag filled with supplies.

"Help me get the sleeping bag?" I ask Cash. His widened eyes turn to mine.

"I am *not* getting out of this fucking car. I heard a child *giggle* here this morning, Tedster. Nuh uh. I don't fuck around with that shit."

Eden, unable to resist teasing Cash, says, "Oh, that's just Lily. She's actually very sweet."

Cash is dumbstruck, but fire ignites my veins, for even if it was a joke, she's just somewhat admitted she can see them. I'll have to press her on that more later, because I find it fascinating and really fucking hot that she can speak with the dead.

"Get out, both of you."

I slap him on the shoulder. "Thanks. We owe you."

"Yeah, you fuckin' owe me, weirdos," he mumbles as I help Eden out. We pull the bags from the trunk, and I wave to Cash, his tires kicking up gravel as he whips his car around and speeds away. The glowing red of his taillights bounce down the road, two demonic eyes winking at us through these hallowed woods, until we're both alone with the ghosts.

TWENTY-SIX
EDEN

SHE CAME to me in a dream, the ghost who brought me here. Freshman year of high school, I'd had such grand aspirations to start anew, to experience the world for the first time with some semblance of normalcy. But the second I'd opened my mouth at Seattle Prep, everyone knew I was different. I didn't understand pop culture references, had never played a sport, had never read a book that wasn't religiously affiliated. The things I did like once I found my freedom deviated from the mainstream, which only cemented my place at the bottom of the social structure.

I wasn't about to change for anyone, and so I stuck my metaphorical finger to the world and knew I could go it alone, no matter how much it really *did* hurt me, deep down.

It was Halloween night that I dreamt of her. A girl similar in age and appearance to myself, wandering alone in the foggy woods, purplish rings around her eyes from exhaustion. She was crying, calling out for help, for anyone to notice and extend a hand to her. That gauzy white dress and those black eyes still haunt me, but I'd answered the call and the lure of the dead.

Dad had quirked his brow at my sudden need for taxi money, but he'd relented, too sick to ask many questions at the time. The man who drove me to Hangman Hallow had only rolled his front two tires onto the dirt road leading to St. Ignatius before he told me to get out. He'd been muttering Hail Mary's when I exited, and part of me wonders if he saw her, the girl from my dreams, because I'd locked eyes with her wavering, phantom form the second we arrived.

It had taken me hours to walk the dirt road to the asylum, but I wasn't alone. She followed closely, weaving between the trees and thick underbrush, peeking at me with hollow, curious eyes, her long black hair stringy, uneven. Her dress—a hospital type gown—was covered in dirt and blood.

She never spoke to me, not directly, but the closer my feet brought me to the building, the more I *felt*. Her sorrow, her fear, her despair, and her longing. Deep in my chest, in my bones. She was so lonely, and I knew above all what that type of loneliness felt like. I'd explored every facet of the ancient, crumbling building with her peering over my shoulder, and I wasn't afraid, not once.

She felt powerful, even in death, and she kept the more vile spirits at bay.

She didn't need help crossing over, something the media always talks about. Not all ghosts want that, or need it. Some are meant to reside in this plane of existence, and she was one of them. In the years that followed my first trip, she became more peaceful, more gentle. Sometimes she'd even smile at me before disappearing.

And now, as I stand on the stone steps that lead into the desolate haven for the dead, she's keen to see who's behind me.

In the grand foyer of the hospital, moonlight barely blots out the darkness. She stands in the hall directly across from the massive double doors, staring at me unblinkingly, head cocked to the side, dress wavering in a breeze I cannot feel. Gently, I smile at her, my heart at peace with hers. She endured hell and torture here, but she found a friend in death, and I found someone I didn't know I would need at the time. She's heard me sob about my father, about being lonely, about the terror my mother foisted upon me at such a young age. She understands pain.

Like me, she just needed a friend.

She evaporates the second Teddy's shoe scuffs over the dusty, unfinished wood floors, but my eyes linger on the spot she just left, a small smile on my lips. All feels calm tonight, the rest of the inhabitants here quiet and curious at the newcomer, their eyes brushing against my skin like cold fingers in the dark.

"Did you see something?" he whispers. It's no use hiding this secret from Teddy anymore. He'll either believe me or not, but with all he's seen, with the way he's so casually comfortable being here, I don't think he will mock me, or think me insane. I suppose I'm in the right place, if that's the case.

"Yeah," I whisper, turning my head to glance at him over my shoulder. He stands tall and breathtakingly handsome, backlit in the entrance by the moon, his teal eyes shining, a smile wavering on his lips, waiting to flash into his trademark grin. His body is tense, his excitement almost childish in nature, like he's giddy to be here talking about all things death and dying.

He's perfect for me, and my heart aches in longing at the thought. I pray I'll still feel this way come morning.

He takes a step forward, duffel bag dangling from one hand, one sleeping bag tucked up under his arm. His smirk is devilish this time as it appears. "Will you tell me what? Or am I still going to be left in the dark here, little ghost?"

I smile softly, nerves jolted at his new nickname for me. It fits. One day, we'll all be ghosts. Hopefully his soul and mine are meant to stay together through death.

Hopefully, we find our way back to one another here, in this place that feels oddly like home to me.

"I call her Eve. She doesn't seem to mind the name. She... she led me here, years ago."

His eyes widen in what looks awfully close to lust, and he steps forward, his frame consuming the light from behind and casting me into his immense, foreboding shadow. I have to crane my neck back to keep our eyes locked.

"Is she still here?" he asks, glancing around the wide, empty space.

I shake my head, still smiling gently. He frowns, cocking his head to the side, his eyes falling to mine. Disappointment swirls there.

"Did I scare her?"

I snort, shaking my head. "No. She just likes to be alone."

His gaze softens.

"Thank you," he whispers.

I quirk my brow. "For what?"

If anything, I should be thanking *him*, over and over and over, for all he did to make my night absolutely perfect, adding in moments I didn't even know I'd want, or need. Having a pizza party in my dad's hospice room? This dress, the makeup, even the ballet flats tied to my ankles? It's perfection, and he is at the root of it.

"For sharing a secret with me."

He reaches out, dragging his knuckles down my cheek, and I shiver at his touch and all it ignites within me. I flash him a grin, unable to resist teasing him back, especially with how alive I feel right now.

"You earned it."

This time, when he grins, it's mordacious and biting, and my heart squeezes.

"C'mon. I have more to earn, Eden Clemm."

My stomach writhes, fraught with nerves, but I take his outstretched hand.

"Lead the way then, Teddy Poe."

WE HIKE THREE FLOORS UP, silent the entire way, both of us listening for any disturbances but hearing none. A strange, nervous sort of calm is taking root in my core, the build up for this night somehow beautiful and transformative, my worries about my dad and the circus fading into nothing because for once, I'm being a teenager, and it feels *so fucking good.*

The old building creaks and groans, winds whistling through the forest outside, and we pause in front of a gaping doorway, Teddy pulling his hand from mine, glancing down at me.

"Wait here?"

Biting my lip, I nod, and he smooths his thumb over my cheek once before disappearing into the darkness. Moments later, soft, golden light begins to flicker into the hallway, making shadows jump and dance along the walls. There's some shuffling, and one or two curses, but he's back, arms outstretched as his hands grip the doorframe, that dark, lurid grin dancing on his devastatingly handsome face.

"Welcome, Miss Clemm," he teases, his eyes alight with mischief. I frown at him, suddenly nervous for whatever it is he's planned aside from the sex. "To one of the best nights of your life."

Brows rising, I scoff, crossing my arms and jutting out my

hip, emboldened here because I feel so at peace, so at home. "*One* of them?"

He steps back out into the hall, taking both of my hands in his own, his warm, rough palms so gentle.

"I don't know about you, but I have a feeling this won't be a one night stand, Eden. Hope you're okay with that. If not..." he trails off, eyes searching mine. Butterflies are wreaking havoc in my stomach as I hold his unwavering, potent stare. His canine teeth appear when his smile broadens, a dangerous glint to his gaze. "Then I suppose you'll have to learn to be okay with it, because if you haven't realized it by now, I'm insane."

Laughter puffs out from between my lips, and I wonder fleetingly if he's serious, if he's subtly sharing something about himself with me. If so...why am I oddly okay with that?

"*How* insane?" I ask, seeking more. He leans in, releasing one hand to cup my cheek before resting his warm forehead against mine. My breath hitches in my throat, and though the night has grown chilly, I am suddenly sweltering in this beautiful dress. Firelight dances upon his angular, chiseled face, and in this moment, everything is perfect.

"Insane enough to follow you through every lifetime."

And then, he kisses me.

TWENTY-SEVEN
TEDDY

SHE'S NERVOUS, but not as nervous as I'd thought she'd be. And with my lips pressed to hers, I've just signed my life away, resigned but happy to devolve into the madness she's stoked to a conflagration within my morbid soul.

Her lips are soft and pliant, her now-familiar scent of lavender, rosemary, and forest swirling amidst the smells of rot and decay and dust. She's frozen, unsure of what to do, and my lips smile against hers. Winding a hand through the soft hair at the base of her skull, I pull her closer to me until our bodies collide, deepening the kiss and garnering a response.

She whimpers into me, and I shiver in pleasure at the small noise, tracing my tongue along the seam of her soft lips as she begins to move them in tandem with mine. Her hands are splayed across my chest, and I know she can feel the erratic thumping of my heart, my excitement like a full balloon ready to burst.

Opening her mouth slightly, our tongues finally touch, and I groan into her, the taste of fruit punch from prom still lingering. She's timid in her exploration of me, and I have to fight back the urge to *really* kiss her; shove her against the wall, sink my teeth into her throat like a vampire, dig my hands into her ass and lift her so my hardening cock can rub against her innocent little pussy.

Breathless, I pull away, the voices screaming at me to do it, to make her mine like a brutal savage, to ruin her in ways unknown so no other human alive stands a chance at making her want them. Sucking in a breath, my eyes flutter open and fall to her ethereal face. Her lips are moist, pursed, her eyes closed. When they open, those twin violets clash with mine in the dimness of the candlelight, and her cheeks bleed crimson.

We both smile in our own way. Her, demure; me, psychotically happy. She shared a secret with me, a big one, and now I'm going to fuck her so thoroughly that they all spill out in screams and moans. Slipping my hands to hers, I pull her into the room, my chest a bubble about to pop as I await her reaction.

Candles flicker in every corner, throwing grim shadows on the derelict walls. The bare mattress in the corner is covered by a massive, plush sleeping bag. On the windowsill, the bottle of strawberry wine is perched with two plastic flutes. I watch her, study her reaction, grinning like a fool when she escapes my hold and wanders further in, at one with the darkness and the dead.

She spins to face me lithely, and a shiver of pleasure rolls down each vertebrae of my spine. She's a dancer, that much Vic let slip. I've seen instances of it before, how she moves with such ghostlike grace. Right now, though, I want her to dance for me. To *really* dance.

"This is..." she breathes, eyes sparkling with happiness and excitement. Shoving my hands in my pockets so I don't stride across the room and kiss her again, I grin in satisfaction, a little calmer now that I've seen her reaction.

"You're a ballerina," I say, nodding to her flats. The shiny, ebony ribbons wind their way up her thinly muscled calves. Her smile falters.

"I used to be."

I shake my head in disagreement, stepping fully into the room. She didn't get the chance to dance freely tonight at prom, too nervous around prying eyes, but here and now, I want to see her. *All* of her.

"Dance, Eden," I command softly, sinking onto the mattress and leaning back onto an elbow. She twists her hands together nervously and shakes her head.

"I don't have music."

"Yes, you do," I press, biting back my smile. Taking another moment to consider, we sit in heavy, charged silence. She heaves a shaky breath, pointed toe skirting through the thick layer of disrupted dust on the floor. Through the window, the melancholy hoot of an owl drifts, and the wind plays in the trees. She closes her eyes and gracefully lifts her arms high above her head, slowly swaying her hips until she pirouettes. She's so poised, her limbs moving with a fluidity reserved for a natural. My cock aches and throbs in my slacks, but my eyes stay stuck on her, the voices all silent as we wait with bated breath for what we know comes next.

Her eyes flick open, stuck in hazy desire on mine, and she brings herself willingly closer to the predator that resides in my soul. She grins, at peace in my presence, and takes one step too far, tripping over the edge of the mattress and crashing onto me. We both fall back as I catch her. I can't help but laugh, her weight atop me reassuring, her hips snug between my legs.

I know, judging by the widening of her eyes, that she can feel me. To ease some of that tension between her brows, I tease her. "For a dancer, you're kind of a klutz."

Her brows drop into a glare, and she pushes against my

chest in an attempt to escape, but I hook my foot around her calf, hold her close, and flip us so I'm above her.

So I'm in control.

Splayed on the mattress with me still between her legs, I shiver again, pleasure curling low in my stomach. My eyes search hers, finding nothing but a frightened sort of innocence there, and I drop down until our noses just barely brush against one another. "Are you sure you want this, Eden?"

She hesitates for a moment but nods, chewing her lip as her eyes flick between mine. This close, pale freckles shimmer across her cheeks, barely visible amongst the ivory. It's fucking adorable.

"Say it," I breathe, lips brushing against hers. She trembles beneath me, one of my hands snaking its way under her dress and up her bare thigh. When I get to her hip, my fingers curl around the bone possessively. "Say it."

"I want you, Teddy."

And that's all it takes for my thin resolve to snap. Shucking her dress up around her waist, my lips crash to hers in a brutal, claiming kiss that leaves her breathless. Winding my arms under her thighs, I yank her hips up, breaking our kiss and ripping her panties from her body.

"What...what are you..."

I chuckle against her, pressing a kiss to her inner thigh, my feast laid bare before me. I almost come from the sight of her cunt alone, that perfect little slit so wet and greedy already, the pearl of her clit begging for the attention of my tongue.

"I have to taste you," I growl.

"T-taste?" she stutters. Does she not know about getting her pussy eaten? Because she's about to find out, and I intend for it to be fucking amazing.

Kissing the soft skin of her other thigh, I laugh against her, bringing my head up slightly to catch her eyes. She's staring at me, mouth agape, shock written into her features. The voices rejoice at her innocence, at the fact that I will be the one to claim it, to show her pleasure she's never known. "I'm going to devour you whole, baby. It's okay to scream if you need to."

Her eyes widen another degree, but I drop my mouth to her bare, silky smooth mound, and close my lips around her clit. Her back arches at the contact, the breath leaving her lungs, and I have to keep her pinned to this earth by sheer force alone. The moment I flick my tongue over that bundle of nerves, she cries out and bucks her hips toward my face, her little hands spearing themselves into my hair and tugging painfully at the strands.

All that serves to do is turn me into a hedonistic beast, and I lave my tongue over her cunt, her taste sweet, her pussy so wet I doubt I'll need the lube I packed just in case.

"Oh...my god," she breathes. "Teddy..."

My eyes roll back, hearing my name whimpered in such a breathy tone, and I sloppily explore her cunt, my tongue diving into her tight channel before I drag it back up to her clit and suck the little nub between my lips, teasing her with quick flicks of my tongue. She trembles and releases a guttural moan.

"What...what are you...doing?" she asks. It's fucking cute, everything she doesn't know, but what's even hotter is knowing I'll be the one to guide her, to teach her how to demand what she wants from me, because no other man, woman—fuck, even *ghost*—will ever make her feel the way I do.

I'll make damn sure of that.

I chuckle against her, pressing a lingering kiss to her clit, raising my head so our eyes meet again. Her cheeks are blotchy, her eyes shining, and I can feel the dewiness of her and my spit dribbling down my chin. "Does it feel good?"

She nods, eyes widening for dramatic effect, and I grin.

"Can I put my fingers in you?"

She swallows, a serious look settling across her features, but she nods.

"Will it...hurt?" she whispers, uncannily honest in her fear at crossing these new and unknown boundaries. Unable to keep my lips from her now that I've had a taste, I kiss her thigh again and shake my head, meeting her eyes from below, her fingers still gripping my hair.

"No, little ghost. I'll make you feel good."

A small smile plays at the corners of her mouth, and she nods. Collecting her wetness onto my two middle fingers, I play in her silkiness for a moment, watching her heavy-lidded eyes before I skim my tongue over her clit. She sucks in a breath, and I slowly ease my fingers into her tightness, slightly worried at the fit.

If she's gripping my fingers like this, how the fuck is she going to take my cock?

I begin a rhythm, slowly pumping them in and out through her slickness, timing my shallow thrusts with the flicking of my tongue. She writhes beneath me, tugging at the ends of my hair until I'm sure I'll have bald patches. I don't fucking care, not when she's making me feel alive for the first time in so fucking long.

Pressing my digits deeper, I'm rewarded with a guttural moan and the fluttering of her walls as her climax builds. A thin band of resistance meets the tip of my middle finger, and a new shiver of icy delight runs through me. I keep the thrusting of my fingers gentle, as deep as that band will allow.

I'm saving her hymen for my cock. The voices want to see her bleed all over me like the little virginal sacrifice she is.

"Mmm," she whines above me, and I quicken my pace, needing to fuck her, but not until she's experienced coming from my tongue and fingers first. I grin against her pussy, and the wet noises we're making are music to my fucking ears. "Oh...Teddy...w- what..."

Her cunt clenches me harder, and I pull away to hastily answer. "Come for me, little ghost, come hard."

"Ahh!" she cries when I scrape my teeth over her clit, thrusting faster until her pussy clamps down on my fingers. She goes rigid, her muscles tightening, and when that band releases, she *does* scream.

She screams my name.

It echoes and bounces off the plastered walls, loud enough to wake the dead and let them know who their new master is. I keep thrusting through her climax, keep sucking her clit until it sends her into another one, her body spasming beneath mine in ecstasy.

Breathless, I pull away, chest heaving as I move above her. She pants on the mattress, the aftershocks of her orgasm zapping through her, those eyes hooded in lust and content-ment. They widen when I bring my sticky fingers up between us so she can see, scissoring them, her slickness stretching between them. Grinning, I bring my fingers to my mouth and suck, moaning as I lick myself clean.

She tastes like a fucking dream, and there won't be a day that goes by where I don't eat her out.

Eyes wide, she watches me in fascination, and I plant my hands on either side of her head, smirking down at her.

"I think you're ready for my cock now, aren't you, good little girl?"

TWENTY-EIGHT
EDEN

BODY STILL WITHERING from the high coursing through my veins, it pushes out all of the fear I'd been feeling earlier. How can any one person make another feel so...alive? *Electrified?* Is this normal, or is this Teddy?

Because the way he's grinning at me after he just licked all my wetness off his fingers stretches those bounds of normality until they threaten to snap. And him calling me a *good little girl?* Why does that have me getting even wetter? I *do* want more, greedily so, and emboldened under his stare that makes me feel seen and womanly and sexy, I slowly slip one side of my dress down my shoulder, his eyes zeroing in on the movement like a tiger prepared to pounce. Slowly—as slowly as I am undressing for him—a wicked grin stretches his cheeks, his eyes glinting with a touch of madness.

He rises up on his knees between my spread legs, ripping off his jacket, loosening his tie with one hand and unbuckling his belt with the other. It becomes a race for him, as excited as he is, and it's then I feel it leisurely pushing through my veins. *Power.* I have power in this situation, over someone as immense as Teddy, and it feels so fucking good. He really is obsessed with me. He held himself in check, because Cash let slip how badly he wanted me.

I think I finally believe it.

So I pause, watching him strip for me, utterly entranced by his dark beauty, his muscles moving sinuously beneath his skin, as taut as a stretched rubber band.

"Eden." His deep voice snaps me from my bemused staring, and my eyes jump up from the bulge in his slacks to his dancing eyes. Chuckling, he nods to my dress. "Fair is fair."

Blushing a little, I say softly, "I...I need help."

Leaving his pants on, he drops down onto his hands to hover over me again, grinning like a fool as he studies me. "You taste so fucking good."

Well...now I'm not blushing just a little. I didn't know I could taste good to someone, but the truth is there in his eyes and in how enthusiastically he did all that with his tongue and fingers. I'm thankful that when I came to the circus last year, Jess told me to go get waxed. Wearing those skimpy outfits makes me self conscious on a good day, especially if I forget to shave my legs or it's time to rip the hair from my nether regions again.

"Thank...you?" I say. He laughs, the sound so beautiful and rich, his grin stretching his cheeks wide. When his smile fades from his face, it still lingers in his eyes.

"I was serious. I want to do that to you every goddamn day. More than once a day. Even if you say no."

A million different emotions hit me at his words, but that subtle threat at the end has my thighs rubbing together, an ache growing between my legs anew.

"You can't make me," I whisper, throwing the line out to see what reaction I'll ensnare. His pupils dilate so quickly that the black consumes the teal in less than a second. He visibly shivers, but I can tell it's not from the cold beginning to seep in from the broken window.

"Is that so?" He quirks a dark brow, and biting my lip to hide my playful smile, I nod. His nostrils flare as he answers my grin with one of his own—albeit one a wolf would wear.

"Eden, I'd hunt you across this entire fucking earth if you ever tried to run away from me. I'd lock your ass here, in this asylum, if you ever even *thought* you could escape me," he says, his voice low, his oaths spoken from the deepest, most wicked parts of his dark soul. "You made your little deal with me, but you were mine long before that, even when I was too wrapped up with the voices in my head to see."

Lightning strikes my veins, because he's just shared something with me, something I'm not sure he meant to. Swallowing hard, I whisper, "Did...Did I earn a secret?"

His smile morphs and grows again, and it's then I understand that he *did* mean to tell me. So he hears...*voices*? Is he schizophrenic? Or is it something like me with seeing the dead?

Am *I* schizophrenic?

"They're obsessed with you," he says breathily. "So please don't make me wait any longer to *really* make you mine."

Shocked, I hide it by smiling coyly.

"Then do it."

"Fuck," he breathes as soon as I taunt him, shaking his head and tearing his eyes from mine. The muscles and tendons and veins winding up his arms are stretched tight, his frame trembling with the exertion it takes him to not claim me right this instant. I...I think I like torturing him, pushing his resolve to the brink, seeing what will make him snap. "You little fucking sadist."

His eyes come back to mine, shining anew in their obsession, and my heart soars.

"You'd really hunt me down?" I ask, studying his reaction.

For some reason, I need to know, need that reassurance that he'd be my knight in shining armor when the day comes. I also kind of want to know if he'd...*play* hunt me down, because I'm not sure why, but I really, really like the idea.

"In every sense, Eden," he swears, and I shiver. With no more hesitation, he begins to pluck at the strings of my corset, loosening them one by one until the bodice slips from my torso. He casts the entire dress aside as I cover my breasts, only the ballet flats still wrapped around my feet. He reaches back, fishing in the bag beside the bed for a moment, coming back with a gold and black plastic square in his hand.

With his other, he frees his cock, and my eyes widen. I skipped school the day Seattle Prep had the sexual education course, because I knew Brant would make my life hell by teasing me. So Teddy's dick is the first I've seen, and as uneducated as I am, I *still* know it's huge.

He tears open the packet with his teeth as he strokes the length, veins winding their way to a soft, purplish tip. Something shiny leaks from the end, an enticing droplet clinging there. He watches me as I watch him, both of us equally as fascinated with the other's reactions. I've even forgotten that I'm bared to him, completely naked.

My brows furrow and my lips pout as he rolls the condom on, cutting off my view.

"Don't give me that, little ghost," he jests, and my eyes bounce to his. Fire simmers there, but his entire frame vibrates in anticipation.

"What?"

"I'll put babies in you someday, but not right now. I have a few fantasies to live out with you before that."

God, he can read my mind, and it's fucking scary sometimes.

"I just...wanted to know what it felt like. Without that, the first time."

His head falls back, his face pointed toward the ceiling as he groans.

"Fucking hell," he mutters.

I bite my smile away, and the smelly rubber hits the floor. I know what we're doing is risky, but I also don't care. I want this to be a certain way, and I'll be damned if I don't get my wishes.

"Cash was right," he says, and I cock my head at him in question. He grins. "Said he bet I wouldn't even use those. So he bought us Plan B as a joke."

I only somewhat know what that is, and only because when Chastity takes it, she's a raging bitch for days after.

His smile fades slightly when I don't respond. "You were really sheltered, huh?"

That's a secret I'm not ready to share, but it's because I don't want to give a single thought to my mother, especially right now, when something so good is about to happen. I shake my head softly, but firmly say, "After."

Intrigue lights his gaze, and he moves above me, centering his hips to mine. It crashes upon me, in this moment. This is really about to happen. Awe and terror wage a war over my heart, and I swallow thickly, my voice squeaking when I speak. "Will...will this hurt?"

His eyes flick to mine, and he shakes his head, dropping down so our noses touch. "It will, but it won't be because I want it to."

I quiver at his words but nod.

"I'll go slow, Eden. You set the pace. You tell me to stop or go and I'll listen."

"Th-thank you..."

He smirks, leaning up to press a kiss between my worried

brows, and then I feel him at my entrance. My fingers dig into my bare chest, needing to sink into something to keep me planted. He rubs his thick tip up and down my wet slit, circling it over my sensitive nub, creating that pool of pleasure deep in my stomach again.

He does this a few times, dragging my wetness all around, igniting sparks of pleasure that center in my core and flare out through my limbs. The only thing I can hear is the pounding of my heart that shakes my frame, and his trembling breaths, the exertion it's taking to hold himself back insurmountable.

"You ready?" he pants. No, I'm not, but I also am, and so I nod. He presses his head to my entrance, slowly easing inside, the stretch something different entirely than when it was just his fingers. It burns and aches, but he eases out, and the pain fades to a dull thudding. He reaches down, circling his thumb over my clit, and I gasp as the pleasure helps soothe some of the pain.

He does it again, gently rocking himself into me, a little further this time, pain and pleasure mingling into something darkly beautiful.

"Was...was that all of...it?" I ask.

He bursts forth with a bark of laughter, and I glare at him. He simply presses a kiss to my cheek and says, "No. That was only the tip, baby. Watch."

Suddenly, he's in me again, but his arms have lifted me until I'm half sitting on his lap, his dick inside me. It's such an erotic sight, seeing us joined in such an intimate way, my pussy stretching to its max as it takes him, and his dick throbbing in time with his heartbeats. "You're doing so good, Eden."

His voice is a darkened whisper, and I watch with rapture as he sinks more deeply into me. It's still not even halfway in.

"Ow," I hiss, fingernails digging into his biceps, brow pinched in the middle. He eases out, keeping his cock in me but relenting slightly.

"Such a beautiful little doll. Fuck, you're so fucking tight," he says, voice husky in desire as he watches the scene between us as well. "Look at you, taking me like such a good girl."

"Mmm," I whimper as he pushes more back in.

"Drool on it, baby," he says breathlessly. Shocked, my eyes catch his, but he nods down. "Open that smart mouth and drool all over my cock before I put it in you."

Oh my god...

My jaw falls open, my body obeying before my mind can comprehend, and I let my saliva drip down in long, wet strings. Some lands on his cock, some on my clit, where it slides to my stretched entrance. He continues to back out and feed me more, and I keep my mouth open, my eyes bouncing from us to his face. He's biting his lip, his gaze on his cock, his head tilted to the side for the perfect view.

"You were made for me," he says with conviction, and I shudder above him. When he's halfway in and I swear I can't take anymore, his eyes find mine. "I'm gonna break your hymen, baby. You're gonna bleed. It's gonna hurt. But I'll make it feel better, I promise."

Adrenaline strikes my veins and chills me to my core, but I nod. I'd rather just get the painful part over with. Everyone says it gets better with practice, and I think Teddy and I will be practicing a lot in the coming days and weeks. At least, I hope so.

Sucking in a deep breath, I release it and nod again.

"I'm ready," I whisper.

He pushes me back onto the mattress gently, hovering over me and giving me another kiss on my forehead, the sweet moment tempered by his words.

"I'm sorry," he whispers, and thrusts—*hard*.

I scream, shocked at the painful intrusion, my body unsure of what to make of this new type of pain. His forehead falls to mine, and his thumb brushes my dewy cheek. "Keep your eyes on me, Eden. I wanna watch you come all over my cock."

He eases out, but slams back in, thumb resuming its circling of my clit, igniting the pain and pleasure duo again. Something warm and wet begins to ease his way—my blood, I think, but I don't care. It's starting to morph, the pain, into simply a dull ache as the electricity begins to fire again, my lower belly clenching, my pussy gripping him in rippling waves.

"Fuck," I breathe, craning my neck. Before, when he'd just been using his tongue, my body kept telling me I was missing something, that I felt empty. As soon as his fingers had sunk into me, that rolling wave of ecstasy had crashed into me and made me feel alive for the first time. It's the same now, only his cock is way fucking bigger than two middle fingers, and it's hitting something pleasurable deep inside me.

"That's my girl," he grits out, canting his hips faster, our skin slapping and echoing in the dark. "Come for me."

His thumb works me faster and with just the right amount of pressure, and my heart begins to gallop. The pain in me is changing...and I oddly want *more* of this new type of pain.

"M-MORE," I whimper.

"What?" he breathes, shocked, his hips stuttering.

"Harder, *fuck*..."

He obeys before I can say please, the head of his cock hitting that spot inside me over and over and over while his thumb circles me faster. My pussy tightens, that ball of ecstasy growing in the pit of my stomach, expanding until it's on the precipice of bursting. "That's it, baby, get tight on me...come, Eden, come for me."

His voice is rough with desire, and the lust there is what I need to send me over the edge. My legs begin to quake, my cunt clenching down on his rigid length in long, awe-inducing spasms. My mouth drops open on a silent scream, no air to be found in order to make a single noise. All that can be heard is the furious slapping of our skin as my eyes roll back.

"Yes, yes, yes," he grunts, gripping my ankles and holding them in the air as he drives into me, my orgasm cresting again.

"F-*fuuuuck*," I sob. He slams into me like a savage, my climax just barely ebbing, my pussy still rhythmically clenching him. When it's slowed, he rips himself out of me and strokes his cock so fast his hand is a blur. Ropes of white, sticky cum splatter my stomach, thighs and cunt. It mingles with pinkish hued blood, and we both pant, unable to catch our breath for a few long moments.

But when his eyes catch mine, he sinks down on top of me, blanketing me with his warmth and his weight. I'm shivering. And holding back tears. Tears he must have seen.

"Eden," he breathes, cradling my skull, tucking me up under his chin. "Eden, fuck, did I hurt you, baby?"

"No," I whisper quickly, shaking my head against his flushed skin, breathing him in and calming further. "That just... it felt so good. And I'm...I'm happy it was with you."

He releases a heavy sigh of relief and squeezes me tighter, pressing a kiss to my hairline, his other fingers trailing up my spine comfortingly. "When you're ready, I brought some wine. Strawberry, to be exact."

My head pops up, my eyes misting over again, but for an entirely different reason this time. "You...really?"

"Of course," he says, smirking. But his smile fades, and his eyes search mine. "Eden...I'm not just saying things when I tell you that...that I'm obsessed with you. That you're mine. You're all I am ever going to want. It's not going to change or fade. Doesn't that scare you?"

The vulnerability spilling from those damning eyes turns

him into a little boy, one the little girl in me wants to hold tightly and comfort forever. I glare at him even as elation soars through me, the aching pain between my legs ebbing.

"No, Teddy. As long as you make me one promise."

He quirks his brow, hand snaking to my ass and giving me a squeeze. "Not fair, you know I'll agree to anything."

I smile. "You'll like this, I think."

His smile is so tragically beautiful that it hurts me physically to behold it. I never want to go a day without seeing it. I'd probably lose my mind and perish into nothing, and thus begins my own descent into madness. "What is it, little ghost?"

"That one day, we get out of the circus together, and we come live here."

He strokes the hair from my cheek, enraptured as he stares at me, our legs intertwined on the soft bed as the asylum groans its assent. All is soft and silent, the candles throwing shadows on the walls as the phantoms hold their breath and await their master's answer.

"*I was a child, and she was a child, in this kingdom by the sea*,'" he whispers, and tears fog my vision, a lump welling up my throat. "*But we loved with a love that was more than love, I and my Annabel Lee*.'"

I snuggle into his embrace, warm and safe and content and so fulfilled I may just burst. His heart thuds a steady rhythm beneath my ear, and I commit the sound to memory. "I think I'm falling for you, Teddy Poe."

I can feel his smile against me as I drift off to sleep, cradled in his arms and safe in these hallowed halls where my demons are too scared to roam.

"I've got ya when you do, Eden Clemm."

TWENTY-NINE
EDEN

PALE, watery sunlight filters in through the jagged, broken glass of the window. There's a storm on the horizon, the air heavy with the chilled humidity of the Pacific Northwest, static roiling in the clouds that roll forward ominously. A ghost of a smile paints my lips, Teddy's arms still securely around me, his mouth pressed to my hairline in a lingering kiss as he snores softly against me. It's so odd to see someone who is so lethal and powerful sleep so peacefully.

I pull away slightly, the desire to study him and commit him to memory overcoming me. My eyes trace the planes of his devastating face, from the sharp arch of his brows, to his straight nose that broadens slightly on the bridge, to his full lips and slightly crooked chin. I love it when he smiles widely, because it makes his grin lopsided and boyish. A part of his soul is still a child, but the rest is of a man who grew up far too fast, a man who knows the darkness of this world but one who isn't afraid of it.

The fact that he's still asleep and not eager to explore warms my soul. In every movie, the heroine awakes to find the other side of the bed empty, whether because the man is making her breakfast or because he's rushed off to work. But Teddy is still here, still holding me as tightly as if he were awake, and everything in the world feels calm and right.

The ache between my legs throbs with every movement, my hips burning, the muscles I used last night not ones I think I've ever used before.

Last night plays on a loop in my mind, moments clinging there that I know in my bones I'll never forget. I may have become his, but he is also mine, and I want to sink into that bliss and never resurface. If we could just abandon all responsibility and hide here for the rest of our earthly lives, I would.

He snorts in his sleep, shifting against me until I feel the hard tip of his cock prodding at the gap between my thighs. Shocked, I go still and hold my breath.

"God, I wanna fuck you again so bad," he rumbles, voice gravelly and deep with sleep. Warmth and joy flood me, and I have to bite my lip to stave my smile. His eyes are still closed as he presses his lips to my forehead and pulls me even closer to his body.

"I couldn't tell," I tease. He pulls his face away from mine, eyes hooded with exhaustion, and grins down at me. The silvery light of an overcast day brushes his skin in hues of gray and charcoal, but it ignites the blue in his eyes, like a black and white film with a hint of color for the audience to cling to. His dark hair sticks up all over the place in messy spikes, and my smile only grows. "Can I show you something?"

I bite my lip as he eyes me. Showing him the asylum was one thing, but there's still so much around here to share with him. Now that he's made me such a life-altering promise, I want to introduce him to every single spot here that holds significance to me. Slowly, he grins. "Of course."

Before I can hop up, the haunting sound of a piano key

being struck sounds to us from somewhere below. There's an old piano in the foyer, but I'm surprised it still works, for the last time I checked the strings, they were coated in dust and a hair's breadth away from snapping.

Eyes flashing open so wide they are perfect spheres, Teddy rises up on his elbow, leaning over the top of me in a protective stance, like a dog growling as it warns off intruders. Grinning despite his tenseness, I smooth my palm up his rigidly flexed arm, but his eyes remain on the open doorway. No other sounds greet us in the early hues of dawn, not that I would expect them. Here, it's never a flesh and bone human. It's always the dead, and if you listen closely enough, they speak to you in ways of their own.

"It's okay," I soothe, but he doesn't relax. "Teddy..."

His eyes drop to mine, his brow crinkled as he hovers above me, this position reminiscent of last night. Pleasure curls low in my belly at the memory, and my cunt aches.

"Ghost?" he asks, and I nod. He releases a sharp breath through his nose and smiles, almost in a proud manner. "Who? Since you seem to know everyone here."

I laugh, sinking down further into the warmth of the sleeping bags, knowing that what I'm going to show him will have me freezing my ass off.

It's strange, talking to someone about this. I've never shared it with another soul. My father is too realistic and literal, and my mother would have happily burned me at the stake in front of her congregation. Add in the fact I had no *living* friends until now, and...well...

"I call her Lily. She's really playful. Doesn't...uhh...belong in the era this place was built, though. She seems more modern."

He rolls to the side slightly, propping his head on his hand

and keeping our eyes locked, fascination bursting through his stunning irises. "Tell me more."

I blush, fiddling with a loose string on one of the sleeping bags, but I lick my lips and answer. It feels...sort of good, to ramble about something I love, something that is intrinsically me. "She's kinda shy, but she's really curious. She plays with the...the nicer spirits here. They don't mind her. She's scared of the basement, though. Only goes down there if I go."

His eyes shine.

"I saw her footprints in the dust yesterday, after we set up the room. After Cash left."

My brows rise in shock. "Seriously? Damn. That...that takes a lot of energy. She must be comfortable around you, too."

His smile is as devastating as a hurricane, but as beautiful as flowers growing from a grave.

"What about Eve?"

I smile, his bare leg brushing against mine, a constant reminder in the back of both our minds that we're still naked together under the covers, but it feels so...*right*. Like this is how every day is supposed to be. I thought I'd be far more self conscious around him, but Teddy has a way of making me feel safe and comforted without even trying. "She can be pretty elusive when she wants to be."

"Does she like me?" he fires back. I snicker.

"I don't know yet. She was a little timid last night."

He grins, rolling to crowd my space, hand finding my hip as he digs his fingers into my flesh. My heart races at the contact, at the possessive glint in his gaze that I understand far better now. He hears voices, and I wonder what they're saying about me. "They don't...watch, do they?"

He smirks deviously, and I roll my eyes.

"No. Everyone thinks that but no. They give privacy to people."

He chuckles.

"Well when I'm a ghost," he says matter of factly, shifting his body so it's atop mine, his hard cock nestled between my thighs, his tip pressing at my sore entrance. "I'll watch *you*."

I shake my head, smile fading.

"I don't want to be a ghost without you," I whisper, my chest swirling with too many emotions at the thought of him gone from this earth. Slowly, gently, he presses a lingering kiss to my lips that leaves me breathless.

"Then we go together, baby. That I can promise you."

THIRTY
TEDDY

I'M HOPELESSLY IN LOVE. Or addicted. Obsessed? I can't tell. I've never been in love, but I know what it is to love someone. I love my mom, obviously, and I love Cash like a brother. But to love another soul? To feel myself burning from the inside out every time I lay eyes on her? It's new. It's beautiful.

It's fucking terrifying.

Terrifying, because there are so many unknowns about our future, and protecting her from her past and from everything at the circus is going to zap me of energy. I know what's coming for her on Tuesday, and the voices have already painted such vivid, gory images in my brain of what I'm going to do to the fucker who paid twenty grand for her virginity.

The voices collectively smirk, smug in their satisfaction that it belongs to me for eternity now.

I won't tell her I know, or how I found out. She will tell me when she's ready. Daniel is just a fucking idiot who likes to leave his laptop open and unaccompanied while he tries and fails to flirt with the girls who perform. He steers clear of Eden because of Vic, but I know that his resolve is thinning. When

Danny boy wants something, his daddy always ensures he gets it.

I can't wait to fucking end them both.

I wonder if Eden would let me hunt them through the asylum. Daniel would shit his pants in that basement, and Dick would cry in a corner. It would be so cathartic.

Her cold little hand clasped in mine, my little ghost leads me through the dark, ominous woods, a game trail marking our slender path. It's drizzling, the storm clouds crowding in over St. Ignatius, but the canopy above is so thick with boughs and moss that it doesn't drip down to us yet. My eyes linger on her form, flip flops on her feet, and my Misfits band tee hanging off her petite frame, the white cloth making her appear even more ghostly.

I say nothing, choosing to instead absorb this moment in all its perfection, her long, black hair still wavy as it cascades down her back. She turns and flashes me a brilliant grin, her cheeks pink, her eyes smudged with her makeup from prom. She is devastating in her beauty. I can't help but wonder what I did to deserve someone like her.

"Almost there," she whispers.

I smirk, for I can hear it—the sound of waves crashing on rocks; the ocean is near, the heaviness of salt in the air filling my lungs with life. She knows this place like the back of her hand, and I ponder in awe how she gets out here so much. Poor Cash will be stuck as our driver for the near future I think, because I have plans to fuck her in every room and on every surface of that haunted building.

I tried to seduce her again before we left on this little trek, but she pushed me away with a giggle and told me to wait. I can't deny this girl anything, even if my cock is still as hard as a fucking steel pipe in my jeans right now. My Eden is a sadist *and* a masochist, I think, and I can't wait to play with her, to stoke those desires into full, engulfing flames. The way I know I'd been hurting her last night, but she still begged for more? Fuck. If perfection does exist, it's in the form of this little gothic sprite, and I'll never let her go.

She turns back to the path before us, and ahead there's a slight break in the trees, allowing the heavy, gray morning light to seep through and blot out the darkness. The cacophony of seagulls and wind and waves grows louder with each step until we break through the dense forest. Dark gray rocks jut out from the trees, holding firm against the power of the ocean as it slowly wears them away. We stand upon a cliff that juts out into the air, the tangy breeze potent on my tongue. And on the horizon, stretching as far as the eye can see, is nothing but more gray emptiness—the edge of this world. My heart gives a painful clench at the majestic, dark beauty of it all. An asylum nestled snug in the mountains by the ocean.

The kingdom by the sea.

She turns to grin up at me, her cheeks flushed from the cool wind, her eyes the color of dark purple lilacs, her hair whipping across her features, and my white shirt clinging to her small frame. She wants me to stare at the breathtaking view, to enjoy it with her—something she also finds stunning—but I can't take my eyes off her right now as our worlds begin to shift and collide in cataclysmic ways.

She is at once both dark and light, yin and yang, life and death, wretched and divine. She is everything to me, an enigma that will satiate the voices in my head until long after my physical body is buried in the ground and my bones are dust. Even then, I'll never stop hunting her, my reason for existence. For if Eden Clemm goes, then so do I. I made that vow to her, and I intend to keep it.

So I pull her close until our bodies clash, wrap her in my arms, and press a lingering kiss to her cold lips. When I pull away, she's breathless, blinking up at me with those perfectly round eyes, our foreheads resting against one another.

"Can this be our kingdom by the sea?" I say lowly against the crashing waves. Her eyes glisten at my quoting of the famous tragic love poem by Edgar Allan Poe. Sinking her teeth into her bottom lip, she nods, hugging me back against the chill.

I just hope against all hope that when we're free of the circus, some semblance of who we are in this moment still lingers in our souls, a drop of peace and happiness amidst chaos and destruction.

"YOU...SAID something last night, something...interesting," Eden says as we meander back to the asylum, still hand in hand. She glances up at me, our arms stretched between us as I allow her to lead the way. It seems she's walked this path dozens of times, her muscle memory taking over as we talk aimlessly about stupid teenage shit. Shit that makes me feel normal for once in my life. This, however, has taken a sharp turn into what sounds semi-serious.

I quirk my brow.

"I'm sure I said a lot of interesting things," I tease. She blushes, and I prod further. "Things about how good you taste, how tight your perfect little cunt is—"

She whirls on me, gasping with shocked laughter, gently shoving my chest with both hands.

"Stop it," she hisses, embarrassed. My grin flashes widely, and I reach down, ensnaring her hips with my hands.

My balls ache. So does my cock. School is going to be fucking torture this week, watching her flounce around in that little skirt with her knee high socks. I'll definitely be fucking her under the bleachers during lunch. And every other chance I can get. Cash will have to get over it and get his dick sucked by Brant's girlfriend some more.

"Fine, what did I say that was so intriguing to you, hmm?"

She can't contain her grin no matter how hard she tries, and when she blinks up at me like she is, I know she wants something. And I know I'll have no choice but to give it to her. Cash would call me pussy-whipped, but it's far more heinous than that. If I could find a way for my soul to bury itself beneath her skin, I would.

"That you'd...hunt me."

Oh, fuck.

A tremble slithers down my spine. The voices perk up from their slumber, satiated after last night, but only just. *Chase her, fuck her bloody, make her scream against you, carve your name into her pretty skin,* they all seethe.

"Yes, little ghost," I say, voice slightly strained. Something flashes in her eyes, some type of understanding that not many would catch onto, but Eden is brilliant, and she sees it in me, how serious I am. "Why?"

Her own coy smirk plays on her lips, a deviousness unearthed before my eyes as the real Eden begins to flourish. Just more proof that we are meant to be, her and I. She can be that child she never got to be with me, and I can give her the protection and care to allow that.

"So...*hunt* me."

My eyes widen for a moment as desire flows hotly through my veins, my cock stiffening in my jeans. At this point, the poor fucker is going to fall off, being teased like this. But the logical side wars with that desire, because as much as I *want* to hurt her, I also *don't* want to hurt her. It's confusing as hell, these two sides of myself, but I know which one will eventually win.

It always does.

"Eden," I warn in a low tone. She pushes away from me with a giggle, creating space between us that feels simultaneously cold and charged, my body humming the same way it does when I hunt down predators to sink my knives into. "Be careful."

Pressing her lips together to stem some of her smile, she quirks her brow higher. "Do I get a head start?"

"Fucking hell," I hiss, dropping my head back to stare at the darkened canopy above me. Every time I think this girl can't get any more perfect, she goes and does shit like this. The sound of her cheap flip flop dragging over the pine needles and dirt has my eyes snapping back down to her, the killer in me awakening and attuned to every sound around me. Saliva pools in my mouth, and my muscles go tense and rigid. "You don't know what you're doing."

My voice is lower, a strained whisper on the breeze.

She crosses her arms and juts her pointed chin up, fighting a wicked smile. She has two little dimples when she does, and I melt at the sight, wanting to trace them with my tongue. Running my hand through my hair, I smooth down all the spikes she created last night while I made her scream my name. An anticipatory chill runs through me, knowing I'm about to make her scream again.

"I know you have secrets I need to earn, too," she says, a serious glint slithering into her cunning eyes. "And I think this is part of it."

Crossing my arms, I release a long breath through my nose, eyeing her up and down. Tattered black flip flops, no panties, and my Misfits band tee. She may know these woods like the back of her cute little hand, but the voices in me want to play, a cat chasing down a tiny mouse and forcing it to submit.

My smirk grows as she waits, wavering before me like the

ghosts she sees, thunder rumbling over the mountains in the distance.

"One," I say lowly. Her eyes spark, her body going rigid.

"Two," I count ominously, taking a threatening step toward her. She backs away a pace, palms open and facing the forest floor.

"What happens if you catch me?" she says, that sultry voice breathless in dark desire. I chuckle, pushing up the sleeves of my hoodie.

"*When* I catch you," I correct, my smile fading, only to be replaced by a stoic, ominous look that I feel taking root in my bones, "then I'm going to fuck you until you beg for me to stop."

Her eyes round at the edges, showcasing more of that alluring, bruise-like purple. She takes another step back.

"Will you stop?"

Her voice is barely a whisper now. Grinning like the psychotic serial killer I am, I shake my head. "Run, little ghost. It's time to play."

WITH A GIRLISH GIGGLE, she turns and flees through the woods, and it takes everything I have in me not to give chase, the slap of her flip flops echoing and then fading. I'll let her think she has the upper hand. The voices are as charged as lightning in a storm, buzzing through me, my body humming with the vibration. When I kill, it's the same feeling, that erotic sort of anticipation at knowing my bloodlust will soon be satisfied.

I won't kill Eden, of course.

Just hurt her a bit.

So I meander down the path, everything around me going still. Those eyes I feel whenever I'm alone in this place begin to brush against the back of my neck, raising my hairs as I focus on the hunt.

I put myself into Eden's mind, sink into her psyche, and allow it to lead me to wherever she thinks she's safe from the demons in my soul. It's the same when I've chosen someone to kill; I think like them, put myself in their position. It's how I am able to remain silent and lethal and undetected. The police have never caught me, obviously, and only three bodies that I am responsible for have ever been found.

My father's of course, and two pedophiles I dumped in the Puget Sound a little too hastily. By the time they were recovered, only dental records could prove who they were, and no one batted an eye once their long rap sheets were read on the nightly news. Poor mom had turned pale as a ghost when I'd smirked in satisfaction at hearing my work broadcast to the greater Seattle area, but she'd pressed her lips together and refused to ask me anything.

I appreciate her more than she knows.

To my right, a pair of mourning doves are roused from their spot on a low hanging branch, the rapid flapping of their wings and startled calls alerting me in the direction I should go. Smiling sinuously, I step off the slender trail and into the bracken. It only takes two steps to find one flip flop, and a few feet later, another one. Crouching low, I hide in the cover of the dewy ferns, listening, watching.

It's odd, though, stalking while being stalked by the dead. They feel genuinely curious at this little game Eden and I are playing. I don't mind if they want to watch me fuck her, so long as they understand she is *mine*, in life and in death.

After a few moments, I slowly stand and continue forward, as silent as a mountain lion as I carefully pick my way over fallen branches and blackberry bushes. My heart steadily pumps harder and harder the more excited I grow, my cock twitching, my balls aching. Through the trees, that little giggle reaches me again, igniting the need to hunt her down until it's flaming through me, and I take off in a sprint toward the sound.

She's crashing through the trees when I catch sight of her, that long, dark hair fanning out behind her, a few random leaves tangled in her silky locks. Eden turns to glance at me over her shoulder as she runs, smile stretching her cheeks wide, her eyes igniting in both fear and raw excitement as she sees me. A screech leaves her lips, followed by a breathless laugh, and she pushes herself to run faster, enjoying this—enjoying being hunted.

And fuck, if I don't love hunting her.

Just to tease me further, she somehow manages to flip my shirt up and over her head, flinging it behind her, my little ghost streaking through the woods as naked and as devastatingly perfect as she can be. A mordacious grin is pinned to my lips, and I push myself harder, sprinting past my shirt that's snagged on a thorny bush of dead roses.

Ahead, there's another break in the trees, and we burst forth into a wide, hilly area that has my breath stalling in my lungs. Eden stops, her chest heaving, her ribs straining against her ivory skin as she turns to face me, her breasts bared to the wild. Cheeks blotchy, skin dewy, she walks backwards with a giggle, weaving lithely between staggered headstones that look as ancient as the asylum.

I'm upon her in a flash, snatching her arm and wrenching her body to mine with a voracious sneer, my other hand ripping my zipper down as both of us struggle to catch our breath. Her eyes have widened, and I back her against a headstone until she's pinned there.

"Do you want me to struggle?"

Fuck, what is she doing to me? No one alive has ever read me as succinctly as her, and it only fans the flames of my obsession into an all-engulfing wildfire, burning through me and decimating everything in its path.

Pressing my body against hers as I free my cock and stroke it until I'm fully hard, I say, "Baby, you can struggle all you fucking want. You're never going to win this battle."

She glances down between us, the purplish head of my dick intimidating in the wan light of day, her eyes widening anew as she audibly gulps. Her eyes spring back to mine, and she whispers demurely, "Never?"

I chuckle darkly in response. "Never. Now put this mouth to good use and suck."

I shove her shoulder, forcing her to her knees, and her brows crunch together in anger. She uses all of her pitiful mite to push against my legs.

"No," she growls.

"Eden," I warn, fisting her hair and yanking her head until her lips are poised right above the tip of my thudding cock. "You wanted to play with fire."

And then, the little shit sticks out her tongue and fires back with sass, "Make me."

The storm that gathers on my face and in my soul is reflected in the widening of her fearful eyes, and I release my cock, pinching her cheeks so hard that her jaw unhinges with a whimper of pain. Towering over her with a triumphant sneer, I twist my hips and smack her cheek with my cock degradingly. "Take me in your mouth and get me all nice and wet for your pussy, or it's going in your ass dry. You choose."

She blinks up at me, drool dribbling over her bottom lip as my hold on her cheeks grows more firm and demanding by the second. In the next breath, she glares, shaking her head in an attempt to free herself of my unyielding grip, but it's of no use. "I'll be nice and give you to the count of ten to decide."

She tries to stand, but she's still pinned by the weathered, tilted headstone.

"One."

She mumbles an incoherent string of slurs, and I grin wickedly.

"Two."

She tries to spit on me, but it only slips down her chin.

"Three."

"Argh!" she whines in sheer frustration, tears forming in her eyes.

"Four."

My voice is deep, as ominous as the black clouds on the horizon. She beats her little fists against my thighs, but the small amount of pain only ignites me further. I relish a good fight.

"Five," I hiss, releasing her jaw and bringing my cock to her puffy, parted lips. When she glares up at me this time, true fear is there, eyes welling with tears that slip over and slide down her red cheeks. I shiver in pleasure at the sight. She begins to shake in my grasp, her tiny pink nipples stiff, goosebumps littering her precious skin.

"Six," I seethe. She must understand I am utterly serious and takes me at my word, opening her mouth, but only a little. "There's a good girl."

I rub the tip of my cock over her lips, tracing the O shape and leaving a glistening trail of my precum behind. She whimpers, eyes flicking from my cock to my face and back.

"You were naughty," I say breathlessly, fully sinking into the sick freak I am at my core. "And naughty girls get punished."

I push the head of my cock into her warm, wet mouth and groan, nearly coming then and there. I'm about to fuck the woman I'm obsessed with in a crumbling graveyard, and no other fantasy will ever top this.

"Take a deep breath," I warn. She sucks in, but before she can get a full amount of air, I thrust my cock into her mouth and down her throat, pinching her nose with one hand and gripping the back of her skull with the other. She flails against me, gagging and lurching, but I pound into her, fucking her throat raw as ecstasy sings through my veins. Her wet little mouth and tight throat on my huge cock has me seething in an erotic sort of rage, the power I wield over her in this moment as addictive as heroin.

"Fuck," I hiss. Her struggling becomes more and more futile, her eyes roll back, and I release her nose and wrench my cock out, giving her a reprieve. A line of foamy spit connects us, and she drags in ragged breaths through what I am sure is a raw throat. Crouching until we are eye level, I grin dangerously at her as she pants and cries. "My little Eden. I'm about to fucking destroy you."

Her chest heaves, her breaths echoing through the woods as more thunder sounds in the distance. Someday, I want her to swallow my cum, but right now, I need to sink into her tight cunt again. Twisting her around until she's on all fours, her fingers digging into the fragrant, moist dirt atop the grave, I line the head of my cock to her entrance. She's fucking dripping, she's so wet, and I laugh mirthlessly.

"Teddy," she whimpers. I feel nothing at the sound of her voice, because I'm too far gone at this moment. The voices demand a sacrifice, and she is it on the altar of the dead.

"Teddy isn't here right now," I hiss, and slam into her. She rocks forward with the painful thrust and screams, but I give her no time to adjust to my length and girth, not like last night.

Last night was the beginning of twisted, obsessive love.

Today is the brutal marking and claiming of a woman that will only ever be mine.

Her cunt ripples against my cock as if stroking it, and I groan again, leaving myself planted so deeply in her that I've found her cervix. Biting back the urge to come right now and paint her womb with my seed, I slowly ease out as she whimpers.

"I warned you," I swear, slamming back in as she cries out. "Not to play with fire."

The sound of her laughter as she sprinted away from me

in the woods makes me shiver anew in delight. She likes to play, and I like to dominate. I ease out again, head cocked to the side to get a better view of my dick in her little pussy. My hands smooth over the pale globes of her ass, my fingers sinking into her muscle with the intent to leave bruises behind.

She moans, the sound mingled with the pain I know I'm giving her, and I can't help but grin. A raindrop pelts my sweltering cheek, the first of many to come, and my hands snake their way to her bony hips as I hold her to me, slowly easing back in, fascinated as I watch my cock disappear into her.

Thunder crashes through the trees and echoes between the mountains, and I know we don't have much time.

"Grab the headstone, baby," I demand breathlessly, enraptured as I leisurely pull out again, this time until just the head of my cock resides in her cunt. She's soaked me, my dick shimmering in her juices, and she begins to tremble.

She does as I command, reaching up, arching her back, my eyes trailing along her spine and committing this vision of ecstasy to memory. Shaking, her dirt-coated fingers wrap around the worn edges of the nameless headstone, and she turns her head to peek at me over her shoulder, her violet eyes as stormy as the skies above.

"You like hurting me," she hisses, both an accusation and a discovery. Bending, I press a kiss to her shoulder, our eyes locked as my lips linger on her soft skin.

"And you like the pain," I retort. "Now grab the fucking headstone and scream my name, little ghost."

Her eyes flare, and at the same moment I thrust back into her, I sink my teeth into her shoulder. She screams as I piston in and out of her furiously, claiming the prize I won. Her sweet, coppery blood pools in my mouth as she sobs, her cunt gripping my cock so hard it almost hurts me in return. Her knees skid across the dirt as I pound into her, her cries and moans music to my trained ears.

"Ow...oh, fuck," she whines, and I feel the beginning of her orgasm. She clings to the old stone for dear life, her cheek now pressed to it because of the force of my thrusts, and I wind a fist into her hair, yanking her head back to watch her eyes spark as she comes undone around me.

"That's it, that's it," I encourage, ramming into her as she sobs, her eyes on mine. "Let me see you come."

Her body goes tense, and her cries choke off in a guttural moan that has my balls tightening in preparation for my own climax.

"Teddy," she sobs, withering around me, her cunt clenching me rhythmically, stroking me from the inside until I can't contain myself anymore.

"Fuck, baby," I hiss, ripping myself out of her and jerking myself just as hard and fast as I'd been fucking her. Ropes of cum paint her back and ass as she collapses with a cry into the dirt. The teeth marks on her shoulder still bleed bright blood, and I fall over her, blanketing her trembling form with my body as she spasms and comes down from her own high. "Good girl, Eden. You took me so well."

"Mmm," is all she manages to mumble, and I smile against her, nuzzling my face in the crook of her neck as more rain cools my body.

"Are you okay?" I ask gently, the voices slinking back into the furthest corners of my mind, satiated and content. Without their demands to brutally claim my woman, my nerves begin to take root. Did I hurt her, scare her? That's the last fucking thing I want, for Eden to be afraid of me—*truly* afraid of me.

But she nuzzles me back, and I can feel her cheek lift in a small, satiated smile.

"I earned a secret, I think."

I chuckle against her, wrapping her in my arms and pulling us back so she's in my lap and we're sitting in the middle of a crumbling graveyard. A few hundred feet away, a massive, imposing raven sits atop another headstone, his keen black eyes watching us. Everything feels so right in this moment, but also as though we've been here before in another life, another time not so long ago. It's strange, but somehow beautiful.

"What secret do you want, Eden?" I'd give this girl anything she wanted, right now and forevermore.

She twists in my arms and blinks lazily up at me, that little smug smirk on her perfect lips.

"Who else do you hunt, Teddy?"

My smile slips from my face as the storm clouds finally close in on us, darkening the shades of her pale features until only her eyes seem to shine. She knows, in her heart. I've sensed it for a while, and I'm not afraid of her knowing my greatest secret. It's undoubtedly going to be used to protect her in the near future.

So I hold her close, my eyes on the raven, and say, "Whoever the voices demand, little ghost. And I'll kill them all for you, before the end."

My eyes drop to hers, and she's smiling up at me.

"I know you will. And I can't wait to watch."

THIRTY-TWO
EDEN

"HEY, LOVEBUG." My father's raspy voice has my face snapping in his direction, my tattered book forgotten as I sit perched on his windowsill. He'd been sleeping so peacefully when I'd arrived late this afternoon amidst a new wave of thunderstorms, and so I'd pulled out *Looking for Alaska* and began to read, attempting to distract myself from the memories of the last twenty four hours.

I don't want to forget them, for they are beautiful and dark and powerful. But if I keep thinking about Teddy, how he makes me feel, that dirty mouth and all he can do with it...I'll be changing my underwear for the umpteenth time today. As sore and bruised as I am, I still want more. If he's obsessed with me, then I am addicted to him, and our twisted tryst has just cemented those feelings for the two of us, I think.

Setting aside my book, I drop my feet over the side and slip down, dizzy as I stand. Cash picked us up from the asylum late this morning and we all stopped in Hangman Hollow for break-fast, but with how much my poor body has gone through, I will need to sleep for two days straight at this point to recover.

Dad pats the side of his bed, and I slip onto it, so tired that I simply fall down next to him and curl into his warm embrace. He holds me against him; his strength is nearly nothing now, and I worry my bottom lip as reality begins to close back in around me. It was nice, having a reprieve from everything, but that doesn't mean the hard parts of life don't exist in the peripherals.

"Are you going to tell me about prom, or keep me guessing?" he says, pecking a kiss to my forehead. Despite the storm that looms in my heart, I smile against him and snuggle in further.

"It was...good."

He chafes my arm with a tired chuckle.

"You're definitely a teenager."

My smile grows, but I hide it against him. It's quiet for a few long heartbeats as soft rain patters the window. I almost drift off to sleep, feeling so warm and content, but his voice rouses me from my impending slumber.

"He seems like a good kid, that Teddy. His mom was sweet."

I blush. Tara stayed after we left for prom, Betsy offering to give her a ride home since Dick doesn't allow her to drive. Now I'm nervous for what the parents chatted about while we were absent.

"She made my dress, and did my hair," I say. There's a smile in his voice when he answers.

"She told me. Said how sweet you were, that she always wanted a daughter. Seems like she raised her son right, in any case."

There's more he's hinting at, and we both know it, but I think neither of us want to acknowledge it. That omnipresent lump builds in my throat like a wall of stone, impenetrable and aching. He's fading from me faster than I can wrap my head around, and when he's gone, I'll have no family left but the dead. I've often wondered if he will return to visit me as a phantom, but I don't think he will. He deserves peace in the next life, and I know he will get it.

"He'll..." Dad clears his throat of his own tears, and mine slips down my temple, wetting his hospital gown. "He'll take good care of you when I'm gone, won't he?"

He states it as a question, but there's a surety in his tone that tells me he knows Teddy will. I swallow hard and nod against him, my whisper rough with tears. "Yes. He will, dad."

He gives me as much of a squeeze as he can muster.

"Just...keep your eye on the future, Eden. I want you to go on to school. Never rely on another person, in that sense."

I know what he means, and I do agree with him. Teddy and I haven't discussed what happens after we get out of the circus, beyond agreeing that we will somehow live at St. Ignatius. Would he want to go to college with me? What would he study? I already know he'd fully support me, just as I would support him. There's a level of surety within our relationship now that I don't think many people find in their lifetime.

He is it, I know it in my bones, and no matter the trials, we will face them as one. I sniff, wiping my dripping nose on the sleeve of Teddy's hoodie. It still smells like him, but mingled with rain and dirt from our little...run through the woods earlier. "I'm sure he will want to get out of Seattle too, dad."

It's quiet for another long moment, only the noise of his oxygen tank and labored breathing sounding in the silence of the room.

"He asked me something when you stepped out yesterday."

This, I perk at, my head popping up, my eyes examining my father's. They narrow as he smiles softly, reaching up to brush a still-damp tendril of hair from my cheek. Teddy had left me at home to shower and get ready so I could come see my dad, promising to come back tonight so we could work on our *Dracula* essays together. I have a feeling those won't be getting done, though.

"What did he ask?" I growl, stomach flipping. Dad chuckles.

"He asked if I knew how perfect you were. And then..." he trails off, his eyes swimming with tears. Tears, because his time on earth dwindles more each day, but also tears because he is a father watching his only daughter become a woman. "He asked permission to be the one to look after you when I'm gone."

My chin wobbles, and my throat burns, and the tears I try so hard to keep in spill over and flow down my cheeks. He brushes them away with his thumbs, holding my face between his warm, papery hands.

"What did you...what did you say?" I croak. He smiles, and for the first time in a long time, it's genuine and bright and filled with happiness.

"I asked if he was up for the task. To which he said, life is boring without a little bit of a challenge."

We both laugh, because his answer is perfect, and I can see how relieved my father is, knowing that I finally have friends who will truly look after me when he is gone. It may have taken the entirety of my life to get here, but it was worth the wait.

I bite my lip, eyes flicking between my dad's.

"I really, really like him," I breathe. He nods, as though he already knows this.

"I can tell. Just be careful, Edie. You two are still so young. Go live life before you get too serious."

I don't bother telling him it's too late for that, that both Teddy and I have already shouldered responsibilities meant for those far older than us. For now, I'll just cling to the hope that one day, it will get better. One day, all of this shit will end, and we can be free in our happiness together amongst the dead.

But if life has taught me anything, it's that things always get worse before they get better.

THIRTY-THREE
TEDDY

"I THINK we're past keeping secrets," Eden grumbles across from me in Literature. We're supposed to be teamed up and correcting one another's *Dracula* essays, the final draft due on Friday. Hers is brilliant, of course, connecting William Brodey, Robert Louis Stevenson, Jack the Ripper, and *Dracula* in a seamless way, tracing back the inspiration for heinous crimes and works of art. Her point being that essentially, everything inspires something—even a murderer.

"Oh, we are, are we?" I tease, underlining a wordy phrase in her essay. Her violet eyes cut to the motion of my pen, her lips tensing in annoyance. Eden is a perfectionist, but so am I. Iron sharpens iron and all that. Just another reason we're meant to be. Sassily, she crosses out a line in my paper, and I have to fight back the urge to laugh.

She's a little brat, I've discovered, and every time I think of her giggling as she ran naked through the woods, my cock swells to nearly its full length and weeps at the fact we're stuck in literal hell at school with not many chances to fuck. I love it, the way she's flourishing into herself with me. I know we both have kinks, obviously, but we now have the chance to learn them together. I don't know their names, or why we have them, but it feels right, everything we explore with one another.

There's no one else I'd want to discover them with anyways.

"Yes," she hisses as our teacher meanders by, only giving us a glance. She keeps tapping Brant's desk, forcing him to wake up and threatening to fail him if he doesn't participate. His poor partner is Eunice, a prim and proper first generation American who doesn't fall for Brant's pleas for help writing his paper. He's offered to pay her multiple times, and she pretends to not hear him as she eviscerates his essay.

"What secret do you want, then?" I answer when the coast is clear, circling a dangling participle. Again, she glares at the stroke of my pen and the red ink that mars her paper she printed in the library this morning, and I bite my cheek to hide my smirk.

"How do you know about tomorrow night?"

I should've known that was coming, but it still jolts me, causing the voices to awaken in barely controlled fury. They gnash their teeth and hiss in my skull, enraged that anyone would attempt to take what's ours. Swallowing down my white-hot ire, I flip to the next page of her essay and answer with caution. "Daniel left his laptop unattended. I saw the emails, and the money transfer."

She's gone still as stone, and I begrudgingly bring my eyes to hers, not wanting to see the pain I know is swirling there. Her lips are parted in slight shock, her face paler than normal, purplish bags that match her irises under her eyes. It does hurt her, knowing those two fucks sold her innocence and trapped her, making it seem like her decision. But what surprises me most is her own wrath, emboldened because I think she knows I have her back, now and forever.

"How much?" she grits out haughtily, returning to her marking of my paper. Furiously, she crosses out a line and writes *Redundant* in bold red ink, the tip of her pen nearly sinking through to the next page in her cute fury. It's kinda hot, her taking out her anger on me in this indirect way. I wish we had time to get back out to the asylum so she could fight me again, so we both could have a reprieve from our lives. Maybe next weekend.

"Twenty thousand."

She rolls her eyes, reaching for her grammar book and flipping it open to the section on punctuation for indirect quotations. I frown. She's far too thorough, and thus is the reason she is valedictorian, and I am not. I don't mind her besting me in academics, though.

I'll put her in her place with my cock later.

"I'll take care of it, Eden. Just go along with it, okay?"

Her eyes snap to mine, frightened and angry.

"No."

I smirk.

"Yes, baby. Don't argue. You know what happens when you do."

Her cheeks flood with crimson, and her eyes water, but there in her slender, pale neck, her jugular pulses hotly, betraying her desire. She shakes her head and sharpens her glare.

"Don't do anything stupid, Teddy. There's too much at stake."

"You think I'm going to let another man fuck you?" I hiss, the voices all pushing forth, rushing against my defenses and nearly making it out. My body trembles with the effort to keep them in check, and her doll eyes widen. I researched him, the man who paid for my little ghost. Killing him will be tricky, and more dangerous than simply ending degenerates.

Mainly because he's the dean of the University of Washington, and his record is spotless. But fuckers like him always have skeletons in their closet. I just have to unearth them within the next twenty four hours, or his death will be investigated far too thoroughly to keep me safe.

Seattle's current chief of police is an old west type of man, one who is good through and through.

One who often laughs at the crime scenes I leave behind, because I've made his job easier, giving justice the comic book hero way.

"Teddy..." she says softly, worry laced in her haunting voice. I glance at her, my anger ebbing, but only just. I give her an unconvincing smirk.

"Not happening, Eden. I don't care what I have to do."

Her throat bobs as she swallows. The bell rings, but we hold one another's gaze still, hers softening bit by bit as the ice around my heart thaws. Everyone jumps up around us, shoving books and papers into their bags and rushing away from the dread of impending finals. And still we sit, the air charged between us again, just as it was in the graveyard. She shakes her head, and her cold little hand falls over mine.

"I can't lose you, too," she whispers, tears wavering in her eyes. I grit my teeth against the desire to pull her to me, to whisk her away to our kingdom and never come back. Before I can respond, the shadow of our teacher falls over us, and Eden hastily pulls her hand away, leaving me cold, my heart rent asunder.

"Aww, I always thought you two would be cute together. I'm excited to read your essays!" she says kindly, one of the few people in this shithole I actually admire. I flash her a grin, camouflaging myself as nothing more than a teen prepared to graduate soon.

"Eden's is excellent. She's cemented her place as valedictorian," I say smoothly, winking at my little ghost. She's not buying it, my act, but I quirk my brow at her and prod her to play along.

Mouth screwed up in annoyance, she says, "I don't know. Teddy might *ruin* my streak."

I snort, for her ire toward me is somewhat scary, but also fucking hot. I have to constantly remind myself she rules the dead, and there's a certain type of power there that I've yet to see.

"Well don't be late for your next class, you two. I look forward to your essays."

We gather our things and stand, and Eden breezes past me, icing me out in her fear. I'm not worried.

Because the gift I have planned for her...well, she'll have to forgive me.

I hope.

THIRTY-FOUR
EDEN

THE MASSIVE MANSION before me is surrounded by a stone wall and wrought iron gate, not unlike the derelict one of St. Ignatius. It's dusk, and heavy storm clouds rumble in the distance, like fluffy, gray cotton balls filled with static and rain. The car rolls to a stop, and though the silence within the cab is unnerving, I'd rather stare at my impending doom than glance at Daniel.

He drove me, wanting to ensure no funny business would occur between now and the time I'm raped for twenty thousand dollars. When we'd left the circus, Teddy's perceptive eyes had followed me, Vic yammering at him to pay attention as he taught him how to swallow fire. Ever since our little spat in literature yesterday, I haven't talked to him, too keyed up and nervous for whatever he's planning.

I know he's a killer, that much is obvious. It should frighten me, but it doesn't, because he's had every opportunity to end me and he's never come close. I speak with the dead, and he creates them. We're twistedly perfect for one another, but if he wants a future with me, he needs to keep himself in check and leave this entire situation alone. There's too much at stake for the two of us, and I won't have him risking his life for me.

"Ride the bus home when you're done. I have work to do," Daniel snaps. Jumping at the sound of his voice, I turn and glance at him, fingers gracing the handle of his car door. A nice car, to be sure. A brand new BMW that I have a feeling this transaction helped pay for.

Sick fuck.

Popping the door handle, I don't give him a backwards glance as I exit and slam the door a lot harder than necessary, treading up the driveway to the little box with the keypad near the gate. Shakily, my finger presses the call button as Daniel speeds away. Releasing a deep breath, I glare through the bars of the gate and to the dozens of windows beyond that spill golden light onto the immaculate front lawn. There's even a damn fountain right in the center of the driveway, and I have to wonder...

If this scumbag can afford a home like the one I'm standing in front of, he couldn't fork over more money to sleep with me?

The speaker box crackles, and I jump at the intrusive noise, heart pounding as the gates slowly begin to open with a heavy groan.

"You may enter," says an androgynous voice, and I stare at the box for a moment, summoning my courage and giving my eyes one final lap around the foreboding mansion.

Teddy? My heart whispers longingly, that wistful part of me praying he does come to the rescue, my knight in shining armor. I've thrown up everything in my stomach today, both dreading this moment and fearing that he *will* come and do something stupid and get himself killed for it.

There's no way he can leave the circus though, right? There's too many people keeping an eye on him, and they'd know of his absence?

My feet propel me forward, my body numb and my mind buzzing as it has been all day. Even Cash's jokes during gym couldn't make me smile, and Teddy knew better than to try.

Swallowing down my fear, I raise my chin and calm my soul. If this is what I have to do to keep Teddy and my father safe, then so be it. I'd do much worse if the need ever arose. It's just...scary, that's all. Just something new, and a little intimidating, but I can do it.

I can do anything for those I love.

"SOON AS I laid eyes on you," the man says sloppily around a mouthful of steak and potatoes. My plate sits untouched, a luxury I hadn't been expecting. He reaches for his glass of wine, some of it sloshing over the sides of the crystalline glass, dribbling down in crimson rivulets and staining the starched white tablecloth below. "I knew. I knew I had to have you."

His home is just as spectacular on the inside as it is on the outside, and I can't keep my eyes from wandering over all the gaudy decor. His dining room is huge, hues of blood red and crimson layered against heavy curtains and an ostentatious fireplace. My eyes sweep back to his, a steady tremble thrumming through my chest. He's horrible, at least in his mid-sixties, with long, yellowed teeth and a turkey neck. His tuft of white hair sticks up against a balding head filled with dander, and his watery brown eyes keep dipping to my chest. I don't have big boobs, so I'm not sure what the fuck he finds so interesting about them.

A sinking feeling hits my gut. I'm barely legal, and childish still in my appearance. This must be his way of circumnavigating a child molestation charge. Find someone who looks the part, and take from them like the greedy, sick bastard he is.

The butler in the corner remains stoic and still, but there's a firm set to his jaw and a rather annoyed glint in his eye. He's easy to ignore, as insignificant as the wallpaper. What I can't ignore, however, is the old woman dressed in black that stands behind the man who paid for me, her eye sockets empty, her hair nothing more than wispy tendrils, her skin wrinkled and worn and decomposing.

She doesn't frighten me, because her wrath isn't meant for me. She's rather intent on the man, and I think she's been haunting him for a while. Perhaps a deceased wife, or even his mother, judging by the dress. Even with the blazing fire in the hearth, there's a constant undercurrent chill in the room. She wavers in and out of my view, leering over his shoulder like a vulture waiting its turn for a bite of rotten flesh.

I have to fight my smile, because as disgusted and terrified as I am to be in the presence of him, I'm just as comforted, knowing the dead feel the same.

Something thumps against the floor above us, rattling the chandelier and splintering the thick silence like an ax sinking into wood. Everyone's eyes jump to the ceiling, and the man grunts, stabbing at more red potatoes and shoveling them down his gullet.

Behind him, the woman's head cocks to the side at an unnatural angle, and a sick smile splits her face, nothing but a gaping hole where her mouth should be.

"Go take that mongrel outside to the kennels, Anders, and leave us be for the rest of the evening."

"Of course, sir," the butler says softly, exiting in long strides. Alone, the man points his knife to my plate.

"You'll need your energy. Richard promised me a virgin, and I don't go easy on virgins."

That queasiness enters my stomach again, and I swallow down my bile, refusing to answer. They only told me I had to let him sleep with me, not that I had to attend a dinner date and be even more humiliated in the process first. So when I say nothing, his eyes narrow, and his moist lips quiver.

He slams his fist on the table, knife sticking up threateningly and clenched in his meaty fist, spittle flying from his mouth. "Speak. Or are you a dumb bitch like the last one, too?"

Last one...?

The woman behind him grows darker, her fury mingling with my own. She loathes him. And suddenly, an idea occurs to me that never has before. I have nothing to lose by sharing this secret with him, because who the fuck cares if he believes me or not? As long as he gets what he paid for, I'm in the clear, and my father will be safe.

A nervous smile has my lips trembling and my heart racing as I sit up straighter. "Were you ever married?"

His chewing slows, his eyes narrowing. He doesn't speak, and I don't give him a chance to.

"She died, didn't she?"

"How dare you speak—"

My lip curls back in a sneer, and I lean across the table, emboldened because...because I know that Teddy keeps his promises, and I know he will never let anyone touch me.

"She *hates* you," I seethe with venom. His mouth pops open, revealing wet crumbs of food still clinging to his tongue. "You feel her all the time, don't you? That chill that hasn't gone away since she died. She hated you in life, and she hates you in death, and she knows. She knows you're a pervert."

"You little cunt—"

"Ah, ah, ah," comes a deep, dark voice, filled to overflowing with malice, the tone one I recognize, because the voices in his head have taken over.

And I'm about to witness him *really* hunt.

I have to bury my smile, difficult as it is, as the man whirls in his seat and gasps. It's not his dead wife he sees, but Teddy emerging from the darkness of the doorway. The lights overhead flicker noisily before we are doused in orange-hued darkness, the only remaining light that of the fireplace.

His grin is dangerous, and the reason I am shaking now is far different than the reason just moments ago.

"I'm the only one allowed to degrade my little ghost," he says smoothly, flipping a knife seemingly out of thin air, the silver glinting ominously.

"Who the hell are you? How'd you get in here? Anders! Anders, call the police—"

But Teddy is on him faster than I can blink, the knife pressed to his quivering throat, choking off his pleas. The madness in Teddy's eyes has my body going rigid and utterly cold, the sneer on his lips and the way he's devoutly focused on his task something otherworldly. If demons exist, they do in him, and their master has let them out to play.

"I make it a sport to slice up sick fucks who hurt little girls," Teddy hisses, spilling a secret to me that I catch and bury close to my heart. "You'll never touch her, or anyone else, ever again."

The man protests, but Teddy grips what little hair remains on the back of his skull and forces the man to face me. Knife still pressed to his throat, his watering eyes go wide with shock as they find mine, but I'm not looking at the man who paid for me.

No. I'm looking at the man who is about to kill for me.

And I'm entranced.

He smiles like the devil.

"You wanna watch, baby?"

Sick fascination swirls into me and floods my veins. I've seen the dead in all forms—decrepit, rotting, and as close to normal as can be. But to watch the soul leave a body? It's always been a curiosity of mine, and so I nod shakily.

"You can't do this, you can't—"

"I already sent your porn stash to every professor, student, even fucking janitor at your school. The news has the tapes, too. No one will miss you, Dr. Williams."

He goes pale as the ghosts I'm fond of, and my smile grows, something about this level of justice giving me hope that someday, Teddy and I will take it for ourselves.

"Your wife is waiting for you," I whisper, my voice hoarse with nerves. Teddy's eyes widen in what I can only describe as lust, his entire body tightening and poised to spring across the table and fuck me over the corpse he creates. The idea alone has my underwear soaked. "She can't wait to drag you to hell where you belong."

Teddy chuckles, the sound dark and foreboding as it bounces off the walls. He pats the man's shoulder. "See why I refuse to share her? She's...*exquisite*."

He breathes the last part, his words spoken from the darkest parts of his cracked and ruined soul, one that is so beautiful it makes my bones ache to behold.

"You freaks—"

Teddy smirks. Time stands still. The ghost of his wife buzzes with sick excitement.

"Yes," he says, sinking his knife into skin and muscle and viscera, thick red blood cascading out as the man's eyes widen in a way I've never seen before. It's the look of someone who knows with utter certainty they are about to die at a monster's hands.

My monster's hands.

"We are freaks," I seethe as tears pool in my eyes, threatening to spill over like his coppery blood. He gags and clutches at his throat as Teddy takes the dripping knife away, his cut so seamless and precise, deep enough to be searingly painful, but not deep enough to kill him immediately. The cut of an expert.

"I'll give you a head start again, little ghost. If you make it back here without getting caught, I'll let you finish him off. But if I catch you..." he trails off darkly as the man slowly bleeds out.

A girlish smile lights my face, and I spring from the chair so fast it skids across the floor, my heart racing, my stomach twisting in fear and disgust but also something deeper and far more heinous than love. Teddy's eyes spark as he flips his knife and grabs the man's wrist at the same time. He forces his hand splayed over the table and drives the blade through all the tendons and bones, pinning him there amidst garbled screams and moans.

"*Run.*" He commands.

And I do.

THIRTY-FIVE
EDEN

THE LAST TIME we played this game, I cut my feet to shit, and Teddy spent no less than two hours diligently and gently plucking splinters from my flesh before washing and bandaging me up. They still ache even in my shoes as I sprint down a darkened corridor, windows along one side allowing scant, icy moonlight to seep in, and mirrors on the other, reflecting that silvery light. Laughter bubbles up in my chest, a giddiness there I feel in my soul.

I was never allowed to be a child. The backs of my hands would be bruised and bloodied if I ever dared to run through the house, or even outside. Running wasn't considered ladylike. Playing make-believe created cracks where the Devil could sneak in and tempt you to sin. Having an imagination was equivalent to being a literal witch, and we all know what happens to witches.

By the time I escaped that hell, I was on the cusp of adulthood and forced to care for my ailing father. I never knew what it meant to be creative, to allow your mind to wander, to feel intrinsic freedom as wind whipped through your hair and your lungs ached for breath.

What Teddy and I have is twisted and sick for sure, but he ignites the child in me and allows her a safe place to play for the first time in my life, and I don't think that's bad, or evil. It's so cathartic, this macabre game of tag we've invented for ourselves, and the prospect of him catching me again makes me giddy with dark excitement.

I hope he always finds me and catches me.

I've seen the dead and dying, spent the majority of my life around things of the past, so now I want to be greedy and taste what it means to live, and live the way I want to.

I take a sharp left down a pitch black hallway, slowing my pace and keeping my footfalls light. Hushing my rapid breathing is far more difficult, because I am not athletic in the slightest, and the only reason I have an A in gym is because Miss Peterson has taken pity on me through the years.

Hands outstretched before me, I creep forward, blind in this darkness but unafraid. Nothing can hurt me here, nothing but Teddy, and the pain he inflicts is tempered with pleasure.

Something makes a soft noise behind me, a footfall or the rustle of fabric, I cannot tell, but it makes me freeze in place. Sucking in a breath, I hold it as my heart pounds and my head grows dizzy, the image of Teddy slicing that fucker's neck replaying on a loop in my mind. It was morbid, and fascinating, and I can tell there's a disconnect in my brain, some sort of short that allows me to witness a voracious murderer at work and not bat an eye.

I've always known I was fucked up deep down, and Teddy holds a mirror to that with a smile.

My hands brush against the edge of what I assume to be a table, and I pause, listening intently again for anything as pure excitement courses through my thudding veins. Swallowing thickly, I run my hands along the table and search for a way out of this darkness, but his voice floats to me in the night air, both taunting and menacing.

"You've cornered yourself, little ghost," he calls from somewhere in the long hallway, and I slap my hands over my mouth to curb the screech and subsequent laughter that spills from my lips. My giggle is met with his threatening chuckle. "You think this game is meant to be *fun*, baby?"

His voice grows closer, and my shaking hands find a door. Giddy, I push the handle down, surprised to find it unlocked. When it opens, more moonlight splinters the darkness, and I make a run for it down another hall, this one dusty and strewn with cobwebs, white, gauzy sheets covering the paintings and decor residing here. There's a chill here that cannot be explained by anything rational, and I know in my bones I've discovered his deceased wife's wing of the mansion. Her presence here is thick on my tongue, her anger and fury in death so potent it frightens me far more than the man chasing me.

The door slams behind me, and I glance over my shoulder, screaming with glee as the tall form of Teddy looms in the darkness, the glint of another deadly knife clutched in his hand. I grin, although he doesn't return it. Taunting him and those voices he talks about is far too entertaining to me to be truly afraid, but there's always some level of fear that curls in my gut when I poke at the killer in him.

Turning forward again, I push my legs harder, full out sprinting toward the door at the other end of the long room—

And trip over a stack of books piled near a covered piece of furniture. I crash to the cold, dusty marble floors, my hands and knees taking the brunt of the fall as I hiss in pain, but he's on me in the time it takes for my brain to comprehend what is happening. Both of us pant, but I laugh and twist and struggle to break free of his grasp, his body wrapped around mine from behind, one hand fisting my hair.

"I win," he taunts breathlessly in my ear, and I can feel the long, hard heat of him against my ass. I buck against him, but he only cinches down tighter. "Have to make this quick, baby."

I smirk, although he cannot see it, and claw my way forward across the floor, his strength so superior to mine that it's pathetic. My muscles strain and cramp, but I refuse to give in. Gritting my teeth as I send an elbow flying toward his face, I growl, "No."

He chuckles, one hand slipping the button of my jeans through the hole before he sinks his fingers into the waistband and yanks them down ruthlessly. I can't help my laughter again, because my struggles make him want to hurt me, ignite that predatory instinct within him, and I want him to take me like a savage, to claim me in ways no one else will ever be able to.

The zip of his pants is loud, and I feel the head of his cock slipping up and down through my wetness as he groans in hot desire. I jump away from him, my laughter bouncing off the walls, and he wrenches me back to him so hard that my palms squeak and skid across the cold floors.

"You think this is funny, Eden?" he hisses. "I just fucking slit someone's throat and I'm about to fuck you bloody, and you're *laughing*?"

"Because," I pant, grinning to the darkness. "I'm...gonna get...away," I say, still struggling, however ailing my stamina is.

His answering chuckle is dark and filled with the madness that must live in his skull every day. It sends a chill of foreboding down my spine, and my laughter dies in my throat, turning to a garbled moan as he buries his cock in me in one brutal thrust.

It still hurts, though not as bad as our first time. He *wants* it to hurt, and I want the bite of pain, even if I don't understand why.

"You'll never escape me, and you know it," he seethes through clenched teeth, and my wetness seeps out around his cock, coating my skin as I release a deep breath, shivering beneath him and becoming pliant in his hold. It feels so good, being filled and stretched by him, the tip of his cock nestled against the very end of my insides, a sensitive wall that he knows how to hit just right.

Face plastered to the icy floor, I grin.

"I let you catch me," I say, pressing my ass backwards, his hips cemented to me. I want to take him deeper, and deeper, and deeper still, want to be so tightly joined that we have no hope of ever coming apart. Because in moments like the few we've created over the last couple of days, I feel complete for the first time in my life.

He buries his face in my neck and inhales deeply, his dick throbbing inside me in time with his heavy heartbeats. I don't want him to move, not yet. I just want him to be buried inside me like this forever, the two of us one for eternity. I know his darkness now, and I want to revel in it, poke at it and examine it until I know just how deeply it extends. In the same way, I want him to know *me*—every facet, every deplorable secret.

"Oh you did, huh?" he breathes, teeth nipping at my throat. I moan, shivering anew against him, my knees aching from this position. I don't understand it, how and why my mind morphs into this realm when I'm with him, but I know he likes it, and I don't have to think; I just have to feel, and he makes me feel more than I ever thought I'd be capable.

"Yes," I whimper as he begins to slowly pull out. Panicking, I press back into him, but he plants a hand between my shoulder blades and pins me down, preventing the motion. My cunt ripples and begs for friction, my orgasm already on the cusp, more sticky wetness spilling between my thighs as my arousal mounts. He's teasing me, and I'm getting pissed.

"Please," I whine, trying to back against him again.

"What a needy little whore," he laughs, but the sound is slathered in darkness, and I know Teddy is gone, replaced by the voices who wish pain and suffering upon me. "At least you have good manners."

I whimper again, clawing at the slippery floor, rolling my hips, but he's pinned me tightly to him, and I only barely manage to make his cock move inside me. It's not enough, and I begin to fill with dread, crying out.

"Please, Teddy," I beg.

"You're lucky we have so little time," he growls. Hope ignites in my chest, and my entire body buzzes with sick excitement. *Fuck me, ruin me, please, please, please,* I chant in my mind. "Next time, you're going to sit on my cock until I think you've earned it, understood?"

I nod without thought and cry another *Please* to the void. He pulls out until just the head is seated in my entrance, shallowly thrusting through my slickness. I moan and try to meet the pumping of his hips, but he's careful not to allow himself to sink deep where I need him most. He laughs, smoothing the cool blade of his knife over my ass cheek, but even the threat of blood and pain won't stop me from begging.

My body goes rigid when the handle of the knife skims over my asshole, pressing against it, both a promise and a threat as the breath stalls in my lungs and my eyes fly open. "If you wanna come, baby, we're doing it my way. Yes or no?"

"Yes," I plead without thinking. "Please just fuck me. *Please.*"

He spits onto my ass, pressing the wide handle of his knife deeper into my forbidden hole until I cry out and it pops past that tight band of resistance, pain flaring through me briefly before he thrusts his cock all the way back in. I'm so full that it's bliss, and I wither beneath him, crying out and begging for more.

"You're gonna take my cock in your ass next, and this little knife will seem so small," he swears, twisting the handle in time with the thrusting of his cock, everything rubbing against that precise spot deep inside me. I don't even have time to worry about the blade slicing his hand apart, and I can't seem to care right now. My legs begin to tremble, and my eyes roll back.

"That's it," he seethes. "Good girl, good girl. Come on your master's cock."

"Oh my...oh my god," I cry out, the squelching sounds of my wet pussy and the slap of his skin against mine echoing in this desolate mansion. I'd been sent here to get fucked by a monster.

I'm just happy it ended up being *my* monster.

"Fuck, fuck, fuck," I chant in time with his brutal thrusts, my orgasm climbing to the highest peak as I hold on for dear life, coasting on the top of that blissful high until he forces me over the edge, claiming me ruthlessly as I fall. My cunt grips him in rhythmic bursts, milking him, pulling him impossibly deeper into me until it ebbs and I'm left a shaking mess. He thrusts hard three more times, ripping the knife and himself from my body. The tool clangs to the floor, and his hot, sticky cum coats my ass, his thumb swirling the mess around my abused hole before he pushes his seed into me.

"Someday soon this greedy cunt of yours will take all my cum, little ghost," he swears breathlessly against me, still pumping his thumb in and out, pushing more and more of the white liquid into my ass as I whimper softly in the darkness. "And you'll thank me after, won't you?"

A grin paints my lips in a flash, and I nod as best I can, cheek squeaking against the polished floor.

"Thank you, *master*," I tease, pressing my ass into him so his thumb sinks further in.

"Fuck me, Eden. You'll be the death of me," he breathes, lips at my ear. My smile broadens.

"As long as you take me with you," I say to the darkness.

And I hope he knows just how serious I am.

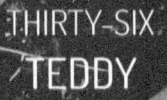

"YOU TWO TOOK YOUR SWEET FUCKIN' time."

The waiflike form of Vic wavers into view amidst the thick evergreens that dot the property of the man I just killed. To Eden's credit, she evaded me for longer than I thought she'd be able to, and he died choking on his blood while I watched, a sick smile plastered to my face the entire time. Hand in hand, we sneak from the house, sticking to the edge of the forest that surrounds the ostentatious mansion, my bloodlust and lust for Eden sated, my voices humming in contentment.

Her hand stiffens in mine, and I tug her after me, knowing she's shocked at seeing Vic here of all places.

"Teddy," she hisses, obstinate as I lead her through the darkness. Vic stands, arms crossed, shoulders pressed against the sturdy trunk of an oak tree. His eyes glow through the darkness, silvery orbs like crystal balls. He'd discovered me snooping through Daniel's laptop, but when I'd shown him what those two fucks were forcing Eden into, we'd formed our plan.

Turns out, I was right in my assumptions about the gaunt

semi-frightening circus master. He is a killer, born and bred in the slums of London, working for a family as their...clean up crew, so to speak. His track record was flawless until the family was massacred, and he fled to the states for a new life.

It ultimately led him to Dick and Daniel, and the old curmudgeon took it upon himself to stay and work there, silently keeping the girls safe from worse fates. He has an obvious soft spot for Eden, so provoking him to help me was rather easy.

We come to a stop before him, Eden glancing between us with worry in her eyes, her brows scrunched together. "What the hell are you doing here?"

Vic raises a brow, a bemused expression on his dry lips. "What's with the tone, little missy?"

I can't help but smirk, staring down at her. That silky, ebony hair is a mess, her pale cheeks are flushed pink, her eyes shining with the remnants of lust. She looks well and thoroughly fucked, and she is. There's no way Vic can't tell.

So teasing Eden a little more won't hurt.

"Thought I fucked the brat right out of you, but maybe you need another round."

Slowly, tremulously, she turns her furious gaze up to me, her cheeks crimson in her embarrassment.

"Teddy," she hisses through clenched teeth, a warning in her tone. I quirk my brow and my smirk deepens, my cock awakening again. I could fuck her until dawn, and still get hard the moment she asked it of me. The way she'd ground her ass against my hips, the way she'd begged me to make her come, the way her tight little ass devoured my knife handle...

"What? Wanna go again?"

She makes a disgusted sound and wrenches her hand from mine, turning her ire to Vic, who's glaring at me with death in his eyes.

"What are you doing here?" she presses again, and he tears his angered gaze from my face, focusing on the wrathful little sprite between us.

"Cleaning up the mess laddie over here made, and keeping you two safe. Now get out of here, and speak of this to no one, understood?"

She glances quickly between us, a terrified glint in her violet eyes. I reach for her hand again, clasping it in mine and squeezing. "It's gonna be okay, Eden. He knows what he's doing."

She shakes her head, mouth open, incredulous look wavering on her slender features.

"No, it's *not* going to be okay. Because Dick and Daniel are just going to keep selling me, idiots, and then what? You're just going to kill everyone who pays for me?"

She has a valid point, and I glance over her head toward Vic. The voices gnash their teeth and hiss at the prospect, keen to sink their canines into anyone who tries to take what is ours. It won't happen. Not as long as I draw breath.

"If that's what it takes, then so be it," he says with finality. Her shoulders droop, and she shakes her head, misery etched into her ethereal features.

"You can't risk yourselves like this for me."

"We'll figure something out, Eden. Just...hold on a little longer," I say, squeezing her hand again. Her eyes find mine through the darkness, and the terror that swirls there is a punch straight to my guts. I know she trusts me, otherwise she wouldn't find it so joyous, me killing for her and then fucking her the way I do. It's the unknown she doesn't trust, and she's already lost so much in her short life.

It would crush her, to lose me in any capacity. The pressing need for us to get the hell away from Dick and Daniel is worse than ever before.

"I should just kill them," I muse aloud, gaze drifting into the darkness of the forest. Vic shakes his head.

"Thought that one through already. Wouldn't work."

"Why?" I bite back, feeling utterly defenseless for the second time in my life. The first was with my father whenever he'd beat my mother or slap me around and call me a fag. I was too young, too weak to fight back. But the moment I loosed the voices like an arrow was the moment I found my strength. Being stuck in this situation makes me feel like a caged fucking animal, and the desperation that begins to take root in me is dangerous.

"Too many connections. You kill them, every paying customer in that joint will start looking for answers. And where would those answers lead?"

"So we kill them and run," I say, ready to do it here and now.

"My...my dad..." comes Eden's soft, sorrowful voice. It's my turn for my shoulders to droop. She's right; we can't do anything right now, and I can't say anything about waiting for him to die before I commit a double homicide. It would ruin her.

"We'll plan, then," I say with surety, holding Vic's gaze, and then Eden's. "Because I'm not going to live my life under their thumbs for much longer."

Vic snorts softly and shakes his head, uncrossing his spindly arms and cupping Eden's cheek. "Let laddie take ya home. Get some rest and put this from your mind for now. Promise, eh?"

She leans into his touch, the fatherly figure she's needed while hers wastes away. A few tears gather and spill over her porcelain cheeks, but she nods all the same, sucking in a calming breath.

"I can't lose either of you," she whispers to the dark. "I've already lost too much."

"You won't, little ghost," I promise with utter surety. But when her eyes find mine, she sees the deplorable lie hidden there. We both know the cost of our budding love is a great price to pay.

We just have to wonder how much, before the end.

THIRTY-SEVEN
EDEN

THE GLOW-IN-THE-DARK BOUNCY ball I bought for ten cents in a vending machine down in Hangman Hollow rolls back to me across the littered floor. The day is foggy and cold, a constant mist that has a chill settling into my bones. Hands dangling off the mattress I lost my virginity on, a wan smile paints my lips as the ball comes to a stop right in front of my pointer finger. Eyes flicking upward from my stomach-down position, I glance into the void hallway beyond the empty door.

Nothing greets me but scant, rainy light for a moment. The longer I wait to flick the ball away from me, the more her energy buzzes and grows, as does my smile. She finally peeks around the door frame, her round blue eyes glassy, her cheeks pink, and her blonde hair long and tangled. She died before she even breathed her first breath, but she's stuck as a toddler.

I don't know how I know, but I do. It doesn't make sense, and maybe it never will, but I'm content with that. Lily is perceptive, and whenever she comes around, so too does Eve. Almost as though they're siblings, Eve keeping an eye on the wild little spirit that roams these dark and sometimes sinister halls.

I roll the ball back to Lily, my smile soft as her eyes shimmer. She wavers like all the ghosts I see, transparent but with touches of soft watercolor here and there. It's like watching a TV tuned to the wrong frequency; you get the static, but you can sometimes make out the words and see the shapes just enough to get the jist of what is happening. That's how it's always been for me, and I've never met anyone else with this ability, so I have nothing to compare it to.

Lily smiles and reaches for the ball, but at the last moment her eyes flick upward, her gaze directed down the hallway. She flickers and vanishes with a girlish giggle, unafraid but wanting to play hide and seek. My muscles tense and I frown, pushing myself up and swinging my legs around so I'm sitting. There's only two people aside from myself who know my secret spot, only two who would know this is the room I now find peace in.

And I know for damn sure Cash would never come out here alone.

So when Teddy appears around the corner, neither of us are surprised to see the other. He gives a firm but somewhat timid smile, his dark hair still damp and slicked back, his scent wafting to me on a breeze that moans through the empty hallways. Clad in jeans and a hoodie with some indie band plastered on the front, he still manages to void my mind of all the things that could go wrong and makes me focus instead on how sinfully sexy he is.

I still hate him for that.

He pulls something forward from behind his back, and a little ball of black fluff with two very pointy ears mewls at me, sharp white teeth and pink tongue splintering the darkness of his tiny face. Two bright green eyes stare unblinkingly back at me, and I fight my smile, my gaze flicking to Teddy's. He waits patiently, not saying anything for once.

All week, I've been a mess. Stressed about my dad, graduation, the fucking murder the man I love committed right in front of me, and Vic cleaning it up. Dick and Daniel haven't said a thing, and neither has the news, and so I've sat on pins and needles for nearly a week, miserable in my anxiety. Teddy has tried to help, but I've pushed him away, and he's given me far more space than I deserve. I can see the hurt that swirls in his eyes growing each day.

But I'm still scared, and I bristle at him.

"You can't bribe me with a kitten, Teddy."

"He's pretty fuckin' cute though."

I roll my eyes, falling back onto the mattress, staring at the ceiling; paint and plaster peel from above and dangle over me, brown stains the shape of puddles blotting out what was once a pristine white.

Teddy sits next to me, his gait silent and unnerving. The weight of the kitten settles on my chest, and I can't help my grin as the tiny thing meows again and hunkers down in the valley of my small breasts, timid but trusting. Reaching up, I stroke my finger through the plush fur atop his little head, and he meows again.

"Where did you find him?" I ask.

He doesn't answer right away, and so I glance at him, struck into silence at the view before me. Teddy sits with his knees pulled up and his arms resting on them, one hand clasping his other wrist, staring down at me with those electric teal eyes and a thousand emotions clamoring in his gaze. In the shadows, his jaw is even more chiseled, his full lips set in a firm line, as though there's a lot he wants to say but isn't. And suddenly, I feel like a little girl, afraid of reprimand because I know I've been unfair to him.

"I was checking out the cemetery. Found him hunkered down in the old mausoleum. Didn't see his mom, so..."

Gently, I cup the warm kitten and cuddle him close, my heart relaxing another fraction.

"So you've been following me," I say, keeping my eyes away from Teddy's. I can't be mad at him when he looks at me the way he is, hurt and scared but also disappointed. Guilt threatens to chew me up and spit me back out.

"I told you, Eden. I'd follow you all over this goddamned universe, across every lifetime."

He's angry, his words delivered to my gut like a sucker punch, and my eyes begin to water. Feeling pushed into a corner, I bite back, "So the space you've been giving me is just an illusion?"

"No," he says in exasperation, and that guilt morphs into a beast from which there is no escape. I don't know how to function around people that actually want to be near me, and so pushing them away feels the safer option.

If I hurt them first, then they can't hurt me.

"I'd never force you to talk before you're ready, but I'd never leave you alone, either. You're...*safe*, with me, Eden. I know you have a lot to process."

My eyes flick to his, and I want to break down and sob, want him to hold me together while I fall apart. I've kept myself going through every trial I've faced, but now I'm just exhausted. Is it so wrong to want to share the burden of life with someone? Someone who understands me in ways no one else ever will? I swallow hard around the lump in my throat, about to speak, but he parts his beautiful lips and beats me to it.

"I refuse to lose you, Eden, especially like this. So talk to me."

His gaze is potent and unwavering, and I tear my eyes away, rubbing under the kitten's little chin. His eyes close in contentment, and a soft purr rumbles through his itty bitty chest.

"I'm scared," I finally whisper. Admitting it tastes bitter coming out, and only serves to stir up more of the emotions I've tried so hard to bury. But Teddy waits with a level of patience I never knew someone was capable of, and I search for the right words amongst the jumbled mess in my brain. "I'm terrified to lose you, to lose my dad. I...I'm frozen, but I know these things are coming, and I know I can't stop them."

He shifts until he's on his side next to me, head propped in his hand, small smile wavering on his lips. "You're never going to lose me. Even if I die, I promise to haunt your ass. Think I can still make you come as a ghost?"

"Teddy," I laugh, rolling my eyes. He chuckles, reaching out to run his long fingers over the kitten. His purrs double at all the attention he's receiving. I bite my bottom lip, returning my eyes to the boy I've fallen for, and the one thing in life I know I can't lose. I've come to terms with my father's impending death, but that doesn't make it any less difficult. But if Teddy died?

I'd happily jump off the cliffs I took him to the other day and join him in the afterlife.

"I'm just worried about what Dick and Daniel will do once they find out about...you know..." I trail off, peeking up at him. His jaw is set, his eyes ablaze with the protectiveness I've come to recognize and cherish.

"If they find out, then I'll take care of it, Eden. I...I've done this for a while. I know what I'm doing."

"Is it because of the voices?" I whisper, holding my breath and praying he shares a truth with me. It's something I've pondered since last Tuesday. How many deaths are those nimble hands responsible for? And why? And why doesn't it frighten me like I know it should?

"Yes," he whispers, eyes holding mine. His hand comes to rest on my lower stomach, a heavy, reassuring pressure. "They can't live without you, either. They've been a little pissed this week."

"Why?"

His grin flashes like lightning.

"They miss your pussy."

"Oh my god, Teddy," I hiss and he laughs. He can never be serious for long, but I love it, how he sees life for all it is and still chooses happiness, even if he finds it in twisted, dark ways.

A lot like me.

His laughter dies down, and my smile fades, and he reaches up to cup my cheek, the little paw of the kitten batting out at a string dangling from his sleeve.

"I've murdered nineteen people, including that douchebag this week...and...and including my father."

Coldness creeps through my veins, and a frigid hand grips the back of my neck as his words sink in. There's a disconnect, a short circuit somewhere in my brain, because the words register, but they don't really mean anything to me. Yet my body knows, and the confirmation he's just shared has my spine stiffening.

"Why?" I whisper, needing to understand in some capacity.

His brows raise briefly, and he looks out the door as he ponders his answer. Clouds move in from the inlet nearby, dark and foreboding ones, and the asylum darkens another few shades. It's peaceful, and quiet, and I wish for the millionth time we could just stay here forever.

"My father...used to beat my mom, amongst...other things. Badly. One night I just snapped. I knew the voices long before then, and they always told me how to do it, egged me on. But ever since that night...I couldn't stop myself anymore. It's a need, just like being with you has become a need."

My blood runs cold at his words. Not because he's a killer, but because I can't imagine anyone hurting his mother like that. She's so kind and soft, and she adores her son. Ever since meeting her, I've wondered what my life would be like if I'd had a mom like her, and it fills my heart with heavy sorrow to know she was mistreated in such a way.

His eyes find mine again, and I offer him a small, sad smile.

"If Dick and Daniel find out, Eden, I'll take care of it. Please...I know I'm asking a lot of you, but please trust me. I won't let anything happen to you."

Our eyes search one another's, and I finally relent with a timid nod. I'm in no way letting go of my anxiety, but at least I understand him better. So with a heavy sigh through puffed cheeks, I turn my face back to the ceiling and speak, searching the stains there for patterns.

"My mom was always super religious. Her and dad were high school sweethearts, from a pretty small farming town. I grew up on a farm, but it was also a vineyard my grandparents owned. When they died...she...she had all of the grape vines burned. I don't remember that, but that's when dad left her. She became way too involved in church, and he was always deployed. I was homeschooled, and had to wear these ugly fucking skirts and dresses."

He snickers, and I glance at him with a coy smile, still running my fingers over the purring kitten on my chest, his warmth seeping into my heart.

"We went to church every day of the week, and things just became more and more zealous. All of my friends started... disappearing. And...umm..." I mutter, fighting for the right words. I know Teddy will understand, but what I fear is his anger on my behalf, because I have a feeling the voices will want to sink their teeth into my mother for what she did to me. So I hold his gaze and find my strength there to speak.

"She would beat me. Lock me up, sometimes for days. If I needed to bathe, or shower, she'd watch me to make sure I didn't...touch myself. I eventually had to sleep in her room with her, because she was so paranoid about *sins of the flesh*," I say, shivering at the phrase and all the abhorrent memories it brings forth.

"I didn't know it, but she was keeping me pure for my husband. When I...when I started my period, she became weirdly happy and nice to me, bought me new dresses, trimmed my hair," I say, blushing.

His stare is unwavering, but the way the edges of his jaw become sharper tells me he's grinding his teeth so hard they may shatter. My heart pumps hard against my ribs, disturbing the peaceful slumber of the kitten. Tearing my gaze from Teddy's, I continue.

"She told me it was time to meet the man God had chosen for me, my husband. I was so confused, kept asking her if dad knew, if this was normal."

I swallow hard, fighting against the need to flee. The emotions these memories dredge up are difficult to bear, seeing as I've spent so long burying them as deeply as possible.

"And then I met him. I was thirteen, and he was forty-something, and she left me alone with him. He...asked me such odd questions. I should've still been playing with dolls...not being...molested by some pedophile," I hiss, my vision swimming with furious tears. I've never even told my father the extent, because he rescued me just in time. But at night, when I'm alone in our house, I still feel those vile hands snaking up my thighs, groping my prepubescent breasts, and those fingers pushing aside my underwear to explore me while I stood there, numb with grief as my childhood crashed and burned around me.

"Eden."

His voice is calm, so deep and gentle and reassuring. My tears spill over and race down my temples, but I look at him. Devastation mars his perfect features, but the fury is simmering there, just beneath the surface and barely contained. Heaving a shaky breath, I continue, lightening my tone for his benefit.

"I sent a letter to my dad, and he came home and took custody of me, but...I still feel guilty, because I never told him the full story. He was already sick. I didn't want to make it worse."

He's deathly quiet, and the entire asylum seems to hold its breath with him. The air around us is charged and tinged with something sinister, and I turn my gaze to Teddy; the emotions that are emanating from his eyes match the storm he's creating with his energy.

I've learned that spirits feed off whatever you put out, so right as I open my lips to issue a warning, something downstairs slams—*hard*, making me jump as my eyes widen. The sound reverberates through the massive, empty space, echoing menacingly. It darkens more, almost to the point where I'm unable to make out Teddy's livid, seething features, and rain pelts the stone façade.

The basement, I've learned, is where the root of the evil of this place resides. The leftover equipment down there is covered in a layer of dust and mold, and rats have eaten away at the fabric and stuffing of chairs and beds. I know it's where doctors with morbid and vile intentions performed lobotomies and shock therapy.

I think it's how Eve died.

"You're giving them energy," I whisper. Slowly, he quirks his brow, and even more slowly, his lip rises into a smirk.

"To whom am I giving my energy?" he asks coyly, that wicked smile cemented in place. I give him a chastising tilt of my head and frown.

"Evil," I say back.

His grin is anything but inviting, and his eyes almost glow through the darkness all around us.

"Don't worry, love," he says, voice rough with sudden desire. "They know their master."

THIRTY-EIGHT
EDEN

"SO," Teddy says after a few tense moments, the storm clouds outside parting briefly and allowing in scant, watery sunlight. The heaviness from before dissipates yet lingers around the edges of my heart, the evil spirits slinking back into their darkened corners to fight another day. "What should we name him?"

I can't help but smile. I know we're in no way prepared for a kitten, or responsible enough with all we have going on in our personal lives, but the selfish little girl in me wants to keep him, damn the consequences. So as I cup his rump and pull him close to my face, nuzzling my nose against his, I grin. "Binx, obviously."

Teddy laughs, dropping his hand over mine, the two of us holding a precious little life between us. "I figured you'd pick that or Jack. I like Binx, though."

I glance at him, his eyes warm swimming pools of lust that I want to sink into and drown.

"Binx can be a guide to the spirits here. I'm sure he plays with them out in the cemetery. You liked the mausoleum."

He smirks.

"Of course I did. Have some...*Cask of Amontillado* plans for the future, I think."

I roll my eyes but press a kiss to Binx's warm, fuzzy head. "I knew you would. You can't actually be related to Poe, though. He never had kids."

He snorts and gently plucks Binx from his resting spot on my chest, leaning over me to set him on the ground. The kitten meows and bats at a dried up bug carcass on the aged wood floors, content to explore. Teddy grips my chin, bringing my attention back to him as he hovers above me, his lithe, muscled bodied tensed as if to strike as he lays himself half on top of me. My cheeks burn, and that's all it takes, this simple movement of him above me for my core to clench in agony at not having him inside me for almost a week.

"My mom did our ancestry. Traced it back to Poe's family. We are related, just not directly."

"Of all the people to be related to, I think he's the most fitting," I tease. He flashes me a toothy grin, his canines biting, desire swirling in his searing gaze. Wherever his eyes grace my flesh, it leaves a burning trail of yearning behind.

But his smile simmers, and his eyes begin to darken again, and I know where his mind has gone before he even speaks. My stomach curls up and withers, my mouth dry as dirt during a drought. I don't like discussing my past, hence why I've never told anyone.

Anyone *alive*, that is.

He brushes his thumb over my chin tenderly, eyes tracing every facet of my face. "Eden...have I ever done anything to...to trigger those emotions from your past?"

I melt beneath him, because I have a feeling no other person would be as thoughtful or caring after such a heavy topic was dropped on their lap. Smiling softly, I shake my head and reach up, my fingers curling around the hand that still holds my chin. He's so warm and strong and sturdy, my anchor in a raging storm that keeps me tethered to this world.

"No," I whisper. "No. When I'm with you...it all goes away. That's why I used to come here so much by myself. This place gives me the same sort of...peace. Release. I don't think about it here, and I don't think about it when I'm with you."

His eyes beam with pride, and he tempers his smile.

"You make me feel the same."

"Good," I quip back, squeezing his fingers. He chuckles, brushing them up the side of my face before sinking them into my hair.

"I know...know how it feels, to be powerless in a situation like that," he whispers, his face clouding over. My heart sinks, and my lips part, but he beats me to it. "Remember that prank a few years ago, Brant and his friends put fish in my locker?"

How could I forget? I'd never witnessed rage so violent before, watching Teddy pummel the kid to a bloody pulp in the hallway before first period. It had honestly frightened me, the way his eyes had gone dark, but I understand it better, now. He was holding back, because he could've easily killed the kid. I nod solemnly. He continues on, and I can hear how the words stick in his throat.

"Miss Goss used that to...blackmail me, I guess. She...well, she took my virginity. In her office. Told me she'd have me sent to juvie if I didn't do it. And she's found ways for it to keep happening, for years."

Tears brim my eyelids, and I feel sick enough to vomit. My skin is cold at his words and all they mean. Yes, Teddy may understand me in this realm, but I'll never understand what it's like to see your abuser day after day, to feel so stuck in a situation that you have to do anything you can to survive.

"I'm so sorry," I whisper. He gives me a wan smile and brushes his thumb over my cheek.

"It's not okay, and what happened to you is not okay. But... if all the bad I've had to endure so far in life has led me to you, then I'd do it all again. Happily."

I smile, a few more tears spilling over and trickling down the sides of my face. His keen eyes watch them, and he catches one with the pad of his thumb, brushing it away.

"Me, too," I say back with conviction. "What...what do the voices think of...of her?"

I'm scared to ask the question, but far too intrigued by the possible answer to keep it locked behind my teeth.

He tilts his head back and laughs, the sound dark yet rich. When his eyes find mine again, they're blazing with barely contained fury and malice and a touch of madness that fights to take over. It doesn't frighten me, because I know I'm a little insane, too. We're meant to be, craziness and all.

"They have a date set for her. She's going to regret every-thing and have...plenty of time to ponder her actions, before she dies."

I swallow hard at how easily he admits he's about to murder someone, but I also know there's nothing I could ever do to stop him, not that I would try. My only worry is him getting caught, ending up in jail or on death row for all the lives he's slaughtered.

But if I were given the chance to kill Malachi Moreau, my abuser?

I would without a second of hesitation. The fact that Miss Goss has hurt someone I love sinks into my soul and festers like a rotting wound. I understand Teddy's fury at hearing my story, because he is *mine* and I am his, and no one will ever touch either of us again.

"Good," I say after a moment, jutting my chin up with conviction. "Hopefully you get to her before I do."

Now he really laughs, and it bounces off all of the walls and echoes down the endless hallways, the asylum sucking this moment in and committing it to its collective memory. His eyes are dancing when they drop back to mine, his grin so wide that his dimples and laugh lines have appeared.

"My murderous little ghost," he murmurs, leaning down to brush his lips against mine. "I'd say I love you, but we both know that's far too trivial for what we have."

My heart stops, and I blink up at him, astonished. His smile has faded into a content but reassured grin, his eyes holding mine as heat tears through me and centers between my thighs.

"What...what do we have, then?" I say quietly.

He looks away for a moment, reaching to wind his fingers through my hand and pin it to the mattress above my head. He does the same with the other, his movements slow and methodical, and he shifts until his body is atop mine, his cock hard as he presses it between my legs and against my aching clit.

"We have madness," he says just as softly, dropping his forehead until it touches mine, his heat flaring through me as my heart begins to race in giddy anticipation. "And that's far, far more powerful than love, I think."

"Why's...why's that?" I say, my breath lost as he brushes his lips against mine again. My back arches, pushing me up toward him, and at the same moment, he rolls his hips languidly, pressing his dick even harder against my throbbing pussy, the teasing unbearable, the clothes between us a hindrance.

Grinning mordaciously, he pushes our hands deeper into the mattress, and that mad glint I've often seen wavering in his eyes grows until it's all I can see, this insane obsession he has with me. There's no severing it, this morbid connection we share.

"Because, little ghost. Love fades with time, and madness..." he whispers against me, rolling his hips again. I gasp and part my legs, wrapping them around his hips and pulling him close, silently begging for more. He chuckles and reaches down, deftly unzipping my jeans as well as his, pushing aside my underwear and finding me soaked and ready for him. "Madness has no cure."

He sinks his two middle fingers into me, and I release a heady moan, grinding myself against his palm as he crooks his fingers deep inside me. Our breaths mingle, our foreheads still touching, this moment so intimate that I find it hard to look away. I am drowning in his eyes, just as I wished to, and he slowly pumps his fingers while circling my clit with his thumb.

"Good girl," he says softly against my lips. "Get nice and wet for me."

"Oh," I whimper, electrified as sparks flare through me from my core, striking out through the rest of my body like splintered lightning. In a flash that leaves my mind whirling, he's up on his knees and tearing my jeans away, throwing them carelessly to the floor before wrenching my panties off as well. Winding his arms around my thighs, he yanks my cunt to his face and devours me, his tongue flicking over my clit as I cry out and sink my hands into his hair.

He tongue fucks me like it's our last night on earth, sucking my clit before teasing my entrance, his rhythm deft, and before I can stop myself, I'm coming on his face with a garbled scream that paints the walls. He gives me no respite as I tremble, my pussy still clenching as he pulls his fingers from me and replaces them with his cock.

"Taste yourself, baby," he says breathlessly, slowly easing into me as I moan, his middle fingers at my lips. I obey, no other thought in my brain as he swirls his sticky fingers over my tongue, and I suck them in just as deeply as his cock is in my cunt. His eyes watch every minute motion I make, and he seems to forget about himself, his cock throbbing inside me, the tendrils of my orgasm still gripping him.

But I always want more of Teddy, and I raise my hips, seeking the delicious friction I know he's capable of inducing. He chuckles, withdrawing his fingers from my mouth and intertwining our fingers again, pressing them deeply into the mattress as he slowly withdraws and sets a leisurely pace.

"Oh, my god," I hiss, for as much as I enjoy the fast and brutal approach, this is somehow a little better, the torture of a promised climax, the way I feel each slow, measured stroke as he drives himself into me with precision and control.

"That's it, good girl," he praises, taking one set of our hands and bringing it to where we're joined. "Feel us. Feel how wet you are for me."

He wraps my hand around his slick cock and I grip him, astonished that something so...*girthy* is able to fit inside me. I hold him as he thrusts into me, and hold him still as he pulls all the way out, the silky head of his cock nestled wetly in my palm before his velvety dick slides back through my fist and into my weeping cunt.

My back arches, and I wrap my legs around his hips again, keeping him planted to me, releasing him to wrap my arms around his shoulders. I never want to let him go, to leave this moment of utter bliss, and by the way he holds me back, I think he feels the same. We fuck for what feels like hours, moving slowly, holding one another so tightly that our limbs go numb and tingly, both of us slowing each time an orgasm draws close, not wanting this to end. For as breathtaking as the climax is, the sheer intimacy in the build up is where I want to live for eternity with him.

We come at the same time, his groans of ecstasy pushing me over the edge as I cry out against him, burying my face in the crook of his neck and inhaling his scent. And trembling, we hold one another against the impending darkness, coming down from the high together but forever stuck in the bliss we've created from our shared madness.

Cuddling as dusk falls over the asylum, I peek out from under his arm, searching for Binx, slightly worried that we haven't heard him in a while. Nuzzling my neck and pressing a deep kiss there, Teddy's deep voice says, "He's fine, baby. Probably playing with your ghosts."

"That's what I'm worried about," I mutter, knowing that some of the spirits here are tricksters. He chuckles.

"Cats are supposed to be super perceptive of that stuff, right? Binx knows good from evil."

I laugh and shake my head. "He's a baby. He still needs his parents to guide him."

Teddy's eyes shine as they find mine. "Are you saying we're his parents?"

"Don't get any ideas. We're way too young," I say firmly. "A kitten is more than enough for now."

"So that's a yes?"

"Teddy!" I giggle, slapping his broad shoulder as he beams down at me. But he waits for my answer, and something tells me he needs one, something to reach for in the future to keep us going through whatever else we must face before the end. "Yes. *Maybe*. Eventually."

"All I ask is for a maybe. The world needs a mini Eden."

"Oh, god. Does the world need a mini murderous Teddy, though?"

He grins and nips at my nose. "Of course. Someone has to be a vigilante when I'm gone."

On cue, the bouncy ball—glowing a pale yellow—rolls to a stop at the edge of the mattress. Teddy springs up onto his arms, hovering above me protectively, eyes focused on the doorway. I smile softly. We're clothed once more, so I don't feel awkward when Lily's timid face comes into view, wavering apprehensively, her round eyes stuck wide on Teddy.

"She wants to play with you," I whisper to him.

"Who?" he asks just as softly.

"Lily. The little girl. She...she seems really attached to you, for some reason," I say, turning my gaze to the side of his face, pondering the connection I feel between the two. He's grinning, still staring at the doorway. When he looks back to me, he's giddy with boyish excitement. I nod my head to the ball. "Roll it back to her."

He pecks my lips with a quick, sweet kiss and hops up, seating himself on the floor with his back to me, plucking the ball from the ground and rolling it to the void beyond. Lily's eyes shine with girlish excitement, and it warms my heart, witnessing this; the master of death playing with a ghost stuck in childhood forever.

My smile slowly fades, though, as I study her eyes. Even with the staticy vision I have of her, the color is still visually striking. Coldness creeps over me, banishing the warmth I felt just moments ago. Teddy cheers as the ball rolls back to him, turning to grin proudly at me. My smile in return is tempered by sinuous fear, but he doesn't notice, too distracted at the moment.

Fear, because Lily has his eyes.

And I have no idea what that means for me.

THIRTY-NINE
TEDDY

BINX RIDES in the pocket of my hoodie as Eden and I meander down the desolate dirt road, hand in hand, the two of us quiet. Something is on her mind, because she keeps chewing her bottom lip and staring at the ground instead of peering through the forest for her ghosts. Mist clings to the mossy trunks of the innumerable trees around us, and scant sunlight the hue of a pale, silvery fish glitters down in patches along the puddle-ridden muddy path.

"How'd you get out here?" she asks, head snapping up quickly. Her face is paler than usual, her hair tangled from our thorough and honestly beautiful fuck-session. I never knew an intimacy like that could be real—tangible— yet I've discovered it is, and I just want *more*. Forever.

I smirk down at her little doll-like face; those violet eyes round and innocent. She's still just a little girl, hiding in the shell of an almost-adult. The voices have added new victims to their long list, bumping Miss Goss almost to the bottom in favor of decimating her mother and the man who molested her as a child. Although I am slightly apprehensive to share what the voices have demanded, I think Eden will understand when I disappear soon and hunt them down.

"Cash was owed a date, so I convinced him to have it at the diner down in Hangman Hollow. He dropped me at the end of the road and he's picking us up there."

Her brows slant and her eyes narrow.

"A date? With?"

I snort, tearing my eyes from hers and glancing around us to ensure nothing follows. The spirits are allowed to.

It's humans and voracious mountain lions I'm worried about.

"Juniper."

She stops in her tracks, our arms going taut between us, and I glance down at her again, our height difference so much more stark when we're not horizontal. It sends that shiver of pleasure down my spine, how little and fierce my ghost is. I wish we had time to play another game of chase, but darkness is about to prevail, and I know the two of us have finals to study for to prepare for our last week of school.

"Juniper? Juniper Wells?" she hisses.

"The one and only," I quip, tugging her along and quickening our pace. She makes a befuddled face but relents, following me silently once more.

"Am I allowed to know anything about that?" she grumbles. I give her a sideways glance and smirk.

"I'm sure she'll shit her pants when you get into the car. The gist of it is...Cash helps her. A lot. With various things. He's just getting what he's owed," I say with a simple shrug. Her lips purse, and she cocks a brow at me.

"You said at prom it was a blow job."

"I did," I say, hiding my laughter. Hearing my innocent little Eden talk so brazenly warms the cockles of my heart.

"So she's prostituting herself?"

I can't fight my smile, and my eyes slice to hers sideways.

"I wouldn't worry about Juni. She just hasn't come to terms with the fact that she's always been in love with Cash. He knows it, and he's wearing her down."

"You two," she mutters, wandering off in her mind again. I give her hand a squeeze.

"You seem...distracted. After what we shared. You...you okay?" I hedge, fucking nervous for her answer. Her face pops up to mine again, and she somehow pales another few shades, the violet veins beneath her almost-translucent skin matching her eyes. She bites her plump bottom lip again, and I worry it's going to fall off before we reach the end of the road.

"I'm...I'm good. Just weird sharing that and...being understood," she says, whispering the last part. She swallows hard, and I wait for her to say more. "And I know you're going to kill him."

My veins become rivulets filled with lava straight from the core of the earth. Fuck, she's perceptive, and it's such a fucking turn-on, to be understood the way we understand one another without even trying. It's like breathing air for the first time.

"Yes, I will, little ghost. Is that going to be a problem?"

Up ahead, there's a break in the trees, and the gray, wet pavement peeks through the dripping boughs. The tempered yellow lines in the middle of the highway become interrupted by cherry red as Cash pulls to a stop right on time.

Eden doesn't bother answering me, but I know by the squeeze of her hand that my newfound resolution to end the lives of those who've hurt her isn't something she will stand in the way of. If anything, I'm sure she'd want to partake. The thought of teaching her to hunt, to kill...it sends a shiver down my spine that has nothing to do with the chill in the air and everything to do with white-hot lust rolling through me at the images the voices conjure up.

Reaching for the handle, I open the back door and allow Eden in first, though she's tense, and Juniper turns in the front seat, her green eyed glare directed at my little ghost. The voices gnash their teeth at her, but I bite my tongue for Cash's sake. For some reason, he's really fucking into Juniper, has been for years. I'll play nice as long as she does.

"How was it, lovebirds?" Cash says from the driver's seat, grinning impishly.

"Great," I say back, settling in and throwing my arm around Eden, pulling her cold body closer to my warmth. "We became parents today."

"To a kitten," Eden adds hastily, elbowing me in the ribs as I laugh. Cash snorts and I grin down at her.

"At the rate you two are going, I'll be an uncle by next year."

He eases back out onto the highway and flips around, and Juniper stews in the front seat, arms crossed and lips pressed thin. Eden doesn't pay her any mind, but I know Juniper has bullied her in the past. Tired and unable to stem the voices as effectively as normal, I begin to pester her.

"How was your date, Juni?"

"Thought I told you to keep your freak mouth shut around me," she hisses icily. I snort, and Eden tenses beneath my arm, fury written into all of the lines on her stunning face. Before she can jump across the seat and throttle her— which would be kinda fucking hot—Binx begins to mewl loudly, discontent in a car for the first time. Juniper whirls in her seat, glaring at his innocent face as he peeks from my pocket.

"You seriously brought that thing with you? It probably has fleas and rabies!"

"Juni, if you want my cock again, you should probably quit being an ass to my friends," Cash chastises. Her face becomes a mottled crimson, her long, acrylic nails digging into her palms as she buries her fury.

"I didn't agree to be paraded around in front of *them*," she seethes to Cash.

Before I can muster a smart retort, Eden beats me to it, and I watch in loving adoration as she defends me.

"You think we want to breathe the same air as you, Malibu Barbie? I can't wait until you get a taste of the real world soon."

I snort, and Cash tries and fails to hide his grin as we speed down the highway back toward Seattle. She whirls in her seat again, thick blonde hair swishing across her bony shoulders, her ire directed at my woman.

"And what do you know about the real world, Eden?" she spits.

The chiming of multiple phones splinters the tense silence between the two quarreling girls. We must've hit a spot of reception, and Eden is quick to fish her cell out of her bag, argument forgotten.

Shame. I was kinda getting turned on by witnessing it.

Cash answers his cell, and Juniper becomes absorbed in her phone as well. Being the only one without any sort of technology, I stare at the side of Eden's face, my guts churning as she turns paler by the second, listening to a voicemail I can only catch snippets of.

When her eyes find mine, they are glassy with tears, and I grit my teeth against the impending wave of foreboding that threatens to consume me.

"What's wrong?" I say softly. Cash glances in the rearview mirror at the same moment, pressing down a little harder on the gas pedal. A tear slips over the brim of her eye and rushes down her cheek.

"My...my dad. He's..." she swallows thickly, and in my peripherals, Juniper sets aside her phone, turning to glance at

Eden with a touch of worry in her gaze, their little spat forgotten. My eyes search Eden's quickly, my heart pierced on a spire and left for the crows to feast upon.

"I'll get you there, Edie," Cash murmurs, taking the winding turns too fast for it to be safe. Eden holds my gaze, lips trembling as she shakes her head.

"He's not going to make it," she finally whispers to me.

The beginning of the destruction of the kingdom we've painstakingly built starts to crumble in that moment, for the woman I love is about to lose everything she's ever fought for.

And there's nothing I can do to stop it.

FORTY
EDEN

THE STEADY, rhythmic beeping of the heart monitor attached to my father's pale finger is the only thing helping me keep time. It's late, well past ten, and nothing has changed since we arrived here a few hours ago. Nothing, save for the fact he can no longer open his eyes, can no longer communicate. His life is now measured in hours instead of days, and a blanket of numbness wraps itself about my shoulders as I stare at the thin man on the bed.

That isn't my father. It can't be. My father was always strong—in shape and athletic, unlike me. He ran every morning, made eggs and turkey bacon to go with his pitch black coffee. And still, the cancer crept into his organs and ate away at him as though it were sport. One day, maybe, this image I have now of my father will fade from my memory, and I'll be able to see him as he was after a run, or when he used to work on his car, smudges of oil caked across his tanned and weathered cheeks.

Teddy shifts beside me in his own chair, the noise as loud as gunfire with how silent we've both been. Cash's mom Betsy left an hour ago at the end of her shift, tears in her eyes, promising to return the moment I needed her. But at this point, what *do* I need? The only thing I want is dying in front of my eyes, and there's nothing I can do to stop it or prolong it anymore.

"This is beautiful," Teddy murmurs, and my sketchbook comes into my line of sight, his strong hand grasping the papers gently. I swallow thickly, eyeing the rendering of an anatomical heart I did for fun while bored in art one day. I've always been fascinated with anatomy, and the heart is so beautifully intricate, woven through with veins and arteries, electricity somehow pumping the muscle that keeps us alive.

It's how my father's heart must look in his sunken chest.

For the first time in hours, I cast my weary glance to the man I love. His eyes are guarded, his jaw set. There's a lot he wants to say to comfort me, I can feel it charged in the air between us. But he doesn't say anything, because he knows that right now, words are useless. Everything is useless against the finality of death, even though I can see the dead. My father won't stick around, nor do I want him to. I've come to terms with his passing, so why am I finding this so fucking hard right now? Why can't I accept what I always knew was the ending for him?

"Thank you," I croak back, unsure of what else to say. He sets aside my sketchbook and reaches for my hands, clasping them in his and giving a hard squeeze. In the background, the harsh breaths rattling through my father's impaired lungs fracture a part of my brain.

It's a sound I know I'll never forget. A death rattle.

"I'm going to go get you some clothes, some food. What else do you need from home?" he asks softly, eyes flicking between mine. Biting my lip, I shrug. What does one need while waiting for something like this to happen?

He gives a small smirk, leaning in and pecking a sweet,

gentle kiss to my forehead before pressing our noses together. My eyes flutter closed, and my heart aches at his kindness; his is a type of love that I will forever drink in like a greedy addict. I can survive the death of my father, so long as Teddy still holds my hand through it all. How I would have ever made it without him, even without Cash, I'll never know. Life has a funny way of bringing you the people you need at the exact right time.

"I'll take care of everything, little ghost. You'll be okay if I leave for a bit?"

I nod against him, reaching out and clutching his frame to me in a tight embrace that he returns, cupping the back of my skull and holding my ear above his steadily thumping heart. When he releases me, the chill of death creeps in between us. He gives me a quick kiss, and he's gone as silently as a ghost.

The minutes tick by slowly. In one hand, my tattered copy of *Looking for Alaska* is open, my eyes skimming the prose I know by heart. In my other hand, I grasp my father's cold fingers. My eyes jump from him to the page every few seconds, my distraction not working as I would have wanted it to.

"I'm here now, dad," I whisper hoarsely, tears brimming my eyes. "I'm here. Just you and me."

He doesn't move, doesn't acknowledge my words, other than to give a pitiful squeeze of my fingers. Sniffing, I wipe the moisture from my cheeks with the sleeve of Teddy's sweatshirt, gazing upon my father with deep sorrow swirling in my heart. He's suffered for so long. He deserves peace, but I think he's still too afraid to let go.

To let *me* go.

Sucking in a deep, calming breath, I grip his hand back even tighter.

"You...you can go now, dad. I'm here. If you need to let go... just let go," I whisper around the hard lump in my throat. "I'm going to be okay. I love you, forever. It's okay to go now."

I wait, watching, searching for his soul to rise above his body, but nothing happens. Tears permanently stain my cheeks, and I return my eyes to my book, rubbing my thumb over the back of his waxy, stiff hand. A smile paints my lips despite the horror I am about to face, and I prop my book on my knee, reading him one of my favorite lines.

"*If people were rain, I was drizzle, and she was a hurricane,*" I recite from memory. My father used to call me that—a little hurricane.

A small smile ticks up the corner of his lips. He raises his other hand, reaching for something I cannot see. My eyes flick to the clock on the wall, ticking down the seconds. The rattle of his final breaths in his labored lungs echoes forever in my ears. The beeping of his heart monitor slows, and slows, and slows.

11:43.

"Dad?" I whisper. But it's silent now. No beeping, no pained breaths dragged in through

a ragged throat. I shake his hand. "Daddy?"

I stand, my book thudding to the floor, icy numbness enveloping me as I call the nurse's station. One is already in the doorway, a young woman I haven't seen yet.

I stare down at him, and he's so, so pale, so frozen in time, his jaw slack, his body still.

"Dad?" I plead. *I take it back,* I want to scream. *It's not okay for you to leave me, not like this, not right now. Please, please I take it back.*

The nurse feels for his pulse, but it's useless. Her wide, brown eyes find mine, and she goes pale as well.

"I don't know what to do," I say, though my voice sounds far off, in another realm entirely.

"Do you need me to call someone, sweetie?"

I shake my head. There's no one to call. I'm the only family he has. He was the only family *I* had.

My eyes fall to his body. It's not him. The man on the bed is not my father. I release his cold hand. No one tells you how fast a body goes cold once the soul has left. The chill seeps into my hand and into my bones for eternity, burning through me like dry ice.

The pounding of feet hits my ears, and I glance up to the doorway. Teddy stands there, face slack. I shake my head.

And we hold one another's gaze through the storm raging in my soul.

My father is finally free, but all I want is one more day, one more hour, one more minute. That's the worst of it, when someone you love dies. You wish so hard for just a little more time, and you'll never be able to get it. It's a type of sorrow I'd never wish upon another person, and one I understand intimately now.

I'll never wish for anything more but time.

FORTY-ONE
EDEN

"WHERE'S BINX?" I ask softly, searching for anything to say to shatter the deafening silence between Teddy and I. Hand in hand, he leads me around the side of his house to the backyard, the darkness engulfing us as we pass beneath the sweeping bows of an aged evergreen and some overgrown shrubs. He'd held me in my father's room as I stared numbly at the man on the bed. Teddy had given me space, and time, but leaving his body there still feels so wrong.

I'll receive his ashes in a few weeks. He never specified what he wanted me to do with them, but I doubt he'd want to be put in some ornate vase and displayed on a mantle. I want him to be free, but I want him to remain close to me. I'm not sure where that place will be, considering how up in the air my life feels at the moment. It's another reason I asked Teddy if we could come to his house instead of mine; I don't want to deal with the disappointment that will follow when I walk into our home and not even his ghost greets me.

Right now, I want to be surrounded by warmth and

comfort, and the only accessible place that fits my needs is Teddy's room.

"With his uncle, of course," Teddy murmurs back, squeezing my hand and reaching over the gate to unhook the latch. It swings forward, giving me a glimpse into an even more pristine backyard and a glowing pool. It's so odd, Teddy living in such an ostentatious home. A prisoner shrouded in finery I know he loathes.

It calms my heart, knowing our kitten is with Cash. One less thing to worry about, I suppose.

We skirt around the house to an egress window, and Teddy hops lithely down into the hole, reaching back up to knit his long fingers around my hips and gently pull me down. With a smirk, he pecks a kiss to my forehead as we stand body to body in the cramped space, and slides open the window, ushering me in before him. I crawl through the frame, tumbling down and landing on his plush bed, keeping my feet up in the air so I don't get any dirt on his sheets. He chuckles as he follows, plucking my shoes off and tossing them to the floor with a soft thud.

His shoes follow, and then we're lying next to one another, staring at the blank ceiling as scant moonlight seeps in through the window. I release a heavy breath, the weight of grief beginning to press in against my chest, snapping my ribs as my lungs implode and carving out a hollow niche where sorrow and melancholy will forever reside.

Teddy cups my cheek, pulling my gaze to his.

"What do you need, little ghost?" he whispers softly, my eyes following the motion of his plump lips. I stare unblinkingly at them, wondrous at how perfect they are, even if his smile is a little crooked. After a moment too long, I shrug, bringing my eyes back to his. A steely glint has entered his gaze, something stoic and austere that I haven't met yet. There's something oddly reassuring about the way he's looking at me, and my shoulders begin to relax for the first time in months.

"I just want to forget, for a little while," I answer just as quietly, throat clogging with tears I will have to shed at some point. His jaw flexes, and his fingers dance against my scalp lightly.

"Then give me control tonight. Let me take care of you so you don't have to think."

My eyes search his, and warmth coils in my gut before seeping through me like fiery poison. My heart thumps just a little bit harder in my chest, and the pulse I feel thudding is between my thighs. What would that be like, to give over something I hold onto so fiercely? The thought is terrifying but somehow exhilarating at the same time. To not have to think? To just exist and be the one cared for? It's a dream I never imagined would come true in any capacity.

And so, I nod, and he smiles in response, his grin tempered by that teflon glint in his gaze.

"Let's shower and get high."

I snort.

"Umm...yeah, okay."

Now he really does grin, that impish, boyish one that reminds me of a happy dog wagging his tail as he chases stray cats.

"Have you ever smoked before?"

I snicker, nodding. "Yeah, last year with Chastity. She said it helps her perform, so I got high in the alley with her before I went on. Giggled the whole time Vic threw his knives at me, and he chewed my ass out afterwards."

He chuckles. "Well this should be fun, then. You think you'll giggle when my hand's around your throat and I'm balls deep in your perfect little cunt?"

He reaches down, cupping my sex hard enough that the

subtle pressure already has me teetering on the edge of an orgasm. Sobering as my cheeks flame, I stare meekly up at him, feeling that inner girl peeking out, wanting to play, desiring to provoke those voices until he snaps.

"Yes," I murmur, blinking slowly up at him. Black engulfs the teal of his eyes as his pupils expand in a heartbeat. He presses his long middle finger harder into my jeans, and my cunt pulses. I need him in me. Need him to make me forget, just for a little while. *Just for a little while.* It's not selfish, right?

His smile fades slowly, a seriousness there that tempers his playful side for a moment.

"You sure?"

I know where his mind has gone, and the tears rush forth up my throat as fast as a tsunami. Barely containing a sob, I jut my chin out, grit my teeth, and nod. "Please. Just make me forget."

He releases me, rolling over and reaching to his desk. When he comes back, a tightly rolled joint is pinched in his deft fingers, that mischievous smile growing once more on his perfect lips. "Hope you don't wanna forget everything."

I roll my eyes, snatching the joint from him. Before I can bring the paper to my lips, both of my wrists are clasped tightly in his inhumanly strong hands, his body atop mine, pinning me to the mattress. Tendrils of dark hair brush against his moon-kissed forehead, and his eyes are as dark as night. Head cocked to the side in a predatory manner, he studies me, and I wonder with a strike of fear if this is what his victims see before they meet their ends at his hands.

At least he's objectively beautiful to stare at. It wouldn't be a bad way to go, having those teal eyes watch you cross from this life into the next.

He releases a soft snort and shakes his head, smirking.

"You're not afraid of me, not at all, are you?"

"No?" I mumble, brows scrunched. Am I meant to be afraid of him? Even in his darkest moments, I've never been truly terrified of him. He wouldn't allow the voices to hurt me, not irreparably. He's too obsessed with me to ever take it too far.

Maybe that's why I like pushing him to the edge so much; I know he'd end himself before he ever risked me.

"Maybe I need to work on being more frightening, then," he teases.

"I did watch you slit someone's throat, you know."

His smirk grows, as does something else. My cheeks flame as he presses his dick harder into me.

"You did so well, too," he whispers huskily. "Now be a good girl and go get in the shower."

I hate that his cheeky demand has me soaked for him already, but I did ask for this. I've never willingly surrendered my control to someone before, but of all people to give it to, I know Teddy will cherish it. So with a deep breath, I close my eyes and release everything from the past twelve hours, and nod.

FORTY-TWO
TEDDY

"OH MY FUCKING *GOD*," Cash moans, chucking a rock at the brick facade of an innocent, local library in my neighborhood. Jumping to his feet from the curb, he turns to face Eden and I, currently perched on said curb, both of us wearing expressions of concern at his outburst. He holds his arms wide and glares at us. "You two are about as boring as watching fucking paint dry."

"My dad just died, asshole," Eden growls, but there's dark humor painting her tone. She's used it often this week as graduation approaches. A cover for her obvious pain, but I feel assured she isn't keeping anything from me; I've held her while she's sobbed at least a dozen times, made her grin while going through old photo albums as she prepares his small funeral. She's allowing herself to feel what she needs to, and that's all I can ask for.

Cash fists his hands on his hips, lips mashed together in a half frown, half tempered smile. "Can't use that excuse forever, Edie."

"Fuck off," I say with a snort, leaning back and resting my

palms on the gritty, damp pavement. There's a bitter truth to his statement, but Eden doesn't need that pain at the moment.

"All I'm saying," he says, beginning to pace in front of us, "is that we're seniors for like, two more days. Then we cross that stage, and we're boring. Adults. Paying *taxes*. Can we *please* do something fun?"

At the end of his little speech, he clasps his hands together as though in fervent prayer, pouting down at us. I glance sideways at Eden and cock my brow at her. A little smile plays at the corners of her beautiful lips.

"Fine. Trip to St. Ignatius, anyone?" she asks, standing briskly and brushing pebbles off the back of her tight little jeans. My cock grows at the thought of spending another night out there with her, but Cash—

"Fuck to the no, you little sadist," he says, crossing his arms. She mirrors his stance, jutting out her bony hip and glaring at him, her hair as shiny and black as a raven's wings, fluttering softly in the cool breeze drifting in off the Puget Sound. Everything is so peaceful, despite the sorrow looming in my heart for her. There's a sort of cathartic release when someone who is in pain is finally out of it. It's not something I know intimately yet, but something I can still resonate with, all the same.

The easiest part of grieving is directly after the incident, when the memories wash forth onto the beach and bring with it innumerable gifts.

It's once that wave drifts back out to sea that the darkness settles into the cracks of your heart.

My eyes trace Eden's slender, ethereal form. If fairies were ever real, she was one of them. If witches walked this earth, then she was burned at the stake. And if soulmates exist, she's mine. In every snapshot of life, we knew one another, and there's a future before us that doesn't understand the man-made concept of time. We are eternal beings, and the pain we feel from one life to the next will always be outweighed by good eventually.

I have to believe that, or else what is this all for?

"Well, you come up with an idea, then," she sasses back. Cash glares at her.

"I would, but I'm always too busy being your damn chauffeur."

They both glance at me, and I sit straight, holding up my palms in surrender. "My idea of fun is highly illegal in every country."

Cash huffs, but I catch the spark of intrigue in his gaze. He never wants to partake in the murders I commit, just gets a rush from being an accomplice. It's terrible to indulge him, but I can't help it.

I kinda like the company.

"You choose. Seems like you have an idea already," Eden says. Cash shrugs, but a coy smirk is forming on his lips, and I know that devious look all too well. My chest flutters with excitement, because we're about to do something fun, yet something innocent. Something *normal* kids do.

Something Eden and I need before our lives further devolve into depravity.

"I don't know. Senior prank, perhaps?" he says, grinning like a fool, drenched in an orange-hued glow from the street lamp above. To passerby, we probably look like a group of degenerates. If only they knew one was a serial killer, one saw the dead, and the other was... well...actually a degenerate.

Eden glances at me, biting her lip to hide her smile. She likes the idea, and this time my dick jumps at the same time butterflies flap their nasty little wings in my chest. Eden is too beautiful and fearsome to be a butterfly. She's more of a little vampire bat; tiny, but fierce. Who knew that seeing her happy, of all things, would make my dick hard.

I quirk my brow and turn my attention to Cash.

"Is this where you ask me to steal Dick's school keys and turn off the cameras and security system to Seattle Prep?"

He grins.

"I thought you'd never ask."

DONNED from head to toe in black—because, let's face it, those are the only colors we own—we sneak along the desolate, dark hallways of our school. Of all the illegal actions I've committed in my short life, breaking and entering this building has never even been on my radar. Being here during daylight hours is torture enough.

But, just as I'm finding I like everything, at night, this place is beautiful. Bathed in darkness with fractured moonbeams filtering in through the doors and high windows, the shiny linoleum floors glow. The scent of books and the gym and cafeteria all mingle together in the quiet air, pushed through ancient vents as dust motes float peacefully to the ground, disrupted by us unruly, albeit brilliant, teens.

Cash lumbers ahead, ladder propped on his sturdy shoulder. He's been hitting up the gym a lot more lately, claiming it's to prepare for Basic. I know it's because he wants to impress Juniper. If only he could see how deeply she's obsessed with him, he wouldn't feel the need to be a damn peacock.

Eden's girlish giggle draws my attention and perks up the voices from their slumber as well. The way she laughs when being chased by me, the way that spark ignites into an all-consuming flame when I've managed to catch and subdue her...

A shudder runs through me, and as much as I adore Cash, I really wish he'd give us an hour to ourselves so Eden could play the naughty school girl for me. The voices collectively foist images of me slitting his throat onto my mind, and I grin to the darkness, hoisting the length of rope back up my shoulder. They've gone from desiring to throttle the life out of Eden while I'm balls deep in her, to yearning to slash anyone who gets between me and the only fix for our addiction, best friend or not.

Everyone in my vicinity should be thankful my frontal lobe developed far faster than my peers'.

Eden skips ahead and twirls around, hair fanning out around her shoulders as she releases a laugh, her eyes glinting. My heart gives a painful lurch at how bewitching she is, the muscle in my chest coming alive for what feels like the first time in my life. Maybe it's because she is my first love, but something tells me this is far deeper than that. I want her etched into me, into my bones.

I stole the rendering of a heart she sketched, unbeknownst to her. She reminds me that I still have a heart, despite who and what I am.

Cash and I already booked the tattoo appointment. Hopefully she isn't too pissed at me, but something tells me she will secretly be pleased. Perhaps one day she will let me tattoo her. I have a few ideas in mind, none of them appropriate, naturally.

"Okay, so how are we doing this?"

On cue, one of the seemingly hundred tarps we bought slips out of my grasp and thuds to the floor. Cash jumps and glares at me, two shiny black lines beneath his eyes. Eden looks more like a baby racoon with her eyes smudged, and I dragged the black Halloween makeup across both eyes and the bridge of my nose, satisfied to see how Eden bit her lip when she looked at me after.

"Edie, you go get your revenge, sweet pea. Tedster, tarps and tape. Me," he says, waving a heavy duty wrench with his

other hand, "pipes. Circle back when you're done for the...
cherry on top."

Her grin widens—a genuine one—untouched by sorrow for
the first time in a while. Bringing her feet together, she salutes
him before marching off, twigs, markers, and half burnt candles
in tow. I watch her disappear up the stairs to where the senior
class lockers reside, and Cash snaps his fingers, demanding my
attention. Dropping the remaining tarps and rope, I quirk my
brow at him.

"You two can fuck later, sicko. You have work to do."

"You're lucky I love you."

He winks.

"Let's get these fuckers back, Tedster."

A sinister grin paints my lips. They turned my locker into a
fish market years ago. We'll turn this entire fucking school into
a lake, then.

I continue to smile as I work, because there is another
senior prank I've been planning for years, one Eden will be able
to help me with, now.

It's almost time to teach my little ghost how to hunt.

FORTY-THREE
EDEN

I HAVE *to see you graduate.*

His words are a hushed, melodic, sorrowful song in my head.

My hands tremble, fingers pinching the thin sheet of college ruled lined paper between their sticky pads. This gown is awful, the sun choosing today of all days to shine and illuminate me—a freak only fit for the shadows. Tears of anxiety and loathing and sadness creep up my throat, a thousand emotions fighting to be the most potent.

Is this universe really so sinister that it would take my father before he could witness the one thing that had kept him going for so long? Are coincidences real, or is some higher power pulling random strings and cackling when things go awry at the last minute?

Gritting my teeth, I raise my eyes to the crowd of parents before me, anger pummeling the other feelings into dust, my tongue twisting and splitting like a snake's. For so long, I've walked these hallways with the world on my shoulders, and no one cared. I reached out until I learned that it granted you nothing but stares and eye rolls. I did everything in my power after that point to blend in and survive, but a target was irrevocably on my back.

I shouldn't thirst for revenge, but I do. I want my mother locked away, want Malachi Moreau burned at the stake while I dance around his sizzling body, want Dick and Daniel to be carved to ribbons at Teddy's hands. I want to drive a knife into Miss Goss' heart for hurting the person I love. A normal girl doesn't seek justice of this level, but the moment my father died, a thin band of resistance in my heart was sliced through.

And I think Teddy was the one wielding the knife all along.

I've always been dark in my core, seeking the dead over the living, envisioning all the horrible ways my bullies and abusers would meet their fates, darkness the source where I draw my power.

Our senior prank was mostly harmless, though Brant cried all of first period because of the fake 'curse' I'd placed in his locker, mumbling his Hail Mary's in the halls. The girls were less frightened, their glances in my direction sharp enough to cut diamonds. The poor janitor had been the first upon the scene. Cash had even floated a kayak in his massive man-made lake.

Although that night has quickly become a core memory to me, I need to gnash my teeth one last time at those who made my years here hell, and so I take a deep breath and smooth out the paper, my nails a shiny, glinting black, my eyes lined like a cat's—all Teddy's doing, of course.

When I'd told him I would make a speech, he'd grinned like the devil himself and said he already knew how he was going to do my makeup.

"Hello," I say, voice trembling. A few students behind me snicker, but I pay them no mind, pretending instead I'm in the asylum, or Teddy's room—somewhere that brings me comfort and peace. "Most of you don't know me. Staff included."

I pause, trailing my eyes over the first two rows of seats filled with teachers. Some look away, other's give tight lipped smiles, and a few chuckle. I smirk and continue, my heart beginning to pound, my head swimming, a type of rapture growing in my chest that will explode and bring me the most vengeful pleasure imaginable.

"My name is Eden Clemm, and I'm this year's valedictorian. I moved here freshman year. I've won academic awards, scholarships, essay contests, and my art has been in exhibitions all over Seattle. But very few see that, and even fewer knew my father was terminally ill throughout this high school career of mine.

No. Instead, freshman year, I opened my locker to find used tampons that Ashley DeRoza and her friends had saved for me. No one saw my father battle pancreatic cancer, but they all saw Brittany Whithers steal my bra during gym class and cut it to shreds. When I asked permission to leave school early, Principal Anders didn't even look up from his book. He told me I needed a parent's permission."

I clear my throat, chest buzzing as I eye the crowd again. Some parents are shocked, others still as stone, and a few are shaking their heads in disgust that I've turned their happy little day into a trip down my hellish memory lane. It makes me smile. If I have to relive these memories, then so will they.

"I'm supposed to leave everyone with some grandiose life message, maybe a few tearful quotes about adolescence and leaving it behind. But when I sat down to write my speech, to sum up what it means to me to be standing here just a week after my father's death, all I could picture was how blatantly and unapologetically cruel the majority of you were while I was here. My intent isn't to make you feel guilty," I say, glancing up again, pressing the paper to the podium.

"It's to warn you. Here, safe behind these walls, you're all the kings and queens of your little kingdom. But outside of this kingdom you've built on belittling the freaks, the *Others*," I say, pausing, holding the eyes of faculty and guardians again, "...out there, you will realize quickly that you're nothing more than pawns in a game you cannot control."

It's silent, save for coughs and the subtle buzzing of the microphone as a storm brews in my soul.

"Here, you know your monsters, however insidious they may be. But out there, they know *you*. Just something to remember the next time you feel an inkling to be cruel."

My smile begins to broaden, even if it wavers with the innumerable tears clogging my throat. Eyes still searching the crowd for a face I know I will not find, some slip over and race down my cheeks. But Teddy is behind me on this very stage, and so is Cash, and if I have nothing else left in this world, I know I have them.

And they are more than enough.

My grin broadens. Somewhere in the distance, a raven sings his eerie tune. Storm clouds gather in the distance. And I drop the proverbial other shoe.

"Which is why I am pleased to let said bullies know that the deans, presidents, faculty, and anyone of consequence at the schools you've all worked so hard to finally attend have been notified of your...extracurricular activities. With evidence, of course."

Scant gasps erupt from the crowds, along with outbursts from angry parents, but my voice rises above them all.

"Because if I was able to be a good person despite my circumstances, then it is my hope that when your scholarships and acceptance letters are inevitably revoked, you will find it in yourselves to learn to be wholeheartedly good. Congratulations, graduates. Now your lives can *finally* begin."

"SO, how does it feel to *not* be a graduate of Seattle Prep, eh?" Cash jests, elbowing me in the arm as he drives casually through Hangman Hollow, one hand on the wheel like the cool 80s throwback he is. Rolling my eyes to the dreary day, I bite back my bitter smile and consider how I really feel. Teddy and I both know we don't have much of a conventional future ahead of us, one where diplomas and degrees will be useless. Sure, I'd love to attend college at some point, simply because I am a sponge for knowledge, and so long as I draw breath, that thirst will never be slaked.

We can cross that bridge when we get there, though.

So the decision was easy in some aspects, this last prank symbolic in more ways than one. Legally, there is nothing anyone can do to me, or Teddy. The faculty and board of Seattle Prep simply stripped us of diplomas we never held, and Dick has added to our debts considerably.

That, I could care less about. It's the thought that I've somehow disappointed my father that hurts the worst.

"Fucking glorious," I say, turning to grin evilly at him. His eyes dance and he chuckles with a shake of his head. "They should've killed me when they had the chance."

He sobers a bit, pondering my words before he smirks, the corners of his eyes crinkling mischievously.

"Sometimes dead is better."

My brows raise, and I nod, applauding his turn of phrase.

"Didn't know you were so poetic," I tease.

He gives me a funny look before returning his eyes to the road.

"Didn't think *Pet Sematary* was considered poetic."

It's my turn to give him a funny look. The village-esque town is consumed by gauzy fog and trees slick with recent rain that shimmer in the silvery light as we get closer to the asylum. It's so peaceful here, like being transported into a simpler time where magic was still just one thin veil away.

"What's that?"

He turns his face to me, stunned.

"What's what? You don't know *Pet Sematary*?"

I shake my head gently, feeling that familiar flush of embarrassment creep up my neck. His jaw drops in slight shock, but he whips his attention back to the road as a logging truck barrels toward us on the other side. Hands gripping the wheel with white-knuckled angst, he explains.

"Stephen King? Only the most notable and famous horror author to have ever lived?"

Frowning, I cross my arms, a debate prepared on the tip of my tongue.

"Actually, Mary Shelley was the best horror author, and here's why—"

"Oh, zip it, I don't need you to vomit up one of your scholarship essays, kiss ass. Stephen King wrote *Pet Sematary* and intended to never publish it. Thought it was too horrific a concept, even for a man like him. I'll let you borrow it."

"What's it about?"

He smirks, knowing I'm intrigued.

"A guy who moves and finds this cemetery for pets but things can come back to life there. Jud Crandall's famous line— *Sometimes dead is better.* You'll see why."

It's quiet, and the mist that normally keeps to the trees has drifted over the road in patches that swirl in the side mirror as we rush past them, forever drawing closer to the place I now consider my home. Without my father, I have no need for our little trailer. I'm not sure what will happen to it once I move our few things out here. The only certainty left in my life is Teddy.

And even he can be ripped from me if the universe decides to further torture me.

"Did he say what he had planned?" I ask, voice hushed. Teddy had Cash pick me up to bring me out here, and knowing him, there's some devious plan he's concocted. The closer we draw to the turn off, the more fried my nerves become.

Cash snorts.

"Knowing Teddy, it probably involves fucking or killing." He glances at me and wrinkles his nose. "And knowing you two together, it's probably both."

A chill runs down my spine, one of foreboding, but also one of sick excitement. Teddy unearthed a dangerously dark side within me the night he killed that man.

I've replayed those moments over in my head on a loop since, fascinated with the way he slowly bled out, and insanely turned on knowing intimately the fingers that held the knife.

"It's weird you know all this," I grumble, crossing my arms, attempting to distract myself. He snorts.

"There are no secrets with Teddy. Better learn that now."

"Has he..." I begin before I stop myself. Cash narrows his eyes at me, and I release a sigh. "Has he...slept with anyone at school?"

"Not our school, no. He'd tell you anything you wanted to know, Edie. Don't be afraid of him like that."

I am, though. There's a realm of Teddy's life that's intimidating as hell. This side of him that hears voices, the side of him that kills, that makes such succinct and exacting decisions it's frightening. He lives in a black and white world of his own morbid creation, and he's genius enough to figure out exactly which move to always make.

In the end, Teddy will win the game of chess he's been playing his entire life. He is the king of his kingdom, and truly the master of death. Spirits don't often cower in the presence of someone alive.

But they reverently obey him.

How can I not be intimidated? What if someday he casts me aside for another, someone far more interesting and with far less baggage?

"Quit it," Cash snaps.

"Quit what?" I grumble, glaring through the windshield.

"Thinking that shit. Thinking you're not enough for him. *You* are the reason for every move he makes, now, Eden."

"But won't he ever regret that?" I whisper, staring at my kneecaps through the slits in my jeans.

Cash snorts.

"Teddy doesn't have the capability to regret anything, trust me."

My smirk drips off my face as he slows to turn onto the bumpy gravel road.

And pulls to a stop.

"What—"

"Out. You're causing Giselle too much strain. Teddy freakishly asked me to make you walk, anyways, so...pick you two up tomorrow!" He quips with a dimpled grin.

"To-tomorrow?" I stammer.

"Don't worry. I'm sure he packed you fresh undies and a toothbrush. He's thoughtful like that."

"Gee, thanks," I mutter, hotly embarrassed now. He chuckles and then reaches into the backseat.

"Before I forget, here," he says, presenting me with a neatly wrapped square. The weight of it settles into my palms, and I quirk my brow up at him. He gives me a sheepish look and rubs the back of his neck. "From Juni. As a sort of 'thanks for not ruining my life' gift."

Chewing the inside of my cheek, I nod. I'd spared her on Teddy's gentle command, and we ended up not sending anything to the University of Washington. He may have let slip that her home life is terrible, and college will be her escape. If anyone understands that, it's me, and Teddy knows I have a soft heart, however deep down I bury it. I peek up at Cash.

"Tell her I'm just biding my time."

He smirks. "Of course."

Ripping through the thick paper, a book with a bubbling cauldron on the front comes into view, the title stating *Witchcraft for Dummies*. I can't help but smirk at her twisted sense of humor. "This will come in handy," I say, wagging the book at him. He laughs.

"Just hex Brant for me, will ya? Give him crabs or some shit."

I release a laugh that only Cash can invoke, pop the handle, and step into the haunting woods.

FORTY-FIVE
EDEN

THE WOODS SURROUNDING ST. Ignatius are as much home to me as the building itself. The familiarity of the eyes roving my skin doesn't send a chill down my spine anymore as it used to. Now, it simply feels like a soft greeting after being gone for the day. With each step I crunch over twigs and gravel, my heart releases more tension. We're safe out here, me, Teddy, and the dead who fought for peace.

But then something sinister makes its presence known. Something acrid on my tongue, something vile, yet something that makes my heart race in terrible excitement. I know each of the spirits here, and only a few are as evil in death as they were in life. It's my belief that in order to survive, to remain here wavering between planes, that they need their own poison to keep them strong, to give them energy.

Which is why I pause in the middle of the road, the fog swirling before me and obscuring my view for a moment. Through the dimly lit forest, a tall, dark figure stands in my path. I swallow hard, my knees trembling, my tongue shriveling up like a carcass in the desert. The silhouette of an ax slung over his shoulder sends a shiver down my spine.

A breeze from nowhere and everywhere all at once stirs the forest into a flurry of life; rattling leaves, tittering birds taking flight, boughs slipping across one another in the canopy above. A predator is near.

And he smiles.

"SO WHAT'S WITH THE AX?" I tease, glancing up at Teddy's chiseled jaw as we amble along the road. The corner of his mouth lifts in a smirk, and his eyes narrow in mischievousness. I'd be lying if I said I wasn't nervous. There's still so much at stake, even without my father here. Cash could be implicated in what sounds like dozens of murders. Teddy could end up frying in an electric chair.

I'd gladly throw myself on that proverbial funeral pyre if it ever happened.

But even with all the threats circling us in the darkness, something tells me everything will be okay, in the end. At least, I really fucking hope so.

"For my baby to practice her wood chopping skills," he jests back. I snort and roll my eyes, kicking a rock out of my way.

"Why? Are we going camping or something?"

He bursts forth with his deep laughter, throat bobbing and face thrown with abandon to the sky. My heart clenches at the sight, reaching to be as near his as possible. Almost as though I can't take a full breath until we're in one another's arms, the pull his gravity has on me stronger than every celestial body in the universe.

"No offense, little ghost, but camping doesn't seem your speed."

"We camped in the hospital," I retort. His eyes cut to me sideways, snapping to me so quickly it's unearthly. He hasn't spoken much since we met on the road, and there's an undeniable energy surrounding him right now. Not quite the evil that preceded him, but something akin to it. Something insanely strong yet giddy and sinister.

"And we will again tonight."

"So what's the damn ax for?" I hiss, becoming nervous. I've never been a fan of surprises. The one time my mother had a surprise for me, it was the introduction to my abuser. I try not to let that memory dampen my mood.

He quirks his arched brow at me, forever smirking.

"Nervous?"

I answer him with a frown. He strides ahead of me and turns on his heel, halting me in my tracks as he swings the ax down and leans his weight on the smooth handle.

"Before we go any further, I need you to wear something for me."

His eyes are still alight with mischief, though now that familiar, consuming lust blots out his beautiful irises until only a thin rim remains around the depthless black of his pupils. Crossing my arms, I raise my own brow and purse my lips.

"Wear what?"

Shit-eating-grin stretching his lips, he reaches into his back pocket and produces a black, lacy thong. It dangles innocently from his long, crooked finger, and my cunt clenches.

"I'll reward your obedience," he says, voice lowering at the end, eyes sparking and shoulders tensing. He's coiled like a snake about to strike out, and I'm not quite sure who he intends to sink his teeth into.

Me, or something else.

Some*one* else.

Swallowing hard, I know I stand on the precipice of a decision that will forever alter my life. My eyes find his, and my heart sings, at home here in our kingdom. I have nothing left in this world but him, and I will follow him into death and every other life we're lucky enough to find one another in.

The moment I begin to smile, so does he.

"Hurry, little ghost," he says, tossing me the panties. Snatching them out of the air, I'm confused to find them heavier than expected, some sort of contraption knitted neatly into the flowery lace. When my eyes find his again, his smirk has grown. "I want plenty of time to play while we still have light."

I obey, knowing in my bones he will always give me what I need, and once my jeans are back on, he tilts his head down the path. Confused, and slightly uncomfortable with the strange contraption centered above my clit, I slowly follow.

"Care to explain?" I grumble.

"Thought you trusted me."

"Of course I do," I snap, my nerves mounting. He wheels on me, trapping my cheeks and pinching them with enough force to make my mind a puddle. Bringing those teal eyes level with mine, he grins.

"Good. It's time to teach you how to hunt."

Fuck.

"W-who?" I breathe as he releases my face. He steps aside, half of his frame disappearing into the woods.

"See for yourself."

My eyes flit to the break in the trees, and my heart stutters to a stop in my chest.

Miss Goss wriggles, tied to a tree, tears streaming down her blotchy face as she screams against the gag that's fitted snugly in between her teeth.

Frozen, I lock eyes with the woman—the guidance counselor who only met with me once in my entire high school career, someone I had hoped would see me and extend a friendly hand, but something too selfish to do so.

Those terrified eyes plead with me as she sobs. Teddy steps forward, eclipsing my view of her for a moment before he circles behind me. His presence is an entity of its own, and I feel him all along my back, simultaneously protecting me and provoking me. "You know what she did to me, baby?"

His warm, minty breath fans across my neck, sending shivers racing through my body. I nod numbly, unable to look away.

"Remember that tonight, Eden. Let your rage consume you," he whispers, lips brushing the shell of my ear. In the distance, a clap of thunder reverberates between the mountain peaks. "Let me see the beautiful work of art you make with her blood and screams."

His fingers snatch my waist at the same moment the thong buzzes to life, a vibrator settled with precision directly over my clit. Gasping, I lurch forward, but his long fingers bite possessively into my hip bone.

"Eyes on her, Eden. If you do what I say, baby, I'll give you everything you need."

The vibrator shuts off, and I whine desperately, already aching to be filled, the need to climax as pressing as ever.

"Yes, or no?" he asks, giving me one final moment to bow out. But a slow, vengeful, sick grin begins to stretch my lips. I know what it is to have someone else take sacred things from you.

I hope Miss Goss held her life in such sacred regards, because I'm about to help take it from her.

"Yes," I hiss through clenched teeth, the final stage of my metamorphosis transforming me in this moment.

"That's a good fucking girl," he growls, slipping the handle of his knife into my waiting palm. "Now let me watch my little ghost play."

FORTY-SIX
TEDDY

AT THE EXPENSE of sounding cliché, I never knew a love like this was attainable. Never in my wildest fantasies could I have ever dreamed the perfection that is Eden. If the biblical garden truly existed, I doubt it would ever stand the chance to measure up to the beauty that is my soulmate.

Darkness falls over the Cascades, and a foreboding hush quiets the forest. The familiar rattling of terrified breaths through clenched teeth shatters that silence. A smudge of bright blood mars Eden's pale, ghostly cheek, but a droplet of rain slices the line and blurs the crimson into pink. Our victim lies helpless on the forest floor, bruised and muddied and broken, bound tightly together once more, her clothes torn to shreds.

Eden's transfixed, the only thought in her skull to obey. That level of power over another is fucking addicting, and I drink it in while the voices gnash their teeth and sing their praises of her. Though not athletic, her breathing is steady despite all of her running, save for a slight, excited tremble. She caught her prey, and like a mother lioness, I am about to teach her how to kill and devour.

"Good," I mutter, cocking my head to the side, studying her precision.

"Now, here," I say, squatting next to her, drawing an imaginary line across the base of the dying woman's throat.

Eden doesn't acknowledge me, nor does she waver at Miss Goss' incessant pleas for her life.

"E-Eden, p-please, don't...I'll do...do anything..."

My teeth grit, fury flaring to life in my chest and burning through me like a raging wildfire, but I temper it the best I am able, eyes locked on Eden. Her obedience is my drug, my reward, just as I am Eden's reward. We're sick and twisted, but the moment her father died, I knew my little ghost was finally ready to sink her teeth into revenge that has always been just beyond her reach.

I've found her abuser, and her mother, and the plans I have for the four of us will be a hedonistic, savage retribution.

Eden raises the knife, her eyes wide and glistening, unblinking, those once-lavender irises now as hard and jaded as uncut amethysts. Pressing the tip of the knife to her throat, it sinks in just enough to draw blood.

"Deeper," I command, settling my hand over hers that holds the knife, firming up her grip. She doesn't quiver, and she's not afraid. She is utterly consumed, fascinated in a way that is far from normal, but in a way that further proves she is the only soul in this universe that is made for mine. As though we were cut from the same stardust and breathed into earthly bodies fortunate enough to find one another in this cosmic wasteland.

Blood oozes from the new wound, and Miss Goss wails and wriggles, tied like a hog, bleeding from dozens and dozens of slices that litter her disgustingly familiar body.

The mausoleum is open, there is a tub of salt in my bag, and her blood seeps into the greedy ground of the cemetery at Eden's delicate hand.

The perfect fucking day, if you ask me, and it's only going to get better, my insanity reaching heights I never knew possible. This type of high is far, far more dangerous, and far more fucking addicting. I'll never be able to breathe the same again, feel any semblance of an emotion, if Eden is stripped from me.

I'd slit my own throat from ear to ear with a grin before I let anything take her from me.

Releasing Eden as she continues her slow and methodical cut, I reach into my pocket and press the button, hearing that buzz come to life as she gasps and moans, dropping the knife and falling back into me. I catch her and shut it off, smirking as she whimpers, turning her dazed gaze to mine and blinking as lust overflows from those damning eyes and her bottom lip juts out in a pout.

I peck a kiss to her temple.

"You're doing so good, baby, Keep going, here," I say, delineating where she should sink her knife next. "You want to hit these arteries. Slower bleed."

She continues to pout, batting her eyes at me, maniacal in her lust-infused murdering. Like Pavlov's dogs, Eden will associate killing with unending pleasure. I quirk my brow in warning as a tremble of anticipation seizes my chest. The urge to throw her on the ground and fuck her into oblivion is almost impossible to quell, but torturing myself has always made the climax far better.

Eden will just have to suffer a little longer.

"Do as I say," I command, my voice going rough. Her eyes narrow, her chin jutting out as it does whenever she wants to fight me on something. The voices demand me to punish her for questioning her master, but that will lead into exactly what she wants.

I have zero fucking self control around this damn girl.

"Or what?" she grits out, glaring at me.

"Pl-please," the woman begs, disrupting the mounting sexual tension between me and my reason for existing. My eyes cut to her pathetic form at the same time as Eden, but my little ghost is quicker than I ever could've expected. She snatches the knife from the forest floor, a few dewy leaves flaking off and fluttering to the ground as she harshly presses the tip of the blade to her throat.

"You hurt him," Eden hisses, livid and trembling, twisting the tip of the knife under Miss Goss's quivering chin. Those muddy eyes flit between mine and Eden's, forever begging for a life that is no longer hers.

Because it's mine.

"I-I didn't—"

Eden sneers, pressing the knife in just enough to draw a drop of blood, effectively cutting off whatever lie we were about to hear.

"You're sick," Eden seethes, drawing her own cut this time without any instruction from me. The voices hum like giddy bees in my brain, and my entire body buzzes as I watch this twistedly beautiful scene unfold before me. "What kind of person does that to someone?"

"He raped me—"

Eden lunges forward, driving the knife up through the soft flesh between chin and throat. Miss Goss gapes, the glinting silver knife skewering her tongue as blood bubbles and pools behind her teeth. Her eyes have gone so wide all I can see is the ghostly white that precedes imminent death. She gurgles and chokes on the thick, coppery scented liquid. Eden stares in morbid curiosity and fascination, at war with her differing desires.

Her desire to kill, her desire to revel in it, and her desire for pleasure.

She will learn that killing always wins, in the end. *My little murderer.* A grin paints my lips as she withdraws the knife with ease, turning her bashful gaze to mine.

Miss Goss's death will come far more quickly than I'd hoped, but I'm also about to fucking come in my jeans from watching Eden be so merciless, so unapologetically and crazily murderous.

"I'm sorry," she pouts again, dropping the knife and her gaze. But I'm on her in a flash, ripping her jeans from her waist until they keep her ankles bound. The lacy panties are next, ripped from her slender frame as though I am a bear tearing into its meal. In the next flash, I'm freeing my rock hard dick from my jeans, shoving Eden over onto Miss Goss's limp body, and burying myself in her in one go.

She screams, her pussy clenching and fluttering around me already, but tight as can fucking be, even for how soaked she is. One hand gripping her throat, my other finds her hip bone, and I set a punishing pace, rocking both bodies—one as alive as she will ever be, the other dying in humiliation as she fucking deserves.

"You little brat," I hiss, putting pressure on the sides of Eden's slender throat, studying the side of her reddening face in sick satisfaction as I drive my cock into her so hard it hurts *me.* I can't imagine the pain I'm inflicting on her.

"Is this what you wanted?" I pant.

Unable to moan, she attempts to bob her head, but it's useless, her body as pliant and malleable as a rag doll. The death rattle takes root in Miss Goss's lungs, and a wave of ecstasy rolls over me, one so potent I almost come deep in Eden's tight little pussy. I somehow catch myself at the last moment, slowing yet deepening my strokes to prolong that wave of pleasure I'm cresting.

"You like killing, don't you?" I growl, my fingers leaving her hipbone to circle her slippery clit. She manages to release a guttural moan when my fingers ease their pressure. "You like me telling you what to do, and then you like taking my cock, huh? My beautiful little whore."

I circle my fingers faster, and her pussy tightens and begins to milk my cock.

"Watch her die when you come, Eden. Look how fucking powerful you are," I breathe.

"Fuck," Eden cries, the two women's bodies jostling with my harsh thrusts.

One is enjoying it. One is finally seeing how it feels to be the victim.

Her legs tense, and her back goes rigid, her cunt clenching my cock as hard as her hand was gripping the knife just moments ago.

"Oh my God, yes, yes, ahhh," she wails to the dead.

With a jerk of my hips, I bury myself so deeply in her cunt that I'm kissing her womb, letting each flutter of her pussy bring me to climax as I spill my cum deep inside her.

The forest is hushed. Dusk hangs between the misty mountains. Our ragged breathing calms in moments of such tender peace that I will not forget them, even when I am dead.

Leaning forward until my body blankets Eden's, my cock still hard and buried deep inside, I press a kiss to her still-bruised shoulder from our last romp in the cemetery.

"Sometimes dead is better," she whispers, the words a broken yet forceful sound from her delicate throat. I know without her explanation that she isn't speaking to me, but to the woman who now stares glassily at the darkening sky.

After a moment, Eden twists in my grasp until our eyes meet, her brows furrowed, and her lips set in a resolved line.

"I'll never let anyone hurt you ever again," she hisses with vehemency.

Her statement warms me, ignites me. She's as protective of me as I am of her, and I am confident enough in my masculinity to let her be so.

She's just proven she has the fucking guts.

"I fucking love you, Eden Clemm," I say, eyes searching hers. The answer I know I will find is there, swirling calmly in the depths of her purple gaze.

She blushes, suddenly a demure, innocent teen again.

"I...I love you too, Teddy Poe."

If only we'd stayed forever in our kingdom by the sea.

FORTY-SEVEN
TEDDY

THE DEEP BLUE blanket of the sky, still dotted with white stars, begins to bleed into dawn. Each footfall is silent, my boots —thoroughly cleaned down by the docks this morning—barely kissing the pristine hardwood floors of Dick's home.

I will never see this cage as *my* home.

After putting Eden to bed in the asylum last night, I'd gone back to work, hacking Miss Goss to pieces and tossing those pieces off the cliffs. This cove on the Sound isn't frequented due to the bowl-like area trapping high winds, the frothy white caps hiding deadly rocks. Her flesh and bone will melt there, stuck in the torrents of forever rushing water while fish and birds feast upon her.

Anything too risky—such as her fingers, toes, teeth—I burned behind the mausoleum. I'd intended to cuff her to the walls and bury her alive with wounds for maggots to wriggle into, but alas, my little ghost beat me to it.

And even now, the smile that paints my lips is just as insane as she is.

As I am.

I could never give my heart to anyone or anything less.

A subtle, phlegmy cough has my eyes jumping up, narrowing in the direction of the living room. Before they can adjust to the dim light filtering in through the sheer white curtains, Dick's ugly, smug face is illuminated, the click of the lamp switch as deafening as a gunshot.

My heart stills in my chest, but my finger ticks against my thigh, my hand itching to feel the comforting weight of my knife in my grasp. Eden is safe back at her home, and I'd only returned to slip mom a note.

Eden and I are packing our shit and running away to the asylum.

It won't save us for long, but it will buy us some time. I just need my mom to leave, too, and that's going to be the tricky part.

"Teddy," he says calmly, cordially. Muscles as rigid as a corpse, I say nothing, prepared to slit his throat this instant if he stands in my way of freedom. He won't be the first pedophile's throat I slit, and he won't be the last. "Don't try anything with me, boy. If you think she's safe, you're more naïve than I thought."

My blood curdles in my veins, and my jaw becomes so tight I fear my teeth will shatter.

"If you touch her, I will gut you like a fish and make you eat your own intestines."

His face pales, slowly, but it pales shade by shade all the same as my threat sinks in. He knows what I am, what the voices can make me do. They are me, and I am them, a multitude of souls pressed into one human form, a multifaceted being that understands what this moment means, and far better than the man in the chair thinks.

He is playing the short game.

I play to win it all, and I am fucking patient.

My downfall is coming, far sooner than I'd hoped, but I intend to rise from the ashes, forever the master of the dead. And my life, my heart, my queen will be at my side. She will forgive me for the decisions I make from this moment on. And if she doesn't?

Good thing she fucking sucks at running away from me, but either way, I'd catch her every time.

"She's already being watched." He presses his hands onto the armrests of the chair and pushes his old ass up, raising his eyes to mine, nothing but a feeble, aging man. The easiest kill I would ever make. The voices demand it. But I just can't fucking do it. I've played out every scenario in my head of how a situation like this would go, and every single one will be painful in one way or another.

"What gave it away?" I say smoothly, quirking my brow and feigning nonchalance. He smirks.

"You two made the yearbook. I sit on the approval council. The eyes don't lie, Teddy."

Of all the fucking ways this asshole would figure it out, it would be something as stupid as fucking prom. Eden would be gloating if she could see me now.

"What does it matter to you who I fuck?" I hiss, the more sinister voices pushing forth. Ever so slowly, the walls begin to close in around me. It's hard to drag a breath in through my nose, my chest tightening in familiar panic. His eyes glint in interest, and the despair that comes crashing over me is devastating in nature.

Not again, please, whatever god is in the universe, not again, I beg to nothing.

"It matters who you kill for, Teddy."

"You will not touch her—" I seethe, taking a harsh step forward, my knife flipping open with a sharp click. But his smile stops me in my tracks, and the voices collectively hush and mourn. There is no choice. I've thought this exact scenario through, and I know how it ends.

"I will have her killed, and then your mother, all while you watch. You've become a burden, anyways."

My hand drops to my side, the knife handle slipping in my limp grip. Stomach churning with acrid bile, I fight the urge to vomit. Clear my throat.

And damn myself to hell, all for the woman I love.

"What do you want from me?" I croak.

His lips quiver into an excited, yet tempered, smile.

"You," he whispers simply. Then, more confidently, "Your obedience. Your loyalty. You do as I say."

My teeth gnash, and my heart thrashes in my chest like a shark ripping into its bloody meal. But all I can see is Eden. Her smile, the light within her sad, beautiful soul. I've known her an eternity. I just wish this universe wasn't so cruel as to keep our other lifetimes a secret from us. I want to know her in every single one. I need to know that we always find each other.

Were we the children by the sea?

"And she goes free," I counter. "Her debt is paid."

"Done," he answers swiftly, like a guillotine being loosed upon the neck of its victim. The wind leaves my lungs, and with it the last beats of my aching heart.

He steps forward, and I tense to step back, my eyes bouncing to his. Those thin lips press together in a frown. I'm already disobeying. *Eden*, my heart chants, wrenching itself in two. Stabbed through with hot needles because I am once again betraying her, and burning because I am saving her from a worse fate.

"Prove to me your loyalty." He stands imperiously, shorter than me but somehow more immense than I ever thought him capable. I drop my knife and kick it aside, my joints locking, my bones refusing to submit. But I would submit to her, to my little ghost. Gladly. And is this not submission to her in some form? Can I mindfuck myself into believing *that* to do *this*, to give my body to this greedy fuck?

I have to. Because if I don't, Eden will be gone.

And I promised I would never leave her, even in death. So I sink to my knees and stare up into the eyes of the puppet master, locking the voices away with as much strength as I have in me.

"Good boy," he says.

And the hope Eden had cultivated to life in my chest, a garden of her wrapped around my ribcage and twining around my heart, dies.

FORTY-EIGHT

EDEN

Business as usual. C U tonite.

THE TEXT from Cash's phone is a message from Teddy. One that has me flipping open my phone every ten seconds to read it again, as if I will find something new woven between the little black letters.

Why is he backing out? He'd seemed so eager to do it, to run away and never look back. Is it because he finally realized what a freak I am? We fucking *killed* someone together, and he liked it, and I let him fuck me over her dying body, and *I* liked it, and—

"Quit," his sultry voice says from right in front of me, his pointer finger tapping my forehead harshly. I jump as he materializes from the darkened hallway that leads to the dressing rooms, his teal eyes swimming with warmth but with a guarded edge, as though shark fins are circling the outer ring.

My eyes dart behind him, ensuring no one follows before I speak. When I find his face again, his lips are set in a pressed, harsh line, his jaw is ticking it's so tense, and those bags under his eyes are as dark as the storm clouds over the Sound.

"What's wrong?" I hiss, dread creeping quietly into my veins. It aches, the way my heart clenches, the way my pulse squeezes. I know he's always been able to read me, often better than I think I can read myself, but here and now, something is wrong, and I don't like the way it's making me feel.

The weight of the reckless decisions we've made over these past few weeks settles into my stomach like a burning hot stone. He's killed and I've watched in fascination, and then I've killed for sport, for curiosity...for *him*. Are we about to end up in prison? Or worse?

"My mom—"

"C'mon, kids," Vic says from the ring behind us. I whirl, heart racing, for his approach was as silent as a ghost. He stands beneath the only light that's currently on, and it washes his gaunt face to eerily pale shades, his skin almost luminescent. "Tick, tock. Knives again."

Teddy moves to breeze past me, but before I can whirl and stop him and demand an answer, Daniel storms down the stairs.

Tie askew, hair disheveled, face blotchy with drink, he points a finger at me—at *Teddy*.

"You little fucking freak! You fucking killed him, didn't you? My client! You worthless little faggot—"

"Enough!" Vic snaps, stepping between us just as Daniel comes within a foot of Teddy. Spittle flies from Daniel's lips as he jabs his finger at us and hurls more insults, Teddy pushing me behind him.

"I don't know what the fuck you're talking about!" Teddy yells, a note of desperation to his normally calm tone. It's then I see it, the silver glint of a revolver in Daniel's other hand. My hands fly up of their own accord, sinking into the soft material of Teddy's black hoodie, keeping him cemented from going forward, though I am powerless to drag him back, to push him behind me and protect the only thing I have left in this world worth living for.

"Calm down, you drunken bastard! It wasn't the boy!" Vic yells, shoving Daniel's shoulder. It's enough to make him stumble backwards slightly, his irate attention now directed at the one who became a father to me when mine couldn't leave his bed anymore.

"You," Daniel seethes, pointing the gun at Vic's chest.

"No!" I squeak without thought, jumping around Teddy, who catches me easily and pulls me into him, locking his arms around my torso as I stare in stunned horror.

"Aye. You think I'd let you harm a hair on her head? She's like a daughter to me, you bloody animal."

Daniel smirks, his eyes glazed with drink, his frame wavering as though he's floating in the steady current of the ocean. Time seems to suspend, to still to an impossible degree, the same way it did in the moments before and during my father's death.

Vic glances at me. Tilts his head toward us. Gives me a small, sad smile.

"I've always thought you were a fucking waste," Daniels says.

The gun fires.

Shock encases me as though I am stuck motionless in a block of ice. I blink. Red. So much red. Even more than when I drove Teddy's knife into Miss Goss' throat.

The body of the man who protected me while I was stuck here in this living hell wavers unsteadily, a gaping hole where his face should be. Someone screams. His body thuds resoundingly to the ground. The screaming reaches a fever pitch, threatening to cleave my skull in two, and before I realize that I am the one wailing, I am rushing forward through hot, sticky blood and bits of bone.

"Eden, no!" Teddy screams, his fingers just barely grazing my own as I throw myself toward Vic's dead body. But my knees never meet the ground. A pair of arms wrap around my torso and cinch down so hard my ribs crack. A cool kiss of metal hits my temple, the center fiery hot from the round that just blew one of my only friends to pieces.

It's then, as I'm trapped in Daniel's arms, staring at the life-less corpse, that I realize my grave mistake. My eyes, so wide now they feel as though they will pop from my skull and roll across the floor, land on Teddy's.

The comfort and surety I knew I would find there is gone, replaced by nothing more or less than a type of terror that seizes my heart and prevents it from beating.

"You," Daniel seethes, pressing the gun deeper into my temple, an ache surging where metal and bone meet. "You killed him, you filthy freak, she helped, and so did he."

A knife glints by Teddy's thigh, but can he be faster than a fucking bullet?

A tear rolls down my cheek, followed by another. Reality sets in that this could be it for me, the end of my short, lonely existence.

Even if that's so, I would do it all again, if it meant finding my way to Teddy Poe. I know there's something beyond this life, and so dying...dying doesn't seem so scary to the girl who can see the dead.

But Teddy dying? I will never be able to bear even the faintest thought. When that day comes, I have to go first. I know he will follow.

I shake my head as much as I'm able, fear gripping me

tighter than Daniel. All I can do is push it aside, but when he speaks again, my hope flickers in the cavern of my chest.

And dies.

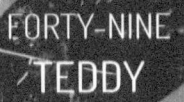

FORTY-NINE
TEDDY

"MOMMY DEAREST HAS BEEN MISSING YOU."

The knife in my grasp slips as it did this morning, before I sank to my knees and damned myself to hell for the sake of saving Eden. I can still feel the delighted shiver of his papery hands on my cheeks as I took him in my mouth at the bottom of the stairs, my mom sleeping peacefully just a few doors away.

And after, I vomited so hard I blacked out.

But all of that pales in comparison to the words Daniel has just uttered, and the truth of it is reflected in Eden's terrified violet eyes.

"You fucker," I seethe, taking a threatening step forward. Eden silently cries, a sliver of hope hidden in her gaze, but one I cannot latch onto, not right now. I have to be calculated, because Daniel's stupidity and drunkenness can very easily spiral, and I will not risk her like that. But at the same moment, the voices have gone absolutely feral in my head, raging, gnashing their teeth savagely, each reaching for the one thing that keeps us sane, the pull so intense I rock forward onto my toes before I can stop myself. "Let her go."

My voice is a hushed growl full of promises of chaos and sickening violence. Eden, pale cheeks blotchy, eyes as wide as they've ever been, tilts toward the command in my tone, her soul bound to mine in ways unfathomable.

Daniel chuckles and shakes his head, twisting the gun, grinding it to her temple, her raven black hair plastering to her dewy forehead and damp cheeks.

"You lost me quite a fucking sum of money. They are paying triple," he says, stepping backwards, taking my life with him. My heart thrashes in my chest like a caged lion, provoked to its carnal instincts of horrific violence. Another step back. Eden digs her heels in, but he drags her raggedy Converse across the smooth concrete floor, a trail of congealing blood connecting her and what was once Vic.

If I move, I risk her. I repeat the words in my mind over and over, shoving back the voices with all of my strength.

"How swift do you think your death will be, if you do this?" I hiss. "You claim to know me. Which means you know it won't be quick. I'll keep you as my fucking pet, I promise you that."

He shakes his head and laughs, dragging Eden back with increasing fervency. I'm scaring him, and I'd rather he run than linger; he wants his money, and I don't want him to be able to hold a gun to her head anymore.

"You can't touch me. He'll sell your mother on the market like the cunt she is."

My body lurches forward, and Eden squeaks in fright as Daniel stumbles in fear and fumbles with the revolver. Heart aching in desperation, I stop, contain my fury, and refocus.

"We're already stuck here, isn't that enough?" I shout, voice rising. The door upstairs slams open, and my face jerks in that direction.

"Down here, keep the kid alive but away," Daniel yells, and the pummeling of heavy footsteps ricochets off the walls.

"Teddy?" Eden says, her voice soft but high pitched in her raw fear, a slight tremble in her delicate tone. The sound of someone begging for life while on the cusp of tears, knowing that death is what is imminent.

And it eviscerates me. I will never be able to scrub it from my skull, that desperate little plea wrapped up in my name. She will haunt me in life and in death, but the difference is, without her, when I relive these darkened moments, I may never resurface. I *need* her to exist. There is nothing else anymore.

Men grab at her, yanking her from Daniel's arms as he points his gun at me, my ears buzzing. My knife clatters to the ground, and I raise my hands, needing to show I'm no threat.

If I am going to hunt my little ghost down, I need to be at my best.

After an eternity, they drag her screaming up the stairs, and the sound is enough to make me go insane from grief. But the moment they disappear and the doors slam closed, I swoop down to collect my knife and turn to sprint to the alley doors at the end of the hall. The moment I'm outside, Cash's cherry red Mustang comes into view, ostentatious on such a dark, rainy day. He waves me toward him, pointing with his other hand the direction they have gone, but I'm still in a full-on sprint and don't need any encouragement.

He throws open the passenger door for me, and I slide in, slamming it closed as he peels out, horns blaring from all directions, his car fishtailing on the wet pavement.

"Fuck!" I scream, slamming my fist through his dashboard, blood spurting from between my knuckles upon impact. He has the wherewithal to not say a fucking thing. "Car?" I hiss, attempting to reign myself in.

"Black Beemer, two cars ahead. You good, Tedster?" he says smoothly, winding in between cars like a snake while maintaining his speed. My racing heart gallops, but slows a fraction with every inch we gain on them.

"No," I grit out.

"What—"

"Her fucking mom. Daniel sold her back to her fucking bitch of a mother," I seethe aloud, the voices all chanting how they'd like to see her die. How cathartic that day will be.

In response, he simply presses down harder on the gas pedal.

"Enlighten me," he says through clenched teeth, narrowly dodging a pedestrian as we near the I-5 corridor.

The Mustang purrs loudly beneath us, a steady rumble I latch onto, my eyes never leaving the taillights in front of us.

"Her mom is part of some cult. Tracked her down a few days ago, but fuck she was hard to find. I couldn't place their compound, but she's high up in their ranks. Tried to give Eden to some fucker when she was thirteen."

Cash glances in my direction, but I refuse to look away. Night has fallen, and rain pelts the windshield, the wipers nearly flying off with the wind from the storm and the speed we're currently traveling.

It's still not fast enough.

Skin crawling in turmoil at not being the one in control, I'm about to mouth off when the car ahead takes a sharp left, fishtailing as it heads for the bay. Cash doesn't hesitate to follow, tires squealing and slipping across the wet asphalt. We wind between warehouses and shipyards, past docks and shoddy, closed businesses, until the world I am familiar with melts away, and we are alone in a jungle of warped steel and broken concrete.

"Get as close as you can," I demand, an idea sparking in my brain as I flip my knife out and settle the blade between my teeth. We're on a straightaway, the beacon of the red lights dimming, when I hear the pedal hit the floor and we're flying. Cranking down the window, I pull myself up by the frame of the car and seat my ass on the windowsill. One arm inside keeping me anchored, I pinch the heavy knife handle between my fingers gently like Vic taught me and focus my eyesight on the black circle.

Gritting my teeth, I reel my arm back, and the second Cash's front bumper noses its way up to their driver's side door, I fling it forward with every ounce of strength in me.

The explosion of air from the tire is deafening, and the car careens sharply to the left, directly in our path. Cash slams on his brakes, locking his arms and pressing himself into his seat. Both cars come to a stop, our bodies settling in the sudden hush.

My heart leaps into my throat the moment the back driver's side door opens, and out tumbles Eden, rushing toward me and stumbling in her haste. Yanking myself out of the window, my feet hit the ground and I'm sprinting breathlessly toward her— my beacon on the jagged cliffs in our kingdom.

But the clicking of another gun has us both stopping in our tracks. Eden's eyes widen and gloss over, and rain races down her pale cheeks, disguising the tears she cries. Her bottom lip trembles, her body poised as though to keep running in my direction, but slowly, incrementally, she changes her posture and turns her back to me, her long wet hair hanging in thick tendrils down her slender frame.

She's only two of my strides away. I could reach her, pull her to me—but I have no weapon. And even I am not skilled enough to beat a fucking bullet. I need to use my brain, and so does she.

The man who stands before us is familiar to me, though only through photos. Malachi Moreau. The man Eden was set to marry as a little fucking girl.

Malachi has three wives currently, I discovered. The youngest was eleven when their sick god told them she was to be the bride of their newest leader. I've only just unearthed these disgusting truths, but I've already made a thousand plans of just how I will torture him. He will be mine for *years* before I show him the mercy of death. A sneer curls my lip as I stare him down, but his eyes are on Eden alone, his bald head shimmering with rain.

"It's time to come home, Eden," he commands, extending his free hand to her, palm up, a snakelike smile on his thin lips.

"Her home is with *me*," I seethe through clenched teeth. His eyes never waiver, never even flick in my direction. Eden's shoulders tense, and she shakes her head at him.

"Why can't she just leave me alone—"

"It is not your mother's choice, but God's," he breathes, fully playing up his reverent bullshit. Eden shakes her head more fervently, her voice thick with tears and high pitched in her stress. The voices seethe and wail and reach for her, punishing themselves brutally for ever thinking we could revel and delight in killing her. The thought had been tantalizing, watching her face go purple while her cunt rippled around my cock, but a life without Eden?

I would become a walking ghost, a body that harbors no soul.

"*Fuck your god!*" I yell. If only they could hear the voices in my head, all in unison, chanting the same sentiment. He would realize demons do exist, and the legion itself is contained within me.

His eyes flicker, but stay on Eden's quivering form.

"You know what happens to disobedient followers, Eden," he warns. Her spine stiffens, and my muscles lock in preparation to spring at this fucker and tear his throat out with my bare hands. He pushes his open hand forward, lowering the gun in a gesture of good faith, when we hear the passenger side door open.

A wisp of a woman appears, her hair pulled back in a tight bun, the strands black but woven through with white, her face bony and severe, her lips wrinkled as though she keeps them pursed in distaste constantly. Her body is wiry, thin but strong, and her icy, purplish eyes cut from Eden to me in a flash.

Her bitch of a mother.

Eden stumbles back a pace in terror, almost within arm's reach now. My heart soars, blood rushing to my head and making it pound in ecstasy.

Hope. Hope is fire, right in the center of your chest, a clenching of muscles that are reserved for a life's most important moments.

"Get away from that filth and back into the car, Eden Marie. You know your place. God does not want—"

"I don't want your fucking god!" Eden screeches, throwing her fists down at her sides and standing her ground. If there wasn't a gun pointed at us, I'd find her fury insanely hot, but all I can focus on is Malachi, ensuring he doesn't try anything stupid.

I'd gladly take a bullet for my little ghost. She's undoubtedly fucking worth it.

She takes another step back, and I can't help but reach for her, my fingers curling around the soft fabric of my hoodie that she stole. The moment I give her a gentle tug, intending to slowly push her behind me so as to not further escalate the situation, another set of squealing tires cuts through the sound of pummeling rain and drowns out the heavy beating of my heart.

I'm about to glance behind me, to shove Eden into Cash's car, when that telltale silver glint catches my eye at the last moment.

Time slows to an impossible speed.

Eden's mother raises her own gun, the barrel pointed directly at my heart.

"No, not him, *please!*" Eden screams. Both of my hands fly up to grasp her arm, but she's somehow faster, pushing away from me—pushing me hard enough that I stumble and catch myself.

For the second time tonight, a gun fires. Eden twirls toward me like a ballerina, but the utter shock etched into her stone-like features has my heart stopping altogether. Her lips part slightly, painted a bright, luscious red. When she closes her mouth and pales another shade, blood seeps from between the lips I've kissed what feels a thousand times.

Her eyes flicker, roll back, and I dive to her, catching her limp form as she falls to the cold ground. In the darkness, my hands rove her body as her lungs rattle and struggle to draw in breath, my hunt for the bullet wound ending quickly.

A pool of blood gushes against my hands, pouring over me from her beautiful, kind, gentle heart.

"No, no, no," I whisper hoarsely, holding her wavering gaze. She stares at me as though this is her first time opening her eyes in this life, with such awe and wonder and trust. A small smile graces her bloody lips. Her cold, still fingers somehow manage to brush against my cheek. Her body is beginning to stiffen, no matter how tightly I press my hands to her wound. I feel every fucking heartbeat, how they grow weaker, and weaker, and weaker still, all while her smile grows.

"I love...you..."

"Fucking stop it, Eden. This isn't it, I've got you, just hold... hold on, for me...please," I beg through my teeth.

She giggles, only to choke on her blood. Cash is screaming at me from somewhere, yanking against my body, but I cannot move.

"Save her!" I yell to Cash. "Fucking save her, *please!*"

I push rhythmically against her chest, keeping her heart beating but only speeding up the amount of blood oozing from her wound. Only killing her faster. My hands still, coated with her beautiful shade of crimson.

Her fingers slip from my cheek, and she swallows thickly, her eyes dimming further. This time, when they find mine, they are sober, and a sob racks my frame, my body hunched protectively over her.

"I'm cold," she says faintly, chin trembling. My forehead falls to hers as I choke on my tears, pulling her into me, releasing the pressure on her chest. If this is to be our last moments together in this life, she will know the peace of death in my arms.

"Shh, little ghost. I'm here," I say, kissing her forehead. A fight ensues behind us, but I can't care, not now.

"Teddy..."

I cup her cheek and hold her gaze.

"Why'd you do that, brat? I'm gonna beat your ass when I get to the other side."

Her eyes close as the widest smile imaginable paints her cheeks.

"It's beautiful over here," she whispers, quoting her favorite book, a book scarily aligned with her in this moment. My eyes trace her ethereal face, death creeping through her veins, her muscles locking, her breathing shallow.

"Not nearly as beautiful as you," I whisper, brushing my thumb over her cold forehead.

"Find me...always."

"Always," I choke, gathering her into my arms. She hums, her cold lips smiling against my throat, leaving a bloody kiss there.

And then, she stills, her final breath a soft exhalation

against my skin. The girl who can see the dead has now joined them.

How funny a feeling, to lose your soul and still be cursed with life, for I will never truly exist beyond this point in time ever again. Edgar Allan Poe was right all those years ago; nothing can ever dissever my soul from hers.

So I smile, knowing that until I can join her, she will be safe, protected by me wherever it is she's gone.

I'm just glad she finds it beautiful.

EPILOGUE
TEDDY

1 Day Earlier

"BEFORE YOU DISAPPEAR AGAIN, will you at least tell me why you're so fond of frequenting an abandoned hospital, Theodore?"

Shit.

Hand on the brass knob for the backdoor, I carefully arrange my facial features and turn to face my mother. She stands at the entryway of the kitchen, bags beneath her tired eyes, arms crossed. Though she appears pissed, I see the spark of mischief in her gaze and relax. If she had to choose between me breaking and entering or killing people, the decision would be easy. How she knows we hang out there is a conundrum, so I search her gaze more thoroughly and roll my eyes when my genius brain figures it out.

"Cash's fucking 'Stang," I mutter to myself. She hides a

tempered smile and wanders into the kitchen, hiding the trembling of her hands as she clenches them near her ribs.

Leaning across the counter, she levels me with that parental gaze I know too well.

"He's put quite a few miles on it in recent weeks. Ever since you and Eden started dating. His mom was...worried."

"We're not doing anything...illegal." *Not yet, anyways.* My eyes dart to the clock on the microwave, and my muscles tense. I'm late, and I have someone very important to meet up with. She frowns.

"You *are* an adult..." she trails off, eyes wandering away. With a sigh, I let my bag slip from my shoulders and hit the floor with a soft thud, the ax nestled safely between rope and duct tape and a few more knives. Ever since Eden shared St. Ignatius with me, I've been planning all the souls I yearn to take out there. Inducing true, real fear in others is what gets me off. There's no better place than a haunted building to chase my victims through.

Rounding the counters, I grip her bony shoulders and pull her into a hug, resting my chin on her head. She's slow to hug me back, warm and familiar but trembling constantly, now.

"Are you cold?" I ask, pulling her in tighter, unwilling to accept that maybe mom has the disease that killed her mother before I was even born. It's something I've refused to acknowledge for years, but something that is now glaringly obvious.

"Don't you worry about me. Just...make good decisions, honey. Don't...don't bring Cash or Eden—"

Holding her shoulders, I pull her away and smirk at her.

"Who do you think brought me out there, mom? It's why..." Now it's my turn to trail off, to search for the right words to describe Eden and what she is and what she means to me, but I don't even attempt to, because I know I will fall woefully short.

She grins all the same.

"You two...cut from the same cloth," she murmurs, reaching up to brush her thumb over my cheekbone.

"I never thought I'd find someone so...*perfect*," I admit, uttering the last word. My mom beams but tries to fight it, and her eyes glisten in pride.

"I always hoped you'd find someone worthy of the love I know you have to give. And I know she is worthy. Just...no grandkids yet, please."

A slow, snarky smirk pulls up the corner of my mouth.

"No promises."

She blushes furiously and glares, swatting at me.

"Go get her, you beautiful boy. I love you."

"Love you, too, mom."

"SO," the raspy, smoker's voice alerts me to Vic's approach as I stand before the asylum, staring up into the derelict perfection that is this building. "Little sunshine found this place, eh?"

I nod, not giving him a glance yet, eyes searching the windows for signs of any ghostly faces. It's frustrating, being able to see them but also not. I am man enough to admit that I'm fucking jealous of Eden's gift and talent. Why did I get stuck hearing voices instead?

They all call me an asshole for wishing them away, and Vic elbows me, bringing me back to the present.

"Yeah, a few years ago."

I glance at him. His skin is waxy and pale in the silvery sunlight, his eyes even more sunken, his cheekbones so prominent and striking he's nothing more than a skeleton with skin draped over his frame. My shoulders droop slowly. My mind is a dark, twisted, obnoxious place. It forces me to hyperfixate on very specific things; threats, killing, Eden. When someone is safe for me to be around, they fade into the background, and I miss the glaringly obvious.

With my mom, it's denial. With Vic, I'm just a selfish, self-absorbed asshole. The voices hum in agreement, still pissed at me for my slight a moment ago.

I cross my arms, still studying his face as he glares up into the gaping, empty windows.

"How long do you have left?"

His eyes cut to me so quickly it's unnerving. I can see he wants to deny it, too, but after gritting his teeth, he sighs through his nose, crosses his arms, and drops his gaze to his feet.

"Days. Weeks, if I'm unfortunate enough."

"What is it?"

The side of his face lifts in a smirk, but he doesn't look at me, instead glancing back up at St. Ignatius.

"Lung cancer."

"And you haven't told her?"

Now he turns his ire-filled glare to me.

"After the kid just lost her father the same fuckin' way?"

I frown, pity swirling in my gut. Pity for Eden, and for Vic. She'll take his death hard.

"Sorry," I mutter. He sighs again, his breathing labored and crackly.

"Don't be. I deserve what I have coming for me. I'd prefer a bullet to my head over this shit," he says, motioning to his waiflike body. My frown deepens.

"That's probably what's going to happen."

My voice is low, guarded, but when his eyes find mine again, the truth is there, however abhorrent. He knows Dick and Daniel are onto us for killing that fucker who tried to rape Eden. We've both seen the emails, the gun Daniel bought.

"If I'm going to die, boy—"

"I'll take care of her," I say with surety. He snorts and shakes his head.

"Get her out of that fuckin' place. Don't care how. You stay, she goes, or I'll find a way to eat your fuckin' heart while it's still beating," he seethes. I smirk, sadness coursing through me for a thousand reasons.

I'm going to lose my mom to a disease that runs rampant in our family. I'm going to lose Vic, either to the cancer eating his organs, or to Daniel's stupidity. And in a way, I'm going to lose Eden, because I've known since the beginning, since I first met her eyes at the circus, that I would do anything to get her out of there.

And I know, with a sorrow-laden heart, exactly what it is I will do to free her from this hell. Dick has only ever desired one thing since he took us in, and that's full control over me, my body. Can I not sacrifice myself to save the girl I fucking love?

"Already planned it out," I say lowly, kicking at pebbles. There's no conviction in my tone, because the voices and my body rebel at the mere thought of submitting to anyone, but especially that fucker. Vic's surprisingly strong grip on my arm has my eyes bouncing to his, and he gives me a frown.

"If it's already planned out, don't get fuckin' mopey about it. Man up and do it."

Before I can say anything in response, he releases me and strides back to his car. I assume he's about to open his trunk, where a drugged Miss Goss is hogtied, but he beelines for the backseat instead. Opening the door, he rummages around for a moment, backing out with a shiny black plastic bag.

He stops beside me, a smirk on his lips, and hands me the bag. Unsurely, I take it, knowing what it is without even looking. My heart clenches, and I give one last look to the impenetrable castle of our little kingdom. It will be ours, someday.

Someday, I'll reclaim this haven for the dead with Eden by my side. But until then?

I peel back the plastic and pull the sturdy felt object from the dark depths. A slow grin curls my lips. I'll wait to be the king of the damned for however long it fucking takes, because in this one item is the brutal, honest truth. To save Eden, to save my mom, there is no other option in this world, not anymore. So I hold it high, and proud, displaying it for the dead to see.

A circus master's hat.

THE END.

THANK YOU

Peeks out from behind laptop, That wasn't so bad, right? Like I said, this isn't the end. I love Teddy Poe far too dearly to ever leave his story so tragic. You will see him again, and it will hurt (again), but this is also the story that was meant to be told. I floundered for two years to get his story right. Never before have I struggled so immensely with characters, imposter syndrome, depression—the list goes on and on. And as strange as it sounds, I truly do think Teddy wanted me to know what a taste of madness feels like.

Because now I know, and it fucking sucks.

Writing this story was like digging up a grave filled with all of my darkest moments—and with my bare hands. I am no stranger to grief. Freshman year of high school, I lost three family members suddenly and tragically. Sophomore year, I lost a friend to a sporting accident, and watched a loving, beautiful family bury their child. I was granted a small reprieve from grief until the summer I turned twenty one. My grandfather discovered he had throat cancer, and from the time he was diagnosed to the time he passed, it was only three weeks.

The last words he said to me? *I have to see you graduate college.*

So much of life is a culmination of those devastating moments. Of wanting something so desperately but fate taking it from you, leaving you breathless with grief.

I always knew Teddy's backstory would be tragic. I never intended to dive into it, though. But something kept pulling me back to his origins, and I'm forever thankful I listened to the call. As hard as this book is to read at times, it is my hope that you find peace in knowing you are never alone in your grief, even when the night is unendingly dark.

With that said, I have some thank yous to extend.

To my family, and my husband, thank you for listening to me for two years as I complained and fretted over this story.

To my son Zeus for napping so well for a month, thank you buddy. Mama was able to write the bulk of this book then, and I'll forever cherish those memories of watching you sleep peacefully while I sobbed into my computer.

To my brother. This book is released on your birthday for a reason. Without you answering the call, I would not be here today.

To my best friend Juliann, thank you for your listening ear, your advice, your talks, and your willingness to go on all manner of adventures together. I am forever grateful life gave me you.

To my PA Alicia...I'M SORRY for the long voice notes whether you tell me to stop being sorry or not. I am truly blessed to know someone as kind, generous, and loving as you, even if you don't want the world to know you have a soft spot.

To Charly, this freaking cover. You knocked it out of the park again. I am as obsessed with this cover as Teddy is with Eden. Thank you.

To Nicola, thank you for stepping in at the eleventh hour

and helping me get this book formatted so it can gracefully enter the world. I can't wait to see you next year!

And lastly, to my readers, for sitting patiently by me during one of my darkest nights. You kept me going when I wanted to give in. That is something I will cherish always. I am truly the luckiest person to have you all. Thank you.

DID YOU LIKE THIS STORY? DON'T BE SHY!

LEAVE A REVIEW ON AMAZON, GOODREADS, OR WHICHEVER REVIEWING PLATFORM YOU LIKE BEST. ALSO BE SURE TO FOLLOW ALONG ON SOCIAL MEDIA FOR BOOKISH CONTENT, SIGNING INFORMATION, AND WRITING UPDATES!

Instagram/Threads/Blue Sky/TikTok: @rubymedjoromance

SNEAK PEEK OF FOLIE À DEUX,
THE NOVELLA THAT STARTED IT ALL:

Jameson Stefanov

I GLARE at the thick envelope on my desk as though it is some living entity. Cheek resting along my pointer finger, elbow grinding into the unforgivable black marble, I simply stare. I know what is in that fucking file. But bringing myself to open it? Something my cold fucking heart cannot do.

I'll wait until Tristan gets home, for I cannot make a decision of this magnitude without his approval.

Our empire is in a carefully balanced position, but not fallen yet. We've cousins in New York who'd be willing to help, though the Volkov's interests are beginning to split from ours, likely in thanks to Maksim. If I had any say—any pull against his father—I'd join with him. Gone are the ways of old. Drugs, weapons—they don't pay the same anymore.

Secrets are the knives to twist now. Secrets are the way to bring an empire to its knees. And with our father dead and buried, we are vulnerable to the families who'd use us as a rung on a ladder. Family is the only thing you can trust anymore, and we are fresh out of immediate family.

The door to my office slams open, a furious Tristan in the doorway like some avenging angel. He wears his emotions on his sleeves and paints the most beautiful scenes with his knives. I, on the other hand, crave control and the thrill of power above all else.

I often wonder when our mother was pregnant with us if she felt that duality; the calm, tempered power and the unbridled strength.

I stare into my twin's steely eyes, his face contorted into a sneer, black hair wet from the rainstorm. He doesn't bother to push it out of his line of sight as he stomps forward, boots squelching on the equally black marble floors. I'd be pissed about the mess he's tracking in, but I realize that is simply a tendril of leftover fear of what our father would have done to us if he'd seen such disrespect.

We both bear the scars of his form of child rearing, but most are covered by ink now.

Those who don't know us cannot tell us apart, save for our hair and the differing collage of images forever ingrained in our skin.

We have no resemblance of our mother to remember her by. We are our father's children—his only children. His heirs.

Tristan splays his inked fingers on my desk—mine, because he is too irrational and wild to sit at a desk and crunch numbers. Mine, because he enforces and I command. His cobalt eyes flick to the envelope and back to meet mine as a rumble of thunder claps over the Cascade mountain range. The heat from the roaring fireplace does nothing to diminish the ice in his gaze.

"You rang?" he growls through clenched teeth. I must've

interrupted something...*fun*, for him to be so surly. Judging by the fleck of blood on his cheek, I can only guess at who endured the brunt of his anger today. If the vodka on his breath is any indication, I'd put my bets on a lowly civilian this time.

I nod to the thick, taunting envelope.

"We have a...*problem*."

His eyes flare, pupils blowing wide in the span of time it takes me to say the damning words. A sick smirk curls on his lips. Twin telepathy is real—he knows already, and the savage hunter in him is salivating.

The line of work we were born into does not require ethics or morals. As such, neither of us seem to have them in our daily lives, either. The very same excitement I can see in his eyes, in the way his body hums with charged currents, is the very same excitement that I feel thrumming through my chest at the same time.

We played our cards the best we could, but time has run out.

"Shall I?" I ask. He gives a slight dip of his chin, which I know is the only indication I will receive as his assent. Reaching beneath my desk, the wide, bumpy handle of my favorite knife slips into my grip, and I free it, slicing through the top of the envelope. He upends it, spilling the contents onto my desk like a gutted deer. Our eyes search the documents briefly, but it seems we both know the answer before we have to speak it into existence.

After all this time, she's finally ours.

ABOUT THE AUTHOR

Ruby Medjo is a graduate of the English program at Eastern Washington University, where she cultivated and refined her passion for telling stories. Currently residing in the gorgeous Pacific Northwest, she spends her time reading, writing, drinking coffee (or wine), and teaching her English and History classes. She is blessed to be surrounded by amazing friends and family who continue to push her to pursue her dreams no matter how intimidating. She is still waiting on her Hogwarts acceptance letter, but she is now willing to fall through the stones at Craigh na Dune instead.

instagram.com/rubymedjoromance